A RELUCTANT BRIDE

JESS MICHAELS

THE SHELLEY SISTERS, BOOK 1

At Buns and Roses 2019 the lovely Allyson Wotzka won a chance to dedicate this book. On her behalf, this book is dedicated:

"To my children Ashlyn and Larry Reeves, who have taught me anything is possible."

CHAPTER 1

Summer 1812

Thomasina Shelley stood at the sideboard, plate balanced on her hand, watching the man standing across the parlor by the fireplace. The Earl of Harcourt.

She stared, as she always did when the man was in the room. How could one not? He was tall, with a lean strength and a graceful way of moving through the world. His dark blond hair was always perfectly in place and his brown eyes seemed to take in whatever and whoever was around him and make quick, simple judgments that he never doubted. He was, in a word, *perfect*.

Suddenly she felt an arm come around her waist and she jumped as her sister Juliana appeared at her side. Juliana squeezed her gently and said, "I imagine I know what you are thinking."

Thomasina managed a weak smile as she shook her head. "I would think not."

"You are staring at our sister and her fiancé and wondering how in the world we will manage when we Shelley Triplets are separated at last."

Thomasina bent her head and stole another glance at the man

she had been so closely observing. She had been focusing on him, but yes, her identical triplet, Anne, was indeed standing with him. Harcourt was hers, after all. Or he would be in just one short week when the wedding they had all come to his estate to attend would be held here in the beautiful, wild Lake District.

Anne would become Lady Harcourt. And Thomasina would have to call the earl brother.

"The Shelley Triplets will always be sisters, though, will we not? Society will never let us forget it, spectacle that we are," she said with a shudder, as she tried to focus on Juliana's statement and not her own inappropriate feelings. "And Anne will come to London often, I'm certain."

Juliana snorted a laugh. "She will, indeed, for she has been complaining to me all week about how much she hates this estate."

"She does?" Thomasina said with a tilt of her head. "I cannot imagine why. The land is beautiful, the air is clean, it's quiet."

Juliana chuckled. "Have you *met* our sister? All those things might suit *you* very well, but Anne is already lamenting the idea of being stuck out in the country where there will be no fun to be had."

Thomasina shook her head. She and Anne and Juliana were as close as could be. She adored both her sisters, but they could not have been more disparate in their characters. Anne was the wild one, the one who liked to have fun, sometimes to her own detriment. And Juliana was calm and responsible and even keeled. She fixed situations and smoothed ruffled feathers with ease.

And Thomasina? Well, she was the boring one, she supposed. The *good* one, Anne had often accused with some small amount of disdain to her tone. As if being good was so very terrible.

"Well, she'll grow to like it," Thomasina mused. "I'm sure she will be happy with the earl in the end."

Juliana let out a long sigh. "I hope so. She has been...*odd* in the past month since we arrived here to begin the preparations."

Thomasina pursed her lips. Normally she was very in tune with Anne's moods, but recently she'd felt disconnected. Since her sister's engagement, actually, Thomasina had felt a distance beginning between them. The reason why, she didn't want to explore too fully.

"I can speak to her after the party if you'd like," Thomasina said, shrugging back into the role of beloved sister. One she had perhaps abandoned too long. "Possibly she'll be more open with me if she's struggling, as you believe."

Juliana replied. Thomasina heard her do so, but she didn't fully understand the words because at that moment the Earl of Harcourt broke away from her sister and the others they had been standing with and came across the room toward them. God, he moved with such certainty. Such confidence and grace. It was a pleasure to watch him command a room as he did.

She blinked and dropped her gaze as he reached them.

"Good afternoon, Thomasina," he said. "Juliana."

"Good afternoon, my lord," Thomasina managed to whisper at the same time as her sister. "It is a lovely luncheon."

He smiled and motioned his head at the empty plate she still held foolishly in her hand. "Is it?"

She blushed as she looked at the dish. Gods, she'd all but forgotten, she was so distracted by her sisters and the party and…well, *other* things she would do best not to lose herself in.

"It *smells* delicious," she said, hating how hot her cheeks were. She probably looked like a plum right now. And her hands were shaking, which he had certainly marked because he seemed to notice everything. And *everything* was not good. Not when she got so tingly whenever he was near her.

"My lord, I wanted to ask you about your library—" Juliana began.

Harcourt turned his attention toward Juliana, and Thomasina took her opportunity. "I shall let you two discuss that," she said. "And excuse myself. Good afternoon."

Harcourt blinked at her as she set the plate down on the sideboard and then backed away. His gaze stayed on her, even and cool, all the way until she turned and hurried from the room. Even then she felt those eyes on her, dark depths that one could lose oneself in.

"Great God, girl," she muttered as she staggered through the earl's halls, away from the parlor toward so many other chambers. She needed to find an empty one. One where she could hide for a moment and regain her composure. She tested the first door and found it open.

She hurried inside and shut the door behind herself, her breath short. "You need to *stop feeling this*!" she admonished herself softly.

"Stop feeling what?"

Her sister Anne sat up from her reclining position on the settee in front of the fire, where Thomasina hadn't been able to see her. It was almost as if the floor had come open beneath her as she stared in shock at Anne.

"I, er," she stammered. "I didn't—"

"Oh gracious, you are turning purple!" Anne said, getting up and crossing the room to her. She caught her hands and drew her toward the warmth of the fire. "Take a breath, Thomasina, before you fall over! I'm certain whatever you are feeling, it cannot be so bad as that."

"You would be surprised," Thomasina muttered as she did as her sister required and drew a few long, cleansing breaths. Then she shook her head. "Wait, what are you doing in the parlor? I just saw you at the luncheon."

Anne rolled her eyes. "Oh, I needed a break from it all. I swear, ever since we arrived it's been one thing after another. This never-ending march to my doom."

She said the last with feeling, and all but hurtled herself away from Thomasina.

Accustomed to this high drama in Anne, Thomasina shook her head slightly. "Well, it *is* your wedding celebration, isn't it? You must have expected there would be much to do."

"I suppose," Anne said, plucking at a loose thread on the back of a chair on the opposite side of the room. "I just thought it would be more...more *fun*. There has only been one fun thing here and it—"

Anne broke off with a blush. Thomasina stared at her. Her sister was truly out of sorts. *That* was a rare thing, as Anne normally carried herself with as much certainty and confidence as her future husband did. Now she shifted as she paced the room, worrying her hands in front of her, her lips pinched and her cheeks pale.

Thomasina stepped in her path and caught Anne's cold hands in hers. "Dearest, I realize that marrying must be a rather overwhelming idea. After all, it is pledging your life to one man for the rest of your days. But you will be happy. Harcourt will make sure of it."

Anne rolled her eyes. "Oh, Harcourt! Harcourt, *Harcourt*. That I would marry such a man as *that*."

Thomasina drew back in shock at her sister's dismissive tone. "What—what do you mean? A man such as that? What is wrong with the earl?"

She could certainly think of nothing. Her sister was apparently another story, for she immediately launched into a tirade. "He never smiles, Thomasina. *Never*! And laugh at my quips or jokes? No! He only stares at me like I've carried something unpleasant into the parlor."

Thomasina opened her mouth to interrupt, but Anne seemed to be on a roll now and barreled on. "His finances must be in a *terrible* state, even worse than rumors have named, for he is always hunched over some ledger, utterly distracted. He likes the country over London, so that means I shall be forced to stay here on this dreadful estate with him and his mother, who always seems so nervous and never meets my eyes. Like she has something to hide. Probably that her son has dead wives stacked up in some locked room somewhere and I shall be next."

At that Thomasina could not remain silent, and as powerful defensiveness rose up in her, she shook her head. "Anne, that is ridiculous, you've been reading too many French fairytales.

Harcourt is a good and decent man, and to accuse him, even in jest, of something so terrible is not right."

Anne tilted her head slightly and speared Thomasina with a speculative look. Thomasina shifted beneath it, for Anne often saw her too clearly about mundane things. She certainly didn't wish to be seen when it came to the very complicated feelings she had for Harcourt.

She turned away as Anne huffed out a breath. "You are right, of course. Harcourt is nothing but *decent*."

At the emphasis, Thomasina faced her again with a huff of breath. "You say that as if it were a curse."

"It's just so boring!" Anne flopped back on the settee and dropped her forearm over her eyes. "My life will be endlessly, ceaselessly, lovelessly *boring*, and I shall wither up and die from it."

Thomasina's lips parted and she sat down on the edge of a nearby chair to stare at her pouting sister. "You really think your marriage would be loveless?" she asked. "You don't think you could come to love Harcourt if you tried?"

Anne peeked over her arm at her. "And you say I read too many fairytales! What one have you spun for yourself about my future life with this man? That I will find deep and abiding love for him hidden somewhere in the larder?"

"You could—"

"No, my dear," Anne interrupted. "*That* will not happen. And *I* am not the problem. I have love and passion to share in abundance. The problem is *him*. He is...he's incapable of love, I think. He's made himself so cold to the world, so dedicated to propriety and naught else, that he could not allow himself to melt even a fraction for any woman. And that is what terrifies me."

Thomasina dropped her gaze to the floorboards. She had observed Harcourt over the past month since their arrival. Hell, she had observed him from the moment he entered their house to be introduced as Anne's intended, much to the shock of all three sisters. And yes, often he could be proper and cool, distant.

But there were times when she also saw something else in his gaze. A heated core, a passionate center that he was obviously fighting not to reveal. Those were the times she wished she could approach him. She wished she could take his hand and offer comfort to him.

Those were the times she had to walk away so she didn't do something so utterly foolish and wrong. It would destroy everything if she did. She couldn't do that. It wasn't in her nature to take what wasn't hers.

She cleared her throat, pushed thoughts of Harcourt aside and focused on her troubled sister. Anne needed her now, and that happened so rarely that it was a remarkable situation.

"Anne, you may be correct that Harcourt's nature is not the perfect complement to your own. Father should have thought of your temperament before he made the match," she began. "But your engagement has been announced, the banns read and your wedding is happening in a week's time. There is no other answer than to make the best of it."

Anne lifted her arm and stared at her. "No other answer," she repeated softly.

"I wish for your sake that there were, for I hate to see you so unhappy and so certain your future will be bleak," Thomasina continued. "But I do believe Harcourt is a good man. And if you were just to…to try a little, perhaps you would find more to connect yourself to him than you think. In time you might even be happy with him."

Anne continued to hold her gaze on Thomasina and she sat up slowly. "Perhaps you are right at that," she said slowly. "Perhaps I should regroup and make the best of it."

Thomasina nodded, ignoring the twinge in her heart. After all, she knew that if Anne tried even a little, she would certainly fall in love with Harcourt and that would be the end of that. "It's for the best, I think."

"I only need one thing to do so," Anne continued. "One little favor from my best and truest sister."

Thomasina's brow wrinkled and she stared at Anne. *Best and truest sister* had gotten her into trouble a hundred times in her twenty-two years on this earth. "What do you need?"

"A break," Anne said, clasping Thomasina's hands in hers. "Oh, Thomasina, how I need a respite. Since we arrived it's been hectic, and perhaps that's part of why I feel so overwhelmed. But if you could just help me take a little time away, I'm certain I could return to my duties refreshed and ready for my future."

"A break?" Thomasina repeated in confusion. "What do you mean?"

"The ball tonight. I cannot face such an event in my current state. But if you were to take my place—"

"Anne!" Thomasina burst out, jumping to her feet and backing away from the ridiculous notion that was clouding her sister's mind. "You cannot be serious!"

"Why not? We have traded in the past," Anne said with a shrug that dismissed everything ridiculous in this plan.

"The last time we did that we were fourteen," Thomasina said. "And the larger problem is that tonight is the final ball to celebrate your engagement. It is the ball to introduce you to the society of Harcourt. It is important to your future."

"It is," Anne agreed with a nod. "Can you imagine my partaking in my current state? I am in no condition to make a good impression. But you could easily do so, you have always had more tact that I have."

"The *cat* has more tact than you do!" Thomasina interrupted. "Anne, this is ridiculous."

"It is only one night," Anne said, her voice getting louder and laced with more desperation. "Please, Thomasina, I am begging. I am *pleading* with you. I need your help—will you not provide it?"

Anne's dark green eyes were filled with unshed tears and her lip trembled. For the first time, Thomasina fully realized how desperate her sister was. And a desperate Anne was a dangerous Anne. She always had been.

"Do you *really* think you will feel better if I grant you this boon?" Thomasina asked softly.

Anne nodded. "You would be saving my very life and ensuring my future."

Thomasina stared at her clenched hands in her lap. Pretend to be Anne for a night. Though it had been a long time since she'd done so, she knew she could. No one could ever tell the three of them apart anyway. And if she did it, if she took her sister's place, then for one night she could pretend that it was *her* future that was with Harcourt. She could be close to him in a way she would never dare as mousey, quiet Thomasina the man hardly noticed, especially when compared to the sparkle of his future bride.

It would be a small gift to herself as well as to Anne. She cleared her throat. "I-I would do it if you think it would help."

Anne let out a yelp and launched herself from the settee and directly into Thomasina's arms, almost knocking her back on her bottom on the floor.

"Oh, Thomasina, yes! Yes, you would be helping me more than you know." She kissed Thomasina's cheek hard and squeezed her so tightly that for a moment she couldn't breathe. Then Anne stepped back and looked her up and down. "You will pretend a headache, that will be your excuse for not joining us and why everyone will leave you alone tonight. Your maid won't help, she's as concerned with propriety as you are. But that's fine. You'll just sneak through the adjoining door from your chamber to mine and I'll have Nora assist. My maid has more discretion, after all. But we cannot tell Juliana. God, she would ruin everything!"

Thomasina nodded, but by this point she really didn't care about her sister's plan. All she cared about was that she had agreed to this foolish notion. And that tonight, even for a moment, she would be Harcourt's. Tonight, just for a little while, he would be hers.

CHAPTER 2

J asper Percival Stephen Kincaid, Earl of Harcourt, stood by the side of the ballroom floor feeling decidedly out of sorts. But then, that was his constant state and had been since a year before, when he had taken the title after the tragic death of his half-brother. A year before when the consequences of his father's and brother's bad behavior had become painfully and pointedly clear to him.

He was left cleaning up the mess. And this was how one did it. By standing to the side, watching the ball to celebrate his engagement dance by and trying to remember how to smile so no one would see his misery in the act.

"Small steps," he muttered to himself as he thrust his shoulders back.

"Miss Anne Shelley," his footman intoned, and the party stopped spinning as his fiancée entered the ball honoring her and their future nuptials. He set his jaw as he watched her enter to a smattering of applause.

She wore a stunning gown. It was red, because of course it was. Anne Shelley had never done anything by half. It had a low neckline trimmed in golden swirls of thread and would have been the exact kind of scandal he was trying to avoid at all costs but for another strip of gold fabric between her breasts that kept the world from seeing everything. Her dark blonde hair was bound up high on the crown of her head, with perfect ringlet curls falling from the mound to create an illusion of being tousled.

She was lovely, of course. And she did nothing for him. She never had and he accepted that. Reluctantly.

Only as she lifted her face toward the crowd's adulation and subsequently in his direction, he realized something in a heartbeat. Despite the fact that she had been introduced as Anne Shelley, despite not correcting that notion nor denying the greetings of those around her…it was *not* Anne who stood at the entryway to the ballroom.

It was Thomasina Shelley, youngest of the Shelley triplets. The only one of the three Jasper could immediately identify the moment the sisters entered the room. He had no idea *why* he could pick her from the threesome and not his fiancée or the other sister, Juliana. He had no idea why he sometimes found himself watching her as she read or talked or danced or just moved through the world.

He certainly had no idea why she was gliding though his ballroom, a look of tension on her lovely face, and pretending to be Anne at this, the last of their engagement balls.

But despite not knowing, he couldn't help a stir in his chest. Something that said life was suddenly much more interesting.

Thomasina couldn't feel her legs. Or her arms. They were all tingling out of control and she had no idea how she was keeping herself upright as she walked across the ballroom, forcing a smile at the felicitations her sister's guests called out. She had played the role of Anne before, of course, but she regretted agreeing to it this time. Schoolgirl pranks were nothing like this…monstrosity.

"Good evening, *Anne.*"

She froze and slowly turned to her left to find Harcourt standing at her elbow, his chocolate gaze sweeping over her from head to toe, taking in every inch of the exposed skin her sister loved to display. Thomasina felt almost naked with the top swell of her breasts lifted just above the line of the fabric.

"G-good evening, my lord," she managed to breathe as she let herself look at him. By God, but he was handsome. Why was he so handsome? And he was also observant, which was very dangerous in this situation.

She shoved aside the star-struck response he always engendered in her and tried for the cool smile her sister could easily find. "Quite a gathering," she mused, and wished her voice didn't tremble ever so slightly.

He moved a fraction closer and his hand settled into the small of her back as he guided her toward the edge of the dancefloor. She tensed at the touch, so familiar, so warm, even through the layers of her gown. He had touched her before, of course, when they danced or if he helped her into a carriage.

But this was something else. There was something...*possessive* about his fingers curling so low on her back. But of course there would be. She wasn't Thomasina to him, she was Anne. She was his. He could be a little possessive if he wished to be.

"You look lovely," he said, his gaze sweeping over her face a second time. He was really looking at her, too. So very dangerous.

She dropped her chin even though it wasn't an action Anne would take in the face of a compliment. Her sister did not demur. But it was better than being caught. "Thank you, my lord."

He stared at her a beat longer, then looked off into the crowd. "It is quite a crush," he said. "You must be pleased."

She blinked out at all the people swirling around. Too many of them and it was hot. "Pleased?" she repeated.

"You said you wanted the wedding of the decade," he explained, arching a brow in her direction. "It seems you shall have your wish."

Thomasina swallowed hard and reminded herself that she was

meant to be Anne, who loved to be the center of attention. She could not forget that at her own peril.

"I am very pleased," she said with a forced smile for him. "I hope you are, as well."

His brows lifted, and for a moment it seemed like he was going to say something. Then he looked away and focused on the crowd again. They stood in silence for a moment, though she would not call it companionable. He was too stiff and she too terrified to label it as such. Then he faced her again. "You know who I have not seen this evening?" he asked.

She tilted her head. "Who?"

"Miss Thomasina." He held her gaze. "Where is your sister?"

Thomasina cleared her throat and tried to calm her racing heart. He was bound to hear it if she didn't settle herself. "Er, a headache," she lied. "Poor dear. I tried to talk her into joining us, but she declared it was too painful."

"That sounds serious," he drawled. "I could call for a doctor for her. He could be here in less than half an hour if I send my best horse. I could even go myself if you think it is truly dire."

Thomasina shook her head swiftly. "Oh no, my lord. I promise you it is not serious. She would greatly appreciate your kind concern, I'm sure, but it is not needed. My sister will likely be right as rain tomorrow."

He nodded slowly. "That is good news. But I suppose Thomasina is not overly brokenhearted about missing the ball. She does not like such things, I think. Or at least not as much as you do." He glanced over the crowd again. "Or is it me she does not care for?"

Thomasina pivoted on him in shock. He could not truly believe she didn't like him! The very idea was terrible. "My lord," she said. "I assure you I—she...no, she isn't as comfortable at a ball as An—er, as I am or as Juliana is, but Thomasina thinks only the highest of you. Why would you think otherwise?"

He shrugged but continued to keep his gaze away from her. "I don't know. Only that she flees every room I am in. And she will not meet my stare sometimes."

The blood was draining so rapidly from Thomasina's cheeks that she feared she might collapse right here in the middle of the engagement ball and cause the kind of scene that would be talked about for decades. Especially if her ruse was uncovered. She dragged in a ragged breath and smiled at her sister's fiancé.

"You know Thomasina," she said, waving a hand to dismiss her own actions. "She is shy. I'm certain her behavior has nothing to do with her esteem of you. Quite the opposite."

"Quite the opposite," he repeated, and now the corner of his lip lifted in half a smile. A rare expression, indeed. "And what does that mean?"

Thomasina opened and shut her mouth, for it seemed no matter what she said, she was digging herself in a deeper hole with this observant man. She shook her head and tried to focus. What would Anne do? What would Anne say?

She tossed her hair. "You are suddenly very interested in my sister, my lord."

He shrugged again. "Not at all. I'm glad to hear she isn't terribly unwell. I do like that little mouse."

Thomasina's mouth dropped open. Little mouse? Had he called her a *little mouse*? This time she did not have to force a cold tone as she said, "She is more than that, I assure you."

He smiled again, this time tightly. "Well, then I shall have to get to know her better. Once you and I are wed."

"Yes." Thomasina blinked. Was that right? "Er, no. I mean, yes."

He ignored her stammering as the orchestra began a waltz. "Shall we dance?"

She stared at the dancefloor where the couples were gathering and swirling off into each other's arms. She had only ever danced country jigs and the like with Harcourt. A waltz would require being tucked into his arms.

And yet there was no way to refuse him under her current deception.

"Certainly," she murmured, and took the elbow he offered. Touching him immediately made her very aware of herself, her body and her wayward thoughts. Made her very aware that she wasn't Anne, even if she pretended. Anne was always confident. Thomasina felt anything but.

And yet, as he turned her onto the dancefloor and they began to spin together in time to the music, she felt herself find some of the calm she had been seeking since she entered the room. His fingers on her hip were comforting, his grip on her hand firm but gentle. He was certain in his movements and truly guided her, leading her so that she couldn't falter or fall.

For a moment, she forgot everything but him as she stared up into his face, memorizing the lines of it, the curves of his lips, the angle of his jaw. She searched the darkness of his eyes and wondered what he was thinking, for his stern expression gave no indication of whatever was in his mind.

"You really are lovely," he murmured, and then his eyes widened as if he had not meant to say those words out loud.

Thomasina stumbled, but he kept her upright as they continued to turn to the music. He wasn't saying those things to her. Not really. He meant to say them to Anne. If there was warmth in his expression or if he was drawn to someone, it was to *Anne*. Which was the way it was supposed to be. It would be better for them both if they found a way to care for each other.

And yet as Thomasina stared up at him, she couldn't help but drink in his compliment and his regard and his warmth. She couldn't help but pretend that it was *her* he wanted. And that she could want him in return without it being a harsh betrayal of a most beloved sister.

She took that moment and allowed it, knowing there would never be another.

The music slowed and he released her so that he could bow and she curtsey in return. As he placed her hand back into the crook of his elbow, he said, "You look warm."

"I am. The crowd, you know."

"Well, then let me escort you to the terrace for some air," he said, and smoothly drew her through the crowd to the exit onto the veranda outside the massive room.

She stepped into the cool night air, trying to find purchase again when she felt like her world had been spun directly off its axis. Drawing away from him, she moved to the low stone wall and gripped her hands there as she stared down into his beautiful garden maze.

If only she could gather her thoughts. She had to do so, and quickly.

"You know, that dress reminds me of one you wore the day we went riding in the park this spring," he said. "Do you recall it? Just before we announced our engagement."

Thomasina blinked as she continued to stare out at the garden. Oh God, he was bringing up events that had happened where she had not been witness. Had her sister gone riding with him before their engagement? Her father had been trying to push Anne toward Harcourt, even before the family as a whole met him. It was all a blur now, memories Thomasina tried not to revisit because the entire engagement brought an odd tightness to her heart.

"Anne?"

She nodded, still not looking at him. "Er, yes. Of course I recall it. What a...what a day that was." She silently cursed Anne for never giving more details of her courtship with Harcourt. Thomasina hadn't wanted them, but now she needed them.

"It was," he mused. "I think you fell in love that day."

She pivoted with a gasp and stared at him. "What?"

He smiled. "With my sorrel mare, Ember."

Thomasina reached back to steady herself on the wall's edge and nodded. "Oh yes, of course. A beautiful animal."

"Indeed," he breathed, and moved a long step toward her. He was crowding her suddenly, pressing into her space as she stared up and up at him. "Beautiful," he repeated.

His hand came out. She watched it extend almost in slow motion and couldn't breathe as his fingers fanned across her jawline. He tilted her face up a fraction, his expression focused in the moonlight. Then he slowly began to lower his mouth to hers.

For a wild, wanton moment Thomasina considered allowing the kiss. She wanted it. She could admit that in her own mind even if she would never say it out loud to any other living soul. She wanted his mouth on hers and his hands on her and a great many other reckless things that fit Anne's personality more than her own.

But then the moment passed. And she recalled that this man wasn't hers. That letting him kiss her was wrong, a betrayal. At the last opportunity to escape, she slipped to the side and dodged him.

"I, er, I should go inside," she stammered, her entire body trembling as she refused to meet his gaze. "I ought to check on—check on my sister."

She didn't wait for his response. She merely turned and all but ran from him. And wished, in her deepest heart, that she didn't have to do so.

As Thomasina entered the house, Jasper sagged against the terrace wall, letting his weight press into the stone as he fought for breath. Had he almost *kissed* her?

The plan had been to test her. With his questions about herself, with their dance together, with his lies about rides with Anne before their engagement. It was all meant to see how far Thomasina would go and if she would admit to her ruse at some point.

But the plan had never been to stare down at her in the moonlight and not only want to press his mouth to hers...but *need* it. Not as a test, not as a part of a plan, but because when she stared up at him, her lower lip trembling, her hands clenching against the wall ledge, her gaze reflecting stars...he had longed for her.

Not her sister. Her. Thomasina Shelley.

And it was only her pulling away that had stopped him from taking what he wanted even though he knew it was wrong.

"At least she wouldn't betray her family, even if she *was* lying," he muttered as he stared up at the moon above with unseeing eyes.

But that wasn't why he'd tried to kiss her either. It wasn't to test Thomasina's loyalty.

In the few months he'd been engaged to Anne, he had never felt such a notion with his fiancée. He'd tried to make himself want her, connect with her in some way, but he felt nothing when he looked at her except a faint dread that he was going to link himself to her for the rest of his life in order to garner her fortune and save himself.

But with Thomasina it had been different. No one else would ever understand that. He had friends who joked he might kiss the wrong girl, even marry her, because the Shelley sisters all had the same face. But to him, they were different. Or Thomasina was.

And tonight he had wanted, quite desperately, to kiss *her*.

He slammed his hands against the wall ledge. "Bollocks!" he grunted.

This would not do. He had a job to do here, a duty to his mother and his tenants and his servants and everyone else who depended upon him to fix what damage his father and his brother had done to their standing. He had to refocus on those goals and pull his plans back in line.

And the first step to doing so was to stop thinking about kissing Thomasina Shelley and instead find out exactly why she had played the role of Anne tonight. Only then could he skirt scandal and stay the course he'd laid out.

Only then could he forget what he wanted, swallow it back, and do what he needed to do instead.

CHAPTER 3

Thomasina tripped over the edge of a carpet and careened into the banister at the bottom of the stairs. She steadied herself as best she could, ignoring what would certainly bloom into an ugly bruise on her hip. She continued her mad rush up the stairs, away from the spinning, swirling ballroom and what she had almost done just outside its doors.

The Earl of Harcourt had nearly kissed her. Not in a dream, not in a wicked fantasy she could pretend had never happened, but in *reality*. He had pinned her against a terrace wall and leaned in until his face had gone blurry and her whole body had tingled with anticipation and a load of other sensations she dared not name.

Even now, just thinking about it, her body traitorously softened and her hands clenched at her sides with a want unlike anything she'd ever experienced.

He had done it because he believed her to be Anne. Not that Anne had ever talked about the man kissing her. She always dismissed him as cold, but the way he had moved on Thomasina and the feel of his breath on her skin had been anything but that.

Still, *he* had done no wrong, because he didn't know the truth. She, on the other hand, knew everything and the fact that she had nearly lifted into him and surrendered her mouth was most decidedly wrong. *Wrong, wrong, wrong.* She was a liar and a betrayer and a whole lot of other words that pinged around in her mind like billiard balls hit too hard during a game.

She burst into Anne's room, hands trembling. The only thing to be done now was to demand her sister get up from her rest, her *break*, put on her own damned gown and go back to deal with the consequences of what had nearly happened. Maybe *she* could kiss Harcourt then.

Thomasina's stomach twisted at the thought.

And twisted further when she realized that her sister's room was dark. No fire blazed in the hearth, no candle by the bed so Anne could read one of the gothic novels they all loved so dearly. Her sister's bed was neatly made with no indication anyone had rested on it since that morning.

Anne was not here.

Thomasina shook her head. She'd left Anne here, not more than an hour ago. Her sister had waxed dramatic about taking to her bed. But then, she had been pretending to be Thomasina, so perhaps she had gone to *her* room in order to keep up the ruse.

Thomasina drew a short breath and moved into the next chamber. Harcourt had placed the sisters in three adjoining rooms so they could enjoy their tight bond during the last few days of the engagement. A kindness to be sure.

She entered her own room and it was as empty as Anne's. A brief glance through Juliana's door revealed more of the same.

Her heart throbbed as she trudged back to Anne's chamber, confused and feeling a twinge of dread that could not be denied. Where could Anne have gone? Roaming the house when she was meant to be Thomasina and unwell to boot was not likely.

She leaned against the edge of the bed and her eye caught something in the dark. A corner of an envelope stuck out from behind Anne's pillow. She tugged it out—her name was scrawled across the front of the folded sheet. Her sister's hand, which was normally so confident, was slightly shaky.

Thomasina broke the seal, unfolded the paper and began to read.

Thomasina,

You will know soon enough and I'm sure you will tell the others in a way to make it easier for them. I never wished to marry Harcourt. That was Father's idea to tame me, I think.

But I would have done it until I met Ellis. You do not know him, but he is everything I could have asked for in a husband. Or at least he is a better match than Harcourt. We are going to Gretna Green tonight to wed.

I'm sorry to have involved you with such subterfuge, but at least you can claim with a clear conscience that you knew nothing of my plans. I shall see you when I return, a married woman. Do try to square things with Father. I know he will despise me and you can soften him like no one else.

Anne

She read the note again. And again, trying to make sense of it all. She couldn't, and she could hardly breathe as she stared at the words, written hastily and with so little regard for their dire consequences. Her hands shook and the sting of tears in her eyes was so powerful that she longed to collapse on the bed and dissolve into a cry that could make all this go away.

Only that wasn't possible. Anne had done something reckless, as she was wont to do, and now there would be no escaping the consequences for anyone, especially not herself.

Thomasina clutched the letter to her chest and then spun on the door. She had to tell Juliana. Anne had been right that Thomasina was the one who could calm their father, but Juliana was the one who fixed things when they broke. Perhaps *she* would have a plan for all this. A way to manage what would soon be the unmanageable.

Thomasina threw open the door and raced into the hallway, but she had not made it three steps when she slammed into the very broad, very warm and very hard chest of the Earl of Harcourt.

~

Thomasina obviously wasn't looking where she was going as she careened out of her sister's chamber and into the hallway where Jasper was poised to knock on the door and demand answers for her lies to him that night. She hustled straight into him and he closed his arms around her to steady her so she wouldn't fall.

She gasped, staring up at him with wide, teary eyes and trembling lower lip and his world stopped, just as it had on the terrace when they were in a similar position. There was no denying it now, just as there had not been then: he wanted Thomasina Shelley.

Fuck.

"I'm sorry, my lord," she gasped, shrugging from his embrace and backing away. "I-I don't know why you are here, but I will have to speak to you in a moment. Right now I must find Juliana. I must—I must!"

She was trembling, her fingers gripped around a folded sheet of paper. Her upset was plain on every line on her face. For a moment, he felt empathy for that pain, but then he hardened himself to it. This woman had played a game with him. He was not about to forget it or forgive it. Certainly not until he understood it.

"Thomasina," he said softly.

She spun around to face him. "Yes, I told you, my lord—"

She cut herself off and her hand lifted to cover her mouth as all the color drained from her cheeks. He let her stare at him a moment and then he nodded slowly.

"Yes, I know it's you," he said softly.

Her hand lowered and her lips parted. "You know. You *knew?*"

"Yes." He kept his tone hard and she flinched a little from the weight of it.

Then she stepped closer. "Did you know on the terrace, when you tried to..." She looked around like there were spies in their midst. "When you tried to kiss me?" she whispered.

He arched a brow. "I was testing you."

"Testing me!" she repeated, and for the first time since he'd met this woman months before, her voice raised and there was anger in it. "By nearly betraying my sister with me? *That* is your idea of a test?"

He couldn't help but stare at her in her lit-up, angry glory. Her eyes were brighter than ever, her skin now pink instead of deathly pale, and that flush crept down her neck and into the lovely swell of her breasts. Her hands shook, rattling the letter she still held and she shoved them behind her back as she looked up at him.

"You—" She shook her head. He could see how uncomfortable she was at such hard and heavy emotion. At confrontation. "You shouldn't have done that."

He chuckled now, though he found very little humor in this situation. "You wish to talk to me about should and shouldn't? Where is your sister, Thomasina? Why were you pretending to be Anne? You owe me those explanations."

She stared at him and then at the letter in her hand. "Sh-sh-she…"

She trailed off and her knees buckled slightly. He stretched out a hand and caught her elbow, steadying her for a third time, just as moved by touching her as he had been previously.

She jerked away from him. "We must find Juliana, my lord. She'll —she'll know what to do."

"Thomasina!" he snapped, his tone far sharper than perhaps she deserved, despite her reticence to tell him the truth.

She looked up at him. "Please!" she cried out. "Do not argue."

He held her stare, exploring the pure panic, the abject terror on her face. Whatever she and Anne were up to, it was not going well. And there was a deep pit of dread in his stomach, for he knew whatever had been done would probably affect him and his plans, as well.

"Fine," he ground out. "I will help you find her. But then I will need an explanation. From you."

She caught her breath and then her chin dropped. "And you shall have it, my lord. God help us all."

~

Thomasina paced the parlor, worrying her hands in front of her body. She felt tight, like an overly wound clock that was ready to break. That sensation was only made worse by the fact that Harcourt sat on a chair before the fire, just *watching* her. He had not spoken since he sent his servant to find Juliana. She had waited for him to do so. To question and interrogate and demand and shout. All things she deserved considering the circumstances.

He had done none of them. But he had also not taken his eyes off of her.

She felt his silent disdain for her with every turn she made. It seemed to drip from every facet of his focused regard. And it would only get worse. When he knew the truth, he would detest her even more. He would hate her as deeply as he would surely hate Anne.

The door to the parlor opened and Juliana stepped through the entryway. Thomasina made a soft sound of relief and hurried toward her sister. She was brought up short when their father entered the room behind Juliana.

Oh God, this was going to be even worse. If she didn't get to tell her sister the truth first, she wouldn't be able to convince Juliana to deal with their father. That would fall on Thomasina. *All* of it would.

"What is going on?" Mr. Shelley said, his tone sharp as he glanced from Thomasina to Harcourt and back again. "Harcourt's man Willard came to fetch your sister while she and I were on the dancefloor, telling her that Thomasina wanted to see her. Where is she, Anne?"

Thomasina flinched at his inability to see her for who she was. He had never been able to identify any of his daughters from each other, at least not by mere glance. An inability Harcourt didn't share, apparently, and as his eyebrows lifted, she could see he judged her father for not knowing who she was.

She cleared her throat. "Er, *I* am Thomasina, Papa."

Juliana bent her head and her breath left her mouth in a long sigh. "Oh, I thought you were being strange when you entered the ballroom tonight. *That* is why you were avoiding me. *Thomasina!*"

Her father shook his head. "Great God, you were playing your sister at her engagement ball? What is wrong with you?" He pivoted on Harcourt. "You must forgive them, my lord. I thought they had outgrown such foolish notions as to trade places, but here we are. I'm certain there is no ill intent to the act."

"Are you?" Harcourt said, folding his fingers together and looking past Mr. Shelley to spear Thomasina with an even gaze. "I am far less so. I want to hear from Thomasina about why she would do such a foolhardy thing. I would also like to know where exactly my fiancée actually is."

Thomasina could barely hold herself upright at his pointed, accusatory tone and words. She was going to have to tell the truth now. Tell *him* the truth. In this room where everyone was staring at her, waiting for her to explain herself and Anne, his was the most important gaze. He held her captive with it. There was only him.

She felt Juliana move next to her. Felt her sister take her hand, but she couldn't drag her gaze from Harcourt. Even when Juliana whispered, "Just say something, dearest. You are frightening me."

Her father was less gentle and his sharp "Speak!" broke her state.

She shook her head. "I—Anne asked me to take her place. She said it was just for tonight, a way for her to clear her mind. To get herself into a better attitude for the wedding. But—but—"

Harcourt rose from his seat at last, a slow unfolding of long legs and arms. He moved toward her a step, his voice suddenly gentle. "But?"

She swallowed past the dryness of her mouth, the thickness in her throat, and squeaked, "She ran away."

She held the note out toward him, but before he could take it, her father snatched it. He and Juliana bent over the words, shouting together, but Thomasina could barely hear them, barely registered as they rushed together out of the room, probably to look for Anne. All she could do was stare at Harcourt.

And he stared back, his expression impassive. He didn't look angry or sad or upset. He was utterly unreadable and completely captivating. His gaze flitted from her head to her toes.

"You agreed to this nonsense?" he said softly. She felt the accusation in every word.

"I-I didn't know her plans, my lord, or I would have tried to talk her out of such a foolish thing," she said, and wished he would believe her. Wished, did not imagine.

"Hmmm," was his only response, and he moved another few steps closer.

She braced for him to touch her, as he had done on the terrace, in the hall, but he passed by her, only brushing her shoulder with his own and bent to retrieve the note from her sister.

"Did my father drop that?" she asked, stunned for she hadn't noticed that.

He nodded. "In their haste, they were not thinking to hide the further evidence of your sister's ridiculous behavior." He turned over the note and read it slowly. Finally, he lifted his stare to hers again. "Well, we certainly have ourselves a serious problem here, don't we, Thomasina Shelley? Now I wonder, what in the world do you propose we do about it?"

CHAPTER 4

I n his life, Jasper had experienced a great many betrayals. Living with a father and a brother such as his, he'd been disappointed and deceived enough times that he had learned to harden himself to it. Harden himself to any emotion that could allow him to be hurt in such a way.

And he had. Marrying Anne was yet another method of self-protection. He would receive a fine dowry, enough to help him with the financial problems left behind by the previous two holders of his title. There had never been any emotional attachments to cling to. So the fact that Anne had run away was little more than an annoyance to him. A reminder that one did not allow a gentleman to match one with a flibbertigibbet of a girl.

But when he looked at Thomasina and knew she had taken a part, even a small one, in this deception, his reaction was far more passionate. He was angry with her. Angry that she would not refuse such a silly request or at least look into it further.

Then beyond *that* was another emotion. One he really didn't want to face and yet it kept rising up in his chest as he stared at Thomasina, her gaze firmly on her feet and her lips trembling slightly.

He was relieved. After all, he certainly would not marry Anne now. She might be found in short order, but there would be talk and rumor along any route she took. There was no avoiding the secret coming out. So, if she was brought home, the idea of continuing the match was abhorrent.

Which meant he was free. That also meant those powerful desires he felt toward Thomasina tonight were not quite so terrible as they had been an hour before.

And yet he *wasn't* free at the same time. He needed that Shelley dowry, plainly spoken. A broken engagement would materially damage his ability to find himself a bride of means. This was a scandal of exactly the kind his father and brother had destroyed themselves with. The kind he'd been trying to avoid for years.

So he would be decimated by this broken engagement. And the relief fled.

The door to the parlor opened again, and Juliana and Mr. Shelley returned. Their long faces verified what Thomasina had already said.

"All her things are gone," Juliana sighed. "Her poor maid was shocked."

"I should sack her!" Mr. Shelley fumed.

"You shall not, Father," Juliana said with a shake of her head. "You saw she wasn't involved. But *you* were, Thomasina."

They both focused on Thomasina now, and Jasper watched her shrink a little as accusations flew from both Juliana and her father. Juliana's were kinder, gentler. Shelley's were loud and angry.

She took them all, her shoulders slumping as she apologized and tried to explain exactly what she'd already said. He watched her mouth move while ignoring her words, and thought about how much he'd wanted to kiss her. He still wanted to kiss her, truth be told.

And he really didn't like the slump-shouldered lines of her right now. That she would take all the weight of what had happened when in truth it was Anne who had managed all this. Thomasina had been manipulated. Angry or not, he could see that.

"Quiet," he said at last, the harshness of his tone cutting through the chatter of the Shelley family members. They all fell silent at once, and he marked how Thomasina flinched and wouldn't look at him.

"My lord—" Shelley began.

He held up a hand. "I said *be quiet*," he growled, and speared the man with a look not to be ignored. Shelley shrank back a bit and nodded. "Your daughter has dishonored me."

Shelley gasped at the bluntness of the words and Juliana turned her face at them. But to his surprise, Thomasina's shoulders pushed back and she straightened up a little as she took a long step in his direction. "My lord, please don't be so hard on her."

He arched a brow at that interesting response. So she would not defend herself, but she would try to placate him against any harsh feelings he felt toward Anne.

"And what about you?" He moved on her one step, two, crowding her back a fraction and watching her pupils dilate with what he recognized was a combination of fear and arousal. She'd wanted him to kiss her as much as he'd wanted the same.

And just like him, there was part of her that still wanted it.

"What about me?" she squeaked.

"Should I be hard on *you*, Thomasina Shelley? For going along with such foolishness? For offering your sister an escape route she might not have found without your assistance? Whether you knew it or not, that *is* what you did, isn't it?"

Her gaze held his for a moment, emerald depths, and then her lashes lowered. "You are owed your anger, of course."

"Thank you," he said softly. Then he turned to her father. "And what do *you* offer as recompense?"

"I-I don't know," Shelley stammered, shifting in his place and darting his gaze to Juliana, as if the young woman might have a suggestion. For her part, Juliana just looked tired. Bone-tired, like she had been dealing with messes to clean up for years. Perhaps she had at that, considering Thomasina had also wished to seek her out when trouble came in the form of a folded sheet of vellum.

Jasper folded his arms and glared at Shelley. "Think."

Shelley cleared his throat. "Well, I...I can go after Anne, of course. Try to find her and bring her home."

Juliana spun on him, her eyes wide. "Well, of course you will, Father!"

"You must," Thomasina added, worrying her hands in front of her. "We know nothing about this...this Ellis person."

Jasper hesitated, for that name seemed familiar to him, just as it had when he'd read Anne's note to her sister. He pushed it aside, along with thoughts of uncovering the man who had taken his intended. He would think of that later. Right now he had other situations to deal with.

"The matter at hand," he said slowly and succinctly, "is my marriage contract, Mr. Shelley. Finding Anne will not fix this. I would not accept her as a bride now that I know her nature and how objectionable she finds the engagement."

Thomasina gasped and the gaze that flashed to him held more of that fascinating and captivating anger. He found himself wanting to provoke it just to watch it burn in her eyes.

"Sir, please you must reconsider," Shelley said. "If you do not marry Anne, you will damage all our reputations. I have plans for the other girls, you see, and—"

Thomasina caught her breath and her hands gripped in fists at her sides, all the proof Jasper needed that she did not want to be part of her father's schemes.

Which meant she might agree to be party to his own.

"I don't care about your plans," he interrupted. "*I* am the injured party here, sir. You ought to have brought your daughter under some kind of control years ago, rather than let her be so wild."

Shelley pursed his lips. "Fine. Then what do you suggest. Money, I suppose. To make up for her lost dowry?"

Jasper flinched, for the words, spoken under the guise of recompense, certainly hit the mark Shelley likely intended. They starkly reminded Jasper that he needed the funds. That this marriage was not something he could end so easily. Others depended on him too much.

"No, money will not fix it either," he murmured, and found himself looking toward Thomasina once more. "When you and I first met and discussed the idea of uniting our families, you made it clear I would have a pick of any of your three daughters."

Shelley tilted his head. "And *you* made it clear you did not care which one you were given."

"So you gave me the one most likely to destroy your own future. Thank you for that," Jasper said. "Well, now I think the solution is clear, don't you?"

Juliana Shelley took a long step forward. "Wait...are you—are you suggesting you would merely replace Anne with one of us?"

He arched a brow at her. "Indeed, I am. After all, I made a bargain to marry a Shelley sister. Marry one I shall."

Mr. Shelley's eyes were wide as saucers. "My lord—"

"The wedding is on, sir," Jasper said, forcing his tone to be hard as nails, unbendable as cold steel. "And since Miss Thomasina Shelley was so eager to take her sister's place at the ball tonight, I see no reason why she should not do so permanently."

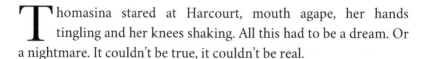

Thomasina stared at Harcourt, mouth agape, her hands tingling and her knees shaking. All this had to be a dream. Or a nightmare. It couldn't be true, it couldn't be real.

And yet everything around her felt too sharp and present to be anything but real.

"You wish—you wish to marry me?" she managed to whisper.

He met her stare, unreadable as always, and shrugged one shoulder slightly. "I wish to marry a Shelley sister, Miss Thomasina."

She ought not to have felt a sting at that response, for she *knew* he didn't truly care for her. Right now he didn't even like her. And yet she did feel it, a sharp tug on the heart that made her eyes fill with tears she immediately blinked away. She hadn't earned those. She refused to let them fall.

"Lord Harcourt," her father said, stepping forward. "This is incredibly unorthodox. How could we ever explain that you were publicly meant to marry Anne and now you are linking yourself to Thomasina?"

Harcourt's lips thinned. "I am not arguing that there will not be a scandal at such an action. I abhor that it has come to this, but it seems like it would be an easier thing to explain than that Anne ran away a week before our nuptials with some man whose full name you do not even know."

Mr. Shelley stroked his chin and Thomasina could see that he was considering the request. Already looking for ways to make it work for his own plans. He wanted a connection to Harcourt's title as much as Harcourt wanted his money. They were the match, in truth. It had nothing to do with her or Anne or Juliana.

But as she watched them talk, hardly hearing their words, hardly hearing Juliana's interjections that they should not be hasty or punish Thomasina for Anne's bad behavior, she couldn't help but watch Harcourt. He was so very handsome. Before this, she had liked him so much. Too much. His face had haunted her dreams, waking her with the sheets twisted around her and her body tingling.

And tonight…tonight when he had held her so close, when his mouth had swung toward hers on the terrace, she had hated herself for wanting to take what should be Anne's. Now she was being offered the chance to do just that and no one could dare hate her for it.

"I'll do it," she said, but her voice didn't rise above the din of the other's conversation. She cleared her throat and said it louder and with more conviction. "I'll do it, do you hear me?"

That stopped them all and three faces turned to stare at her in shock. Well, her father and Juliana looked shocked. Harcourt looked...dangerous. His gaze swept over her and a tiny smile tilted the corner of his lips. She'd never seen such an expression on his usually serious face before. Like he was...wicked.

She shivered as sensations she couldn't control raced through her body and fought to keep her expression calm.

"Thomasina," Juliana said, stepping up to take her hand. "You do not have to do this. Anne's mistakes are Anne's."

Thomasina squeezed her sister's fingers and held her gaze for a moment, for she knew Juliana would sense her peace with this decision if she allowed it. That was one of the lovely benefits of being triplets, that connection of the heart they shared. Juliana's expression softened.

"I did play a part in this," Thomasina said. "Lord Harcourt is right about that. So I must atone for what I did. If I do not, *all* of us will suffer for Anne's bad decisions. This will make it easiest for everyone."

Harcourt stared at her, his eyes searching her. Then he shook his head. "Always so pleasing, Thomasina."

She frowned, for though his words were not insulting, they didn't sound much like a compliment either.

He jerked his gaze away and now looked at her father. "We are finished for tonight. I have nothing left to say to you. We can alter the written agreement together tomorrow and arrange for a special license. Your money and my influence should make that no trouble. Good evening."

He said nothing else, but pivoted on his heel and exited the room. Once he was gone, Thomasina took a long breath and realized she hadn't done so in the entire time he'd been near. He stole the air from the room when he was in it.

Mr. Shelley turned to her, his gaze narrowing. "What a pickle you and your sister have gotten us all into. We are very lucky that

Harcourt has agreed to take any of you after this nonsense. Good
night."

He stomped out and once he was gone, Juliana looked at her.
Thomasina shrugged in response to the question Juliana hadn't
asked, and her sister sighed as she moved to the parlor door and
quietly shut it.

"Thomasina," Juliana whispered.

"I know you are disappointed in me," Thomasina said softly.
"And I know I have helped create yet another mess for you to
manage. I'm sorry about that."

"*Anne* created a mess," Juliana said with a frown. "And I'm sure
she would be far less apologetic about it if she were here. Selfish,
selfish Anne."

As Juliana paced away, Thomasina watched her with concern.
"Anne follows her heart. Often it is my favorite thing about her. In
this case, I hope it isn't a mistake, for I have no idea who this man is
that she's marrying."

Juliana turned. "Yes, her impulsiveness...well, it is frightening. I
fear this will convince Father to abandon her entirely, despite the
danger she might have put herself in."

"I agree." Thomasina shivered. "If she is not a benefit, he might
see her as a detriment, better left to be cut away."

"I will talk to Father again about seeking her out and finding out
who this man she ran away with is. Perhaps you will press Harcourt
to do the same."

Thomasina's breath caught. "Me, talk to Harcourt about it?"

"Well, yes," Juliana said with a humorless chuckle. "You are
apparently his fiancée now and will be his wife in a week if he and
Father have their way. Oh, Thomasina, is this *truly* what you want?
Or is it just your way to make everyone happy?"

Thomasina hesitated. She had never spoken to anyone about the
very wrong feelings she'd been having toward Harcourt. The idea of
admitting her attraction to him all along made her feel a little sick
to her stomach. So instead she shrugged. "I am not so silly as our

sister, to not recognize a good match when I see it. If it also accomplishes alleviation of this terrible situation, then it seems like it's a good outcome for everyone involved."

Juliana stared at her a beat, two. Then she nodded. "If you say so. Now I should go speak to Father. Try to soothe his ruffled feathers, since I'm sure he's crashing about his chamber drinking and cursing that he had daughters and not sons."

"Oof, I'm sorry that duty falls to you," Thomasina said.

Juliana's smile faltered a fraction. "It always does. I am accustomed to it. Now go to bed if you can. There will be little rest for any of us for a while, I fear."

Juliana left the parlor and Thomasina sank into the nearest chair as her knees gave out at last. She covered her face with both hands. Twelve hours before she had been working on acceptance that Anne would marry Harcourt, and that would be the end of that.

Now everything was turned on its head. And she had no idea if her terror was more powerful...or the joy that she ought not feel and which could not lead to anything good.

CHAPTER 5

Thomasina had not slept even a wink, and her body reminded her of that fact with every step as she walked through the long halls of Harcourt Heights. During the time they'd spent here, she had already developed an affection for the place. It was beautiful and the staff was nothing but kind to her and her family. But now she looked at it with a different eye. She would be lady of this house in less than a week.

That thought made her a little dizzy, and she stopped at the entrance to a parlor and leaned on the doorframe to steady herself.

"Are you well, Thomasina?"

She jerked her head up at the voice that came behind her. Harcourt's voice. Slowly, she pivoted to face him as heat crept into her cheeks. God, but he was handsome as he stood there, just a few feet behind her, dressed perfectly. He was always impeccable from the perfect knot on his cravat to the bright polish on his boots.

"I-I am," she said. Lied. And tried to smile.

"You are up early," he said.

She shrugged. "It was difficult to sleep after all the excitement of last night," she admitted, for there was no point in lying. Not anymore. "I hope you don't mind that I decided to take myself on a small tour of the estate."

His gaze flitted over her face and then his expression softened just a fraction. "Why would I mind? It will be your home soon enough. You must be curious about it."

She nodded. "I am, I admit. Though I was already madly in love with it after all the weeks we've spent here preparing for the—" She cut herself off and dipped her head. Then she continued, "Still, it is different now that I know it shall be...it will be mine."

He seemed to ponder an answer to that statement, but then he merely extended an arm. "Shall I take you on a more guided excursion?"

Her lips parted at the kind suggestion. One she could not have earned. But he didn't seem to feel any kind of frustration in being forced to show her around. If anything, he looked a bit more relaxed than he normally did.

"I would very much like that, thank you." She reached for the crook of his elbow and hesitated for a moment. Once she touched him, she knew how her body would react. She only hoped she could hide it as she slid her fingers around the warmth of his hard bicep and tried to recall how to breathe again.

He guided her into the room that she had not yet entered and said, "The house has been part of our legacy for twelve earls. This lake country used to have some importance when it came to invaders and the like, thanks to its position so close to the sea. It was established, as was our line, very early."

"You must be proud of that fact," she said as she released his arm to regain purchase and walked around the parlor, looking at the decorations and furniture.

He snorted out a laugh, and she faced him to find him looking at her incredulously. "You mustn't sport with me. I know you are fully aware of the scandal that follows my family."

"As of late, I suppose there have been rumors," she said carefully. "But that doesn't erase the history of your family in total, does it?"

He seemed to ponder that a moment. "Sometimes it feels like it does."

The words, said so quietly, were definitely a glimpse into his soul and for a moment she realized just how much weight this man had to bear. He was correct that she wasn't unaware of the rumors to which he referred. His father had been a well-known libertine, his brother was whispered to be even worse. The brother had died in a duel, for heaven's sake. Over an unpaid debt of honor, so the story went.

And now Harcourt was trying to repair it all. Do the right thing. Her dowry would help him, and she felt a bit of pride in that, as well as her own responsibility to assist him if she could as their futures merged.

But for now, she saw the discomfort on his face. The expression that said he hadn't wished to share so much. And to make him more comfortable, she shifted the subject.

"You must be bored doing this again. Especially so soon after the last time," she said, and reached out to take his arm as he guided her up the hall to the next doorway. They only peeked inside to look at yet another parlor.

He glanced at her. "Last time?"

She sucked in a breath as they entered the music room. "Oh, a lovely Broadwood grand!"

He nodded. "Yes, my mother plays...or did some time ago." He frowned and she noted that. She had not talked much to Lady Harcourt. The woman was often distant and separated herself from the party. But certainly they would talk soon. "Do you play?"

"All accomplished ladies must play, or that was my father's thought on it. We all learned under the tutelage of the odious Miss Bertha Granger, who rapped knuckles when one played the wrong note."

He smiled a little. "Did it have the desired effect?"

"To make us good at it?" She shrugged. "Well, Juliana is a virtuoso, Anne despises it all and *refuses* to be any good at it, and I am somewhere in between. So mixed results."

He wrinkled his brow and then watched as she slid her fingers along the keys of the piano without pressing them. "What did you mean when you said I did this last time?" he asked.

"With Anne," she explained as she moved to the window and looked out at the estate grounds and the sea in the distance. A sense of peace overcame her, and she drew a long breath as she enjoyed the view.

"Your sister made it very clear she had no interest in my estate," he said, suddenly closer, and she turned to find he had moved on her and was now just an arm's length away. "I never gave her a tour like this."

Her lips parted. "I—oh."

"But you seem to feel differently about the place," he said, and stepped even closer to look out the window at her side. She made herself look again but the peaceful feeling fled when his body heat was curling around her and all she could feel was him.

"I have been here nearly a month," she said softly. "And I do very much love this estate. I love the sea views and the high hills. I love the house and all its hidden rooms and passageways. Anne adores London and all its excitements, and I certainly do not hate the city when I am there. But give me a country living and I could be happy all my days, I think."

"Happy all your days," he repeated, his voice suddenly rough. "Then I grant you that wish, for I also enjoy the country a great deal and am here more often than not."

She forced herself to glance up at him with a slight smile. "Well matched, then."

He was looking at her mouth now, not her eyes, and her body stirred as it had on the terrace. Only this time she had nothing to make her stop when it came to his kiss.

But he didn't kiss her. He took a long step back and said, "Perhaps you would like to see the library, though I assume you have visited there many times during your journey, as I believe you to be a great reader."

"I am," she said, trying to calm her racing heart and maintain the light interaction that seemed to make him most comfortable. "But I never resist when it comes to a library. Please lead the way."

He did so, letting her ooh and ahh over the fine room, and even made recommendations amongst the books she hadn't read before. A few more parlors and gathering spaces came next, and then he took her through a massive, carved door that led into what had to be his study, judging from the large desk facing the door and the papers and quills spread across it.

"Oh, it has a lovely view of the garden," she said as she moved to the huge picture window beside the desk.

"Yes, when I remember to glance up from my work to look at it," he said with a faint smile that faded immediately. "But I spend a great deal of time here, dealing with that scandal we discussed earlier."

"Well, you shall not be alone in it now, at least," she said, turning away from the window and leaning back against the cool glass. "As your wife, I will take on your sorrows as well as your name. Perhaps I can be of some help in alleviating the troubles."

"I'm sure you can," he muttered, his voice rough as he turned away and moved to the sideboard, where he fiddled with the bottles of liquor despite the early hour. He didn't pour anything, but she could see he wished to. Was it because the thought of marrying her was so...unpleasant?

She certainly hoped not.

She moved toward him slowly and cleared her throat. "I had a question for you, actually. Something I would very much like to address."

He faced her and sighed. "Yes, you and I have a great many conversations to share, I think, considering what will happen in a few short days. We might as well begin them now. What was on your mind? I will try to be as honest as I can be and hope you will be the same."

She bent her head at his reminder that she had not begun this at all honestly.

"It is about last night, at the party," she said, and forced herself to look at him even though she didn't want to. "And today, I suppose, too, when you found me in the hall."

He wrinkled his brow. "What about it?"

"Today you said hello to me as Thomasina and last night you claimed you knew who I was almost immediately after my entrance into the ball."

"Not almost immediately," he corrected, though not harshly. "Immediately."

She shifted. "Very well, immediately. You know I have lived my entire life being a bit of an anomaly. Everyone is always staring at us, the Shelley Triplets. A rarity, indeed. But I don't know anyone who can recognize me apart from the rest. What do you do to recognize me instantly?"

He let out a soft laugh and shook his head. "You think I have some trick that keeps you all separate."

"You must," she reasoned. "Something even those closest to us do not know."

"Thomasina," he said slowly, like he was letting her name roll around on his tongue. "I could not tell Anne from Juliana to save my life. The only one I can identify without assistance...is you. I *always* recognize you."

She stepped away as her lips parted in pure shock. He always recognized her? What did that mean? Was it a compliment or curse? The way he looked at her right now it didn't feel like a curse, that was for certain. It felt like a caress. Something sweet that connected them in a way she had never dared hope for.

But then he broke the stare and walked away, back to his desk.

She shifted, and then words fell from her mouth that she had not intended nor wished for. "Do you hate me for my part in all this, Harcourt? More to the point, will you forgive me for it?"

~

J asper stared at Thomasina, her chin lifted, her back straight as she tried to put up a front of strength and calm. But he saw her hands trembling at her sides, saw the way her breath moved short. His answer mattered to her.

He pondered the question a moment, rolling it around in his mind. Then he drew a deep breath. "The world believes me to be a very proud man," he said slowly, uncertain why he didn't give her a shorter answer, but needing to explain himself somehow. "Perhaps not in the best sense. I am considered harsh by some. Cold by most. And I suppose that I do often make a judgment on someone and then never change it. I have learned, sometimes the hard way, to believe it when someone shows me who they are through their actions."

She nodded. "Then you must think very ill of me."

Her voice cracked when she said it and her lashes fluttered down, accepting his censure before he had even given it. Once again, he found he didn't like that response. He would rather have her fight him, argue her case and her cause, than simply accept that she deserved punishment for a crime she'd only had a small part in.

"I don't," he said, a bit sharply. "Please look at me."

She did so, lifting her gaze, making him lose himself in green depths for a moment.

"I was not happy with you last night," he said. "Mostly because one thing I like about you, Thomasina, is that you seem to have more sense than most people. That you would trade places with your sister was a confusion to me. I don't like being confused, because it means I cannot read a situation, and that can be dangerous. But in the end, you thought you were doing something harmless, didn't you?"

"I thought I was helping Anne," Thomasina said with a shake of her head. "I thought if she had a night to herself, a break from all the chaos of the upcoming wedding, that perhaps it would clear her head and help her be more ready for what was to come. I certainly didn't think I was abetting her escape with...with... Honestly I don't know how to describe the man she fled with in such a cowardly fashion."

He smiled. There it was. That flash of hotter emotion, that moment of defiance of her sister. Even of him, as she explained herself.

"Yes," he said softly. "As I've thought more of what happened last night, I could see your thoughts. I could recognize that you weren't working against me, but *for* her. And I cannot fault that kind of loyalty in a sister. I wish I'd had the same in my own sibling."

He flinched as he thought of his brother Solomon, dead for almost a year. He hadn't spoken to him for a full year before that horrible day.

He never would again.

He blinked and turned away so as not to be vulnerable in front of her.

"At any rate, I don't hate you for what you did," he said, fiddling with papers on his desk.

"Thank you," she said softly, and she moved to him. She reached his side and her hand came up slowly to settle on his forearm. "I appreciate your grace in a situation where you have been wronged."

He glanced down at her hand on his body and wished for a wild moment that it were on his bare skin. He heard the catch of her breath and lifted his stare to her face. Her gaze was a little unfocused now. Unsteady with desire she likely didn't fully understand.

Desire he very much wanted to cultivate.

"Perhaps it all worked out for the better anyway," he murmured.

She licked her lips and his groin tightened with increasing need. Damn, but she was a temptress without even knowing it. And in less than one week she would be his, body and soul. He could drown in her if he wanted to, use her to forget his troubles.

He shook his head at that. Christ, he sounded like his father or his brother. Pleasure had always been first to them. Over duty. Over decency. He couldn't allow that, no matter how much he wanted this woman.

He stepped away from her and broke the contact. "There is only one thing I demand from you going forward," he said as he settled into his chair and looked up at her.

There was no mistaking the flash of hurt that he'd pulled away, but she erased it from her face quickly enough. "And that is?"

He leaned forward. "Do not lie to me again, Thomasina."

She considered that a moment, then nodded. "I won't. And I hope I can expect the same from you. This is not the match you wanted, Harcourt...*Jasper*."

His breath caught, for that was the first time she's said his given name. Now it hit him in the gut like a punch and made that wanting, that out-of-control longing, all the stronger.

"I know this isn't your choice," she continued, oblivious to his reaction. "But if we can be honest with each other, I hope it will not be one you regret."

He jerked out a nod and then dropped his gaze to his work. "I realize we did not finish our tour, but I should probably focus on this now. Perhaps we can reconvene at a later date and continue. After all, there is no rush."

He glanced up and saw her lips purse a fraction. Once again, though, she shoved whatever her reaction was aside and nodded. "I understand. But I do have one thing to ask you before I leave you to your business."

His eyebrows lifted. "Very well, ask away."

"My sister," she said, worrying her hands in front of her suddenly. "I know she has done nothing to deserve your help or protection, but I am very worried about her running off with some stranger we know nothing about. Are you planning to do anything to help find her?"

He saw her true terror and couldn't help but empathize. With his own brother, he had started off the same way, wanting to help him. In time, he had learned Solomon didn't want or need his help. But Thomasina didn't see it that way when it came to Anne. She still had the capacity to care.

And in truth, he had his own questions about Anne's escape and the person she had run away with. He'd been mulling over her letter all night, thinking about every word choice. If she had met this Ellis person here in Harcourt, it seemed like a coincidence, indeed. He didn't believe in those. Especially when that name...*Ellis*...seemed so damned familiar to him.

Yet he wasn't ready to share that with Thomasina. If Anne's lover had something to do with him or, God forbid, his late brother or father's bad dealings, he needed to find that out without her interference.

"I will think about it," he said, ducking his head so his message for her to go would be clear. "Good morning, Thomasina."

Her mouth opened and shut, and for a moment he thought she might push. But instead she went to the door and hesitated there, watching him for what felt like an eternity before she finally whispered, "Good day, my lord."

Then she was gone and he flopped back against his chair with a long exhalation of breath he hadn't realized he'd been holding. He got up, going to the door she had just exited. He could smell her perfume there, some intoxicating combination of oranges and honeysuckle.

He tugged the bell, and in a moment his butler, Willard, appeared. "May I help you, my lord?"

"Is Reynolds on the estate?" he asked, returning to his desk.

Willard nodded. "Yes, sir. I believe he was dealing with some of the issues regarding the special license."

Jasper barely kept himself from flinching. He had reached out to several staff members early in the morning, including his man of affairs, Reynolds, about the shocking change to his engagement status. Still, he hated that the news was circulating in the staff already.

Scandal was his constant companion, he feared.

"Should I fetch him?" Willard asked blandly, seemingly unaware of Jasper's heightened state.

"Please."

The butler left and Jasper paced the room. His mind was racing, bouncing from topic to topic and returning often to Thomasina and their uncertain future.

"You wanted to see me, Harcourt?"

He turned and forced a smile for his man-of-affairs. Reynolds had been a friend to him for years, long before he had inherited. Reynolds was a little more than a decade older than Jasper, and had seen far more in the world thanks to his time serving in His Majesty's Navy. He was the man Jasper trusted most.

"How go the preparations for the special license?" he asked.

"I only started a few hours ago," Reynolds said with a bemused smile. "But your influence and Shelley's money will get you what you desire, I'm certain."

"And the talk?" he asked, this time softer.

Reynolds shrugged. "Not very loud for now. But as I inquire more and the servants begin to whisper…"

"Of course," Jasper said with a shake of his head. "That blasted woman will cause me nothing but trouble. In truth, I'm pleased to make the trade with her sister for my bride. Thomasina and I seem better matched."

Reynolds cocked his head. "You've certainly talked about the younger triplet more since your engagement."

Jasper pushed to his feet and paced away from the smirk of his longtime friend and employee. "You are being ridiculous. At any rate, *that* isn't why I asked you to join me. I didn't share with you the contents of the note Miss Anne left her sister before she fled me like I was a monster at her heels. I would like to do so now."

Reynolds shrugged. "Very well."

"She ran off with a man with the name of Ellis. I do not know for certain if it is a first or last name. But I keep coming back to it. It is so familiar. And I have begun to fear that her finding a…well, I hesitate to call him a gentleman…but a man willing to thwart her very public engagement to be rather suspicious."

"You are always suspicious of something," Reynolds drawled.

Jasper pursed his lips. "The world has given me a great many reasons to be so. At any rate, do *you* have any theories as to why that name rings in my head?"

Reynolds paced the room, and Jasper watched as his mind spun on the question. The man had a memory like no one he'd ever known. "Wharton Ellis is the shopkeep near your London estate," Reynolds began.

"No, I doubt *that* is who my until recently intended ran away with," he said with a chuckle as he thought of the ancient shopkeep with a wife of over sixty years and a gaggle of beloved children and grandchildren.

"Ellis Crowley owned an inn you stayed in once in Scotland."

"We're reaching, I think," he said.

Another hesitation as Reynolds continued his search of memory. Then his eyes widened. "Wait. Wait."

"What? You thought of something?"

"What was the name of your brother's second in the duel that—" Reynolds cut himself off, and Jasper flinched.

"The duel that took his life?" he asked, as if there were another. "Maitland, I think. Er…oh God. *Ellis* Maitland."

Reynolds nodded. "He had a bad feel to him when he came to tell you about the particulars of the previous earl's death."

"He did at that." It was Jasper who paced the room now, fisting his hands at his sides. "I knew my brother had involved himself in far worse than mere reckless gambling and carousing when I met Maitland. But I paid him for his support of Solomon."

"Far more than I thought the man deserved," Reynolds said.

"Perhaps, but I hoped it would silence him on spreading rumor and innuendo. Also so he would not return." He ran a hand through his hair. "Christ."

Reynolds shook his head. "You know, he was asking so many *odd* questions when I had him come back to your London home for the payment delivery a week or so later."

"He was?" Jasper asked, spinning on him. "About what?"

"Something about your brother's travels. About any furnishings or knickknacks you wanted to rid yourself of, especially any new ones."

"Why didn't you tell me?"

Reynolds shrugged. "Because it is my duty to keep those kinds of silly questions out of your sightline. You were managing a great deal as you took over the title, and I knew you wouldn't be interested in selling off wares to a man like that. Had you spoken to me about wanting to get rid of things, I'm sure I would have brought it up, but you were storing most of the previous earl's items."

"Yes, here, actually," Jasper said.

"And if it is Maitland who Anne ran away with, that means the same man showed up here," Reynolds said. "It seems like quite a coincidence, as you said."

"Do you think he wanted something of Solomon's?" Jasper asked, the sick feeling in his stomach rising.

"Perhaps," Reynold's said. "It's possible, of course."

Jasper ran a hand through his hair as he thought of Thomasina and her worry over Anne. Now he felt the same concern for his former fiancée, whether he was angry with her or not. "And instead he very well could have found Anne. If she has involved herself with—"

Reynolds held up a hand. "Now wait. We have no idea if *her* Ellis is the same as your brother's second, do we?"

Jasper drew in what he wished was a more calming breath. "I suppose not."

"Ellis is common enough as both a first and last name, as we have already determined by my little exercise trying to recall where you knew it." Reynold's reached out and placed a hand on Jasper's shoulder. He gave a squeeze. "Let me make inquiries. I'll find out if Maitland is even in the area. If he isn't, then your fears can be assuaged."

"Yes," Jasper said, though his racing heart didn't calm as he pondered the horrible possibility that his brother's history had once again come to destroy Jasper's future. "I would appreciate that, thank you."

"And I will be discreet as I can be about it, of course," Reynolds said as he got up and made for the door.

Jasper laughed even though there was nothing funny about the entire situation. "You can try, my friend. But this is all a powder keg now and someone has already lit the match. An explosion is imminent. I will just have to bear it."

Reynolds' concern was clear, but he inclined his head and exited the room to begin his investigation. And as he left, Jasper immediately rested his head in his hands.

There was nothing left to do now but wait. Because that was his life. Waiting and reacting to whatever terrible turn came next on the road of a life that was never meant to be his. Including the bride who would take his name in a few short days.

CHAPTER 6

It was early evening when Jasper stepped into the parlor where he had first found Thomasina that morning. He stared around the room, recalling how she had stood just there looking at that miniature or smiled at him from that place by the fire. It was odd how he already associated her with his home, that he was already making memories of her in this space.

Probably foolish of him, considering their circumstances.

Ones he was sharply reminded of when Thomasina's father entered the parlor behind him with a wide smile.

"Good evening, my lord!" he said with a jolly laugh like all was right with the world. Jasper supposed it was, after all. Shelley was in no worse a position aside from the loss of Anne. A fact that didn't seem to bother him as much as it did Thomasina and Juliana.

"Mr. Shelley," Jasper said with much more coldness. "You have the paperwork, I assume?"

Shelley produced a pile of folded sheets from the inside pocket of his jacket and motioned Jasper to join him at the sideboard, where a servant had left quills and ink for the very duty they were about to perform.

Jasper looked over his shoulder. "Thomasina won't be joining us?" he asked.

Shelley laughed. "Why would she? Anne didn't join us the first time."

Jasper pursed his lips. "Perhaps if she had, her hesitations would have been clearer and we could have avoided all this nonsense."

Shelley shrugged. "In the end you have not made a bad trade, you know. Thomasina is much more biddable and pleasing than Anne."

Jasper clenched the pen tighter as he swirled his name into the marriage agreement. Nothing had changed from the original document save Thomasina's name. The settlements were the same, which was all that mattered.

Or should have been.

He straightened up as he watched Shelley join his name to Jasper's on the paperwork.

"Why not offer Thomasina first if you believed her to be more agreeable?" he asked. "Or was it to prevent your wild child from ruining all your other options?"

At that, Shelley glanced up at him, and then he shrugged once again, as if he had put little thought into the matter. As if the young women were substitutable, even if they had different personalities.

That their father would think so was...disappointing. Heartbreaking. There was no wonder Thomasina seemed driven to please. To make peace. It was a survival technique and Jasper understood those, even if his own was far different.

"Thomasina is shyer than her sisters, more uncertain of herself," Shelley explained. "And Juliana runs my household, so I would not wish to give her up until the very last moment possible. Anne seemed the best option for your bargain of the three and now it is Thomasina who fits the bill."

"Are they so interchangeable to you?" Jasper asked, stepping back from his future father-in-law with a scowl.

Shelley's smile faded a fraction. "You ought not to talk, my lord.

After all, you did not recognize that Thomasina was taking Anne's place any more than anyone else in that room did, including me."

Jasper set his teeth and growled, "Actually, I did. I realized it was Thomasina the moment she stepped into the room last night. I honestly do not know how anyone could mistake her for Anne. She moves differently, she tilts her head differently, she carries herself completely differently."

"Made a study of my youngest, have you?" Shelley said, his brow arching. "And found yourself differences where I assure you none exist. But those feelings do tell me that you are not entirely unhappy with your change in circumstances. If you are trying to pretend upset in order to extract something extra from me, I will not negotiate. You are getting a fine settlement and a bride of the Shelley fortune, and *that* is what you asked for from the beginning."

Jasper wrinkled his brow. The man was truly only about the business being done. His daughters could have been prized horses or barrels of whisky to be traded and he would have had the same disregard. And every time he saw that, Jasper couldn't help but think of his own family. His father overly emotional, his brother driven by passion.

At least he'd known they cared enough to fight, whether it was physically or for something that mattered. He'd never really appreciated that fact until now.

But he pushed it all away and forced his strong reactions down deep where Shelley wouldn't see them. Where they wouldn't distract from the reality of Jasper's situation.

He extended a hand reluctantly. "I am not trying to renegotiate, sir, I assure you. Our documents are signed, at any rate. And my man Reynolds has informed me that the special license will be ready for us before the wedding on Saturday."

Shelley seemed satisfied and shook Jasper's hand firmly. "Excellent."

"I assume you plan to send someone to Gretna Green after Anne," he said.

Shelley wrinkled his brow. "Why?"

Jasper stared at him a moment. "Because she's run off with some unknown man, a potential villain. Don't you want to know her whereabouts? If she reached her destination? If she wed as she thought she would?"

Shelley shrugged. "I'm sure she did, for that was the plan and Anne has a way of getting what she wants. The gentleman may not be as elevated as I hoped for her, but I'm certain we'll determine his credentials soon enough when she returns with him."

"You're so certain she *will* return?" Jasper asked.

Shelley nodded. "Of course. She and the new husband will no doubt want to convince me that she still deserves her part of the dowry settlements."

"You think this is all about the money for her, for this man, and that doesn't trouble you?"

"Why? Money makes the world go 'round, after all." Shelley glanced over his shoulder, not a care in the world. "I would like to have a moment before supper, so I shall leave you. Good evening."

"Good evening," Jasper muttered, troubled by the lack of concern the man showed. But perhaps he was right that Anne would make her return, a new husband in tow, soon enough.

He pushed those thoughts away, and the thoughts of Thomasina's true terror when it came to Anne's safety, and turned toward the still-drying contracts. He would have Reynolds collect them in a while and then it would all be finished. His future locked, once again, in stone.

He was about to turn and leave the room when Willard stepped into the parlor. "I'm sorry to disturb, my lord, but you have had a missive delivered and the messenger said to convey its importance to you."

He held out a folded sheet of cheap vellum, and Jasper found his heart leapt at the look. This was about this Ellis person. This was about Anne. He knew it before he took the letter.

"Thank you," he managed to mutter as he turned the message in his hand. "Tell Reynolds to join me as soon as he can. And close the door, please."

Willard nodded and did as Jasper had asked. Once he was alone, Jasper turned the note over and looked at the seal. Cheap black wax held the pages shut, with an image of a man's fine profile on the seal. He wrinkled his brow at the strange calling card and broke the wax.

There were no more than a dozen words slashed across the sheet in a wild hand. He read each one over and over, his heart sinking. He heard the door open behind him and held the letter toward the intruder without even waiting to see if it was Reynolds there to greet him.

"It *is* Ellis Maitland," he said softly, his fears about Anne's whereabouts as strong as ever.

Reynolds groaned, and the rustle of papers made Jasper straighten his shoulders.

"Make the horses ready when you've read that enough times for it to sink in. We have a meeting with this man in the morning over in Beckfoot, and I want to get there tonight to try to discover just what the hell is going on. And maybe, just maybe, get a leg up on the bastard."

~

Thomasina stepped into the parlor where the families were to meet for their pre-supper drinks and small, private "celebration" of the new engagement. But she found there was no one in the room yet save for Lady Harcourt.

Jasper's mother stood beside the window, staring out at black nothingness as she ran a finger along the edge of her glass. Thomasina's heart leapt. She hadn't spoken much to the woman since her arrival here. Lady Harcourt was more taciturn than even her son and Thomasina had never been able to read her. Anne had simply been terrified of her, going on and on about how cold and disconnected she was.

For a moment, Thomasina considered bolting from the room and not coming back until she had the support of someone, *anyone*, else.

"No," she whispered to herself, and forced her shoulders back in an attempt to be braver than she was. "Good evening, my lady," she said in what she hoped was a breezy, friendly tone as she swept into the room and toward her future mother-in-law.

If she had hoped to garner as welcoming a response, she was immediately disappointed. Lady Harcourt turned and gave her a bored look with flat, empty eyes. "Which one are you?" she asked.

Thomasina swallowed hard and shifted with discomfort. "I am Thomasina, my lady. Your son's newly intended."

Lady Harcourt made a little sound in her throat and returned her gaze to the window. "Very well. Good evening, Miss Thomasina."

"How are you tonight?" she asked, continuing to force herself into an attempt at polite conversation.

"Tolerable," Lady Harcourt said without looking at her.

Thomasina clenched her hands at her sides. "Wasn't the weather lovely today? With all the rain recently—"

Lady Harcourt pivoted on her, those dark eyes spearing her again. "I have no desire to prattle on about the weather with you, foolish girl. If you are trying to make some kind of good impression on me because I am your future mother-in-law, then let me be frank with you. I don't care about your marriage to my son except for the dowry it will provide our house. Honestly, I assume he doesn't care either since he switched between the two of you so easily."

Thomasina took a long step back. "I-I am sorry, my lady."

"All I want from your match is for you to exercise more self-control than your terrible sister did. I have borne enough whispers in my life. If you can manage not to bring even more scandal to our family, then you and I will have nothing further to say to each other."

Thomasina swallowed past the lump in her throat at such bluntness, at the edge of cruelty and dismissal this woman portrayed. She did not cry, though, which she congratulated herself for. She had a feeling that would only set off this woman even more.

"I do beg your pardon," she whispered as she backed toward the door. "I understand you perfectly, and I assure you I will do my best to bring no shame to your family once the wedding has been held. Good evening."

She pivoted and ran from the room, blindly seeking a refuge where she could have a moment. She'd never believed she would encounter such coldness from a woman she didn't even know. And if she had felt its underlying cause was some protectiveness of Jasper, she might have understood it and even respected it given the circumstances.

But it didn't seem Lady Harcourt cared for her son more than anything else. She couched her concerns about the marriage in terms of scandal, not Jasper's happiness or comfort.

And for a moment, Thomasina's heart swelled for him. Was that how his mother behaved with him too? She rarely saw them interact, after all. It seemed he was utterly alone in the world.

She was about to go upstairs, to seek out Juliana for a discussion on the subject, when she heard Jasper's voice in the foyer. She moved toward it, toward him, and stopped at the edge of the circular entryway to the home.

"Reynolds will take care of those arrangements," he was saying to Willard as he pulled his gloves over his hands. "I assume we will be back by supper tomorrow. I will try to send word if that changes."

"Back?" Thomasina said, stepping forward.

Willard and Jasper exchanged a brief look, and then the butler inclined his head. "I will do as you say, my lord. Safe travels."

He exited the foyer and Jasper took a long step toward her, his dark eyes as blank as his mother's had been a few moments ago. She shrank from that similarity, the ability to feel nothing that she certainly didn't share. Sometimes it seemed she felt everything.

"Eavesdropping?" he asked, though there was no coldness to his tone.

She shook her head. "No, my lord. I was passing by and overheard you speaking. It is not the same thing."

"No," he agreed. "I suppose not."

"You are leaving?" she asked.

His gaze darted from hers, and her stomach immediately clenched at the break of their connection. "I am," he said. "Business has called me away, but only to a town not too far from here. We will arrive very late tonight. My business is to be conducted there tomorrow morning and then we will return, assuming my meeting doesn't require me to stay another day."

She stared at him as he recited these facts swiftly and with no particular inflection.

"What kind of business takes you away just five days before your wedding? And if you are delayed, what will happen then? Unless this is your way to repay me for my part in Anne's escape, by running away from me?"

His lips parted and he stared at her a moment, then he surprised her by holding out his arm to her. "Why don't you walk with me to the stables where my man is preparing our horses?"

She drew back and stared at him a moment. His expression had softened somewhat and he no longer looked so severe or cut off.

"Very well," she said, and touched his arm, just folding her fingers into the crook of it. How she hated herself for how strongly she reacted to that simple act. How much she noticed the heat of him and the hardness and the scent of sandalwood from his shaving soap.

How she hated that this touch moved her, when it clearly did nothing for him. She was an exchangeable piece of his plan, just as his mother had said earlier.

She shook her thoughts away as he led her from the front door and down around the house to a long path that led to the stables in the distance. They were silent a few steps, almost companionable except for her racing thoughts.

Then he said, "I would never abandon you, Thomasina. I recognize you don't know me well, but I honor my obligations. Certainly, I would not create a bigger scandal either for you or for myself."

She supposed those words were meant to comfort her, but they yet again reminded her of that utterly unpleasant encounter in the parlor a few moments before.

"Yes, your mother made it clear that you both abhor scandal."

They were almost to the stable now and Jasper stopped in the path, releasing her and running a hand through his hair. The action mussed the usually perfect dark blond locks and gave him a rather rakish look. His frown, however, was not rakish. "You encountered my mother," he said. "Alone, I assume?"

She nodded. "I found her in the parlor before supper."

He shook his head. "May I guess from your tone and expression that Lady Harcourt was cold as ice and cruel as a blade?"

She flinched and turned her face. "I-I—"

"We won't lie to each other, remember?" he said, and now he reached out and took her hand. Her bare fingers rested against the black of his leather riding gloves, and she shivered as he stroked his thumb against the webbing between her thumb and first finger.

"She was not kind," she admitted at last.

He let out his breath. "Well, she can be unkind, yes. I would give you some excuse that she has had a difficult life and that is how she handles herself. But it sounds very flat, I think."

"How do *you* handle yourself?" she asked.

The moonlight flickered off his face and she saw the surprise at her question. He stepped a little closer and tilted his head to look at her. Reading her. Judging her.

"I'm not sure I handle myself very well, Thomasina."

She wrinkled her brow at the suddenly sad tone to his voice and the expression of it in his eyes. That he was hurting truly surprised her somehow. He so often portrayed such an icy exterior that to see there was a heart beneath it gave her hope. Earned or not.

He lifted his other hand, and suddenly the leather-clad fingers were sliding along her jaw. He tilted her face up and she obeyed, mostly because she could scarcely breathe when he looked at her that way. The same way as the terrace. The same way as the parlor. Like he wanted her. Not just any Shelley sister and the dowry that came with her. *Her.*

"When I return," he said, his voice suddenly low and hypnotic and rough. "I want to discuss our marriage with you."

"The wedding plans," she said, shocked that she could find enough air to make words. "Yes, of course."

He leaned in, closer and closer, and her eyelids fluttered shut as his breath stirred her lips. Then his mouth was on her at last, the culmination of what felt like such a long time of waiting. The pressure was gentle but persistent, and she gripped her fingers against his forearms as she leaned into him and his kiss.

He gave a little shudder and then his lips parted, his tongue tasting the crease of her mouth and forcing her to open to him. Which, of course, she did. He drew her tighter against his chest, the kiss deepening and sharpening until the only thing that mattered in Thomasina's world was his lips on hers and his arms around her.

And in that moment, he broke away. He was a little breathless as he said, "No, Thomasina, not the wedding plans. I want to talk to you about our marriage. And what we will both desire it to be."

Her lips parted at that unexpected statement. Then she nodded. "Goodbye, Jasper."

"Goodbye," he repeated, then released her and walked away without looking back.

CHAPTER 7

Beckfoot was certainly not the worst town Jasper had ever been in, but it was far from the best. The comings and goings of the small boats and larger crafts, moving goods and people back and forth to Scotland, sometimes surreptitiously, made it a transient place. And transient places were sometimes rougher than others, for no one had much to lose.

Jasper sat at a rundown tavern just beside the small docks that ran along the western edge of the city and nursed an ale as his thoughts turned, rather dangerously, to Thomasina and the kiss they had shared the previous night.

He'd thought of her almost constantly since then, a thud in the back of his head that kept bringing him back to her taste and her smell and the sound of her sharp intake of breath when his mouth met hers.

He shook away the memories and refocused on matters at hand. He was supposed to meet with Ellis Maitland here at any moment. Reynolds sat just a few tables away, slouched down with his face covered by a low-brimmed hat, watching for any trouble, so he wasn't utterly alone. But Jasper knew there was no safety in a wandering mind.

Especially considering what they'd discovered about Maitland since their arrival the night before. There was no doubt he was the one who had seduced and taken Anne. Several people had recognized her description and mentioned she was with a man named Maitland. The previous morning he had put her on a small boat with another person and then disappeared into the town. No one could say much about his movements since.

Jasper glanced toward the door and straightened to full attention as the man himself stepped in. Ellis Maitland. It was *definitely* the same one who had come to him a year ago to report that his brother had been killed in a duel. At the time, Maitland had put on a good show, expressing what had seemed like genuine empathy, giving details with even a glitter of tears in his eyes.

Now there was none of that. Maitland had a confident expression as he sauntered into the bar. Like a cat who'd gotten into cream and didn't give a damn if everyone knew his triumph.

Maitland was a handsome man, no one could deny that, with broad shoulders, longish dark hair and a dimple in his cheek when he smiled, which he did at Jasper. Jasper didn't return the expression as he slowly got to his feet.

"Mr. Maitland," he drawled, ignoring Maitland's outstretched hand of greeting. "I never thought I'd see you again. I certainly never thought I'd hear you stole my fiancée and spirited her away to God knows where."

Maitland flopped himself into the seat across from the one Jasper had abandoned. "I would wager you didn't, Harcourt. Funny where life takes us."

Jasper fought the urge to simply pummel this man and sat down. Punching him was what Solomon would have done, all emotion and no reason. Jasper had to be better.

As much as it pained him.

"You have some explaining to do, Maitland," he growled. "Start talking. I have no time for foolish games."

"And I have less than you do," Maitland snapped and the smile fell away and revealed the hardened man beneath.

"Then tell me why. Why have you done this and what do you want?"

"Your brother and I went a long way back," he said, motioning for a barmaid. "Your best whisky, darlin'. It's on the gentleman." He winked at Jasper as he sent her on her way. "I mean, you must have discovered some of his...less savory interests since he..." There was a beat's hesitation. "Since you buried him."

Jasper pursed his lips, for this subject was a sore one, indeed. Yes, he knew his brother gambled in hells of the worst kind, that he smuggled goods against his own country, that he invested in ridiculous schemes, including a tunnel under the Thames four years before, which had turned out to be some kind of underhanded way for him to hide money he'd gotten from an unnamed source. In the end, the tunnel had truly collapsed, though, and Solomon had lost it all, along with several of the diggers.

Jasper's brother had been a fool and a sometime villain, and now his friendship with the man sitting across from Jasper came into sharper focus.

Jasper despised Maitland for that. For casting a harsh light on the shadows he tried his best to ignore.

"So, you were friends," he said with a shrug that didn't reflect his feelings on the matter whatsoever. "What the hell does that have to do with Anne or with me?"

"He owed me something," Maitland said, glancing up as the barmaid brought his whisky. He took a long slug and motioned for her to bring another before he continued, "He owed me more than *you* could ever imagine."

"You were settled nicely for your help with my brother," Jasper said. "I now question that decision."

"I'm sure you do." Maitland shifted, almost as if he was uncomfortable. "But I want something else."

"And what is that?"

Maitland looked at him speculatively. "Your brother took something of mine before he died."

Jasper flinched and shoved down the riot of emotions that rose up in him at that statement.

"There isn't enough cash in your coffers to make up for it," Maitland continued. "I *need* it back, and Anne is my...she's my way to make certain that you take me seriously and work very hard to find what I want."

"Took something of yours?" Jasper said, and thought of Reynolds' words about Maitland wanting to take any objects Solomon left behind. Had he been looking for this mysterious item even then?

Maitland leaned closer and a glint of desperation entered his stare at Jasper's confusion. "Don't play like you don't know, for I'm certain you must have come up with some record by now. Your brother took a treasure that...it doesn't matter what or why."

"Treasure," Jasper repeated, and almost laughed but for the danger of this situation. "I assure you, Mr. Maitland, I know nothing about a treasure. If I did, I wouldn't be in the very public position that I am now."

Maitland's jaw set and his fist flexed on the table. It took a moment for him to respond, like he was trying to rein in his emotion. "That is a very sad story for you, my lord, because you see, I will not return your Anne to you until you get me what your brother stole from me."

Jasper shifted. He had to play this very carefully. If Anne was near this man—which by all accounts she had been, though not now —she was in danger. Whoever Maitland's associates were, they could be no better. Right now Maitland felt she had value.

But if the bastard thought she didn't, then perhaps he would release her.

"You needn't give her back," Jasper said carefully, and tried not to flinch as he thought of what Thomasina would say about his cold dismissal of her beloved sister. She would hate him, even if he tried to explain why he was doing this.

"What?" Maitland's mouth dropped open in shock and for the first time his confidence in his plan seemed to falter.

"Keep her," Jasper clarified. "You see, she has no value to me. I am marrying someone else, one of her sisters. I never cared about her—I care about her family fortune. So *you* may keep her."

Maitland stared for a moment, seemingly stunned by this turn of events. Then he shook his head. "You're more of a bastard than Solomon was. Who would have thought that was possible?"

Jasper held steady, although his stomach turned. "Perhaps that is true. And so is this: I don't know a damned thing about a treasure. If my brother had it, he likely got rid of it one of his drunken nights when he didn't know his head from his ass."

Maitland lunged to his feet, flipping his chair back in the process and causing every head in the bar to turn toward him. Slowly, Jasper got to his feet too, readying himself for attack even as he flicked his wrist at Reynolds to keep him away. He didn't want the interference. Not yet.

"You'd best rethink your position, my lord," Maitland hissed. "Because you might not give a damn about Anne Shelley, but if you force my hand I will have to find a pressure point that *will* matter to you. You can bet your life on that."

He pivoted and stormed out of the bar. Reynolds shot Jasper a look and hurried after their foe as Jasper righted Maitland's abandoned seat and sank back into his own chair with a long sigh. That had gone badly and now he had more questions than ever. And more fears when it came to Anne.

He sat for half an hour watching the door, waiting for Reynolds. When his man of affairs returned to the bar, Jasper almost sagged in relief. Reynolds took the seat Maitland had left and met his eyes. He shook his head slightly.

"Gone, eh?" Jasper said. "You couldn't track him?"

"Just for a bit," Reynolds said softly, apology in his stare. "I think he knew I was tailing him. He disappeared into a crowd and then he was smoke on the wind."

Jasper scrubbed a hand over his face. "He won't be found again unless he wishes to be, I'd wager. My brother involved himself with a much more dangerous set than I gave him credit for."

"I think that might be true. Did Maitland give you any clues about Anne's whereabouts?"

Jasper's heart sank. "No. I tried to persuade him that she meant nothing to me and couldn't be used as a bargaining chip. Hopefully he'll abandon his plot for her and allow her to escape. My stomach turns at the idea that he could...he could hurt her."

Reynolds nodded slowly. "It is a possibility. But we know she's not with him right now—she got sent off in a boat with someone else. Let me do some research here, send some resources to Scotland and track them if I can."

Jasper swallowed. "Yes. Do that. I must do everything I can to find her. She's only endangered because of me. And Thomasina is..." He trailed off as he thought of the fear in his new fiancée's eyes every time she considered her sister's fate.

Reynolds gave him a strange look but said, "I will do everything in my power to discover her and return her if I can, my lord."

"Then I will go home," Jasper said as he got up and tossed some blunt on the table for the barmaid. "And marry the woman whose fortune will pay for it all. Like the fucking bastard that I am."

Reynolds' forehead wrinkled at that statement and he cocked his head. "You weren't the bastard in this, Harcourt," he said softly. "You're just trying to clean up his mess."

Jasper bent his head because for a moment an image of his brother popped into his mind. Not as a thirty-year-old wastrel Jasper had come to resent, but as an eight-year-old with a crooked smile and a fishing pole. The older half-brother who had taught Jasper to climb a tree and do a cartwheel.

He shook those thoughts away and cleared his throat as he

regained his composure. "Keep me apprised of anything you discover," he said. "I will head back now."

Reynolds nodded, the pity clear on his face. "Very good, my lord. I will keep you informed of anything I hear."

They left the bar together. Reynolds headed up the street after their goodbyes, and Jasper made his way to the man who was holding their horses. But as he swung up on Ember and urged her in the direction of home, his mind wandered. This time not to his brother, but to Thomasina, waiting for him back in Harcourt Heights. To all he would have to conceal from her to protect her from the nonsense his brother had created.

And to the fact that seeing her was all he wanted to do right now.

∽

Thomasina flicked the tines of her fork across the beef filet once more, breaking up the fibers halfheartedly as she glanced up the table to the very empty seat at the head of it. Jasper's seat.

Jasper, who had left last night and promised to return just before he kissed her senseless. And yet she felt a powerful fear at the sight of that empty chair. And at her memories of his haunted expression as he rode away from her.

"You are so forlorn, Thomasina," her father said with a chuckle. "Seems I have made you a love match after all. I suppose you will thank me for it."

Juliana huffed out her breath and Lady Harcourt glanced up from her plate with a frown. Heat flooded Thomasina's cheeks at her father's uncouth comment and she balled her napkin in her lap.

"Not at all, Father," she said. Lied. He wasn't wrong about the forlorn part, after all. "I am simply tired after all the excitement of the last few days. Might I beg off the rest of supper?"

He blinked at her. "You want to leave in the middle of supper?" he blustered. "Did I not raise you better?"

"Doubtful," Lady Harcourt said into her glass, loud enough that Thomasina couldn't doubt she wished to be heard. Her future mother-in-law seemed to teeter between complete disconnection and abject disdain when it came to her.

And that only made her churning stomach even more unsteady. She glanced at Juliana and found her older sister watching her carefully. For a moment that unspoken connection felt very strong, that bond of a long-ago shared womb that had always united she and her two sisters. How she missed Anne in that moment and her smiles and unspoken jokes.

Juliana smiled at her gently. "Let her go, Papa," she said, using that tone she always used to soothe him when he was angry or frustrated with one of her sisters. "She will have little opportunity to herself once Lord Harcourt returns from his errand. You cannot begrudge her an early evening when she will be solving so many of your own problems in just a few days."

For a moment their father seemed to consider that logic, then he shrugged. "Go then, daughter. Go read in your bed by candlelight. Your eyesight will not be my problem once Harcourt takes your hand. Go on."

Thomasina cast a quick smile to Juliana and one to her father. Then she nodded toward Lady Harcourt. "My deepest apologies, my lady," she said softly. "I hope I will be in a better humor tomorrow."

Lady Harcourt arched a brow. "As long as you do not humiliate us on Saturday as your sister did, I really do not care."

That elicited a small gasp from Juliana and even Mr. Shelley jerked his head up at the rude comment. But somehow Thomasina managed to blink back tears at the set down and exited the room. Once she was out of anyone's view, she rushed up the stairs like the very hounds of hell were on her heels and scurried into her chamber. She slammed the door behind her, turning to lean her forehead on the cool surface as she tried to calm her suddenly racing heart.

She stretched her fingers against the wood to bring feeling back into them and then looked up at the bell pull. She needed to ring it, to bring her maid Ruby to help her get ready for bed.

"I don't want to see anyone," she whispered.

"Even me?"

She started at the deep voice that came from the shadows behind her and pivoted to find Jasper standing at her dressing room door, watching her.

She moved a few steps toward him before she stopped herself. He didn't want her to throw herself into his arms. Even though that was just what she wanted to do right now.

"My lord," she gasped, lifting her hands to her chest so she wouldn't do something as foolish as reach for him. "You are here."

"I am here," he repeated softly, and entered her room in one long step, closing the dressing room door behind himself and shutting them into what now felt like a very small chamber. He looked around. "Had I known your sister was going to act a fool, I would have given *you* the biggest chamber of the three connected ones."

Thomasina found herself smiling a fraction despite her continued shock that he was in her bedchamber. And he was looking at her bed, then her, with an expression she couldn't read. It didn't seem angry or accusatory, though. If anything, he looked...he looked lost. He looked sad.

Her heart ached for him.

"How was your excursion?" she asked.

To her surprise, that sadness in his gaze deepened before he jerked it away and hardened himself to her inquiry, locking her out from what she'd seen. But she couldn't unsee it. Jasper Kincaid, Earl of Harcourt, had something lurking beneath the surface, something broken that called to her. That made her want to smooth the line of his frown away. That made her want to help him.

"I don't want to speak about that," he said, his voice rougher.

She shifted at the tactic being used to put her off. And at the questions she continued to have. But they could wait.

"And why are you in my chamber?" she asked, her breath coming short. "Instead of joining the rest of the family for supper upon your return?"

He looked at her again, his eyes trailing over her slowly, with a heat she didn't fully understand but that created an answering clench in every muscle in her body. That made her ache in very inappropriate places. That made her want more of his kiss, as she had been dreaming of since he left her the night before.

"I don't know," he whispered. His voice cracked a fraction. "I don't know why I'm here, but I-I needed to be here. In your room. With you, alone. Even though I shouldn't. Even though it's wrong. It goes against everything I'm trying to…"

He broke off and shook his head. "So I must ask you, since you might have more sense than I do in this moment. Do you want me to leave, Thomasina?"

CHAPTER 8

Thomasina couldn't breathe as she stared up into Jasper's face. His expression had changed again in the firelight and now he wasn't hiding what he felt. It was written in every line of his mouth and eyes. The same expression that had been written on that beautiful face before he kissed her.

He wanted her, somehow. Wanted to touch her just as she longed for him to do the same. He was asking her to give him a reason to walk away. To go back to propriety. But in this moment, she wasn't strong enough to save them from themselves.

"I don't want you to leave," she whispered.

He let out a shaky breath and nodded. "Very well. But before we...we proceed, I do want to talk to you about something."

She swallowed hard, her uncertainty filling her throat with a lump that she could barely speak beyond. "Then do so. We promised we would be honest with each other, Jasper. I know that is important."

His gaze flitted away at that statement and he fiddled with a loose thread at his wrist before he said, "I mentioned to you before I left that we needed to have a conversation about our marriage. It would be best to do this now before…before anything else clouds both our judgment."

She shifted a little. "I have thought about that statement quite a bit since yesterday, but I'm not certain what to say on the subject. After all, I've never been married, so I don't know the kinds of expectations you might have of me. I will try to be a good countess, of course. It isn't something I specifically prepared for, but my father always hoped for good matches for all his daughters, so I know about running a household."

He shifted, and she thought she heard him curse beneath his breath as he turned away and paced off toward the window. He looked out for a moment and then said, "I don't doubt you are more than capable of being a fine countess, Thomasina. You have already been kind and thoughtful toward my tenants and my staff during your time here. It isn't those sorts of things to which I refer."

She tilted her head. He seemed very uncomfortable but she couldn't place why. "Just say it, Jasper. I'd rather have you tell me something I do not like honestly than to hide the truth from me."

Once again he shifted and then shook his head. "I'm talking about our expectations of each other when it comes to our…our connection."

She blinked. "Our connection."

"I did not seek love in a marriage partner, is what I mean," he said, smoothing his hands along the front of his jacket. "I certainly have seen love matches work out, but they can be *messy*. I do not wish for a life that is messy—I'm trying to get myself out of just that sort of thing right now, thanks to my brother's bad behavior."

That was an entirely unexpected admission. Jasper had never spoken to her or in front of her about his late brother, nor of the persistent rumors that surrounded him and his untimely death. But there it was, blurted out as he ran a hand through his hair with an uncommonly wild expression to his dark eyes.

"The notion of love is fine, of course," he continued. "For fairytales. But I do not want to go into this arrangement with you misunderstanding why I am doing it."

She cleared her throat and tried to ignore the sting his words created deep within her.

"My lord," she said, folding her arms. "I am well aware of why you are marrying into my family. My dowry will refill your coffers, your title will please my father's desire to be linked to an important family. It is a business arrangement, just as it was when you chose my sister for your bride. I am not a fool."

Relief seemed to wash over him, and once again she was stung by how happy he was that she accepted his lack of affection for her. As if she had a choice in the matter.

"Of course you aren't," he hastened to say. "You are, in fact, wonderfully intelligent. It is one of my very favorite things about you."

She stared. He had a favorite thing about her? That was very confusing given what he'd just said about not wanting an emotional bond.

"You know, you could have simply taken me aside tomorrow and had this conversation," she said. "You didn't have to slip into my bedchamber and wait for me to tell me you couldn't love me and only wanted the barest connection with me when we wed."

She went to turn away and he caught her arm, pivoting her back. "You have misunderstood me," he said, his voice quiet, his breath warm and sweet. "I tell you that I do not seek love so there will be no confusion. But I *don't* want the barest of connection with you, Thomasina. What I would like, what I want more than perhaps I should, is far deeper than that."

She shook her head. "I'm very confused."

"I know, because I'm bungling this," he said with a tiny hint of a smile. Such a rare thing on his normally serious face and she was struck silent by it. "The night you pretended to be Anne, when I almost kissed you on the terrace...you wanted that, didn't you?"

Her lips parted at his demand that she confess her most terrible desire. Her betrayal of her sister, even if Anne had clearly not given a damn.

"Jasper—" She tried to tug away, but he kept her close.

"Please don't run," he said. "I won't judge you. I cannot, if truth be told, because I *knew* it was you, Thomasina. I *knew* and I wanted to kiss you so badly that I could hardly maintain control over myself."

She stared at him, at that renewed flare of desire that burned in his gaze. She felt every flex of his fingers against her arm, and the wall of his body heat curled around her and made her want to sink into him and disappear forever.

"Yes," she whispered, her voice cracking. "I wanted you to kiss me. I hated myself for it, but I wanted that so badly that night."

He smiled. "And when I did finally kiss you right before I left, did you want...*more?*"

"More kissing?" she asked.

He nodded, a jerky motion. "I—yes. More kissing, but did you also ache, deep within yourself, perhaps in a way you don't fully understand? Did you want something more than the kissing, something that keeps you awake at night, something that makes you...*need?*"

She was shocked to find he had exactly described her constant struggle since he kissed her. Her mind had flown so many times to what might have happened next. What would happen on their wedding night, an act that had only been described in the barest of details by scandalized female figures who mostly seemed to see the act as one to be borne, not enjoyed. And yet when Jasper touched her, she wanted to know more.

She wanted to feel more.

"Thomasina." Her name was a prayer, begged from his lips, filled with far more meaning than it ever had before.

"Yes," she burst out. "I wanted more. I want more now."

"Good." His shoulders rolled forward in further relief. "I want to touch you and taste you and pleasure you. I want to explore that need, that passion. Do you think you could do that even if you knew I might not ever offer you my heart?"

She shivered, aching to give him exactly what he had just denied he could return. Aching to give him the body he wanted over anything else.

But she had one tiny hesitation. One thing she had to know. "Did you...did you ask the same of my sister?"

He flinched at that question, as if it were abhorrent. "Never," he reassured her. "Wrong as it may be, I never wanted Anne. I want *you.*"

She had spent her life feeling interchangeable with Anne and Juliana, part of a unit and not an individual. But this man...he saw her as more. That didn't seem to be a lie or a manipulation. When he said he wanted her...she believed him.

And in that moment, she couldn't say anything but, "Yes."

His mouth dropped against hers and his arms came around her, dragging her against him as he devoured her with far more passion than he had allowed in the driveway the day before. He tasted her, coaxing her lips to part, delving inside to tease and explore while her legs shook.

He pushed her back toward her bed, and she shuddered as he leaned her against the high edge so she no longer had to support herself as he kissed her and kissed her until her entire world condensed down to their mouths and tongues and lips. Finally he broke away, staring down at her, his breath as short as hers, his hands shaking as he lifted them to cup her cheeks gently.

"I want to touch you, Thomasina," he whispered, his voice broken and cracked and raw.

She blinked up at him, this man who looked like the one she would marry in a few short days, but also seemed different. Jasper had never let her see past his cool façade, but right now his walls were down. He was passionate and heated and driven, and all his energy was focused on her.

He also seemed to expect an answer to his statement, and she struggled past the lump in her throat. "Aren't you already touching me?" she asked with a nervous laugh.

"Intimately," he said, letting his hands slide down her throat, across her collarbone, down her shoulders and arms.

She felt the pressure, the heat, through the fabric of her gown, and suddenly and shockingly wished that it wasn't between them.

"If you don't want me to," he continued, "if you want to wait until we are properly wed, I will walk away tonight and be pleased with just being able to kiss you as I've fantasized about for far longer than I should have. But I cannot express to you how much I want to touch you until I feel you flutter with pleasure."

She felt how wide her eyes were. It was almost as if she couldn't blink anymore. What he was describing was not something one *bore*, that was for certain.

"You would...claim me?" she asked with uncertainty.

He smiled again, but this time there was something a little pained to the expression. "I would very much like to do that, but I think once I start, I'll never want to stop, and that would make the next few days rather awkward. So, no. I would not...er...claim you, as you put it. Just pleasure you. Touch you but leave you untouched."

"That makes no sense," she said, and found herself smiling even though this entire situation was fraught with odd emotion and desire and a great lack of understanding on her part. Why in the world had no one educated her better?

"No, this kind of sweeping thing never does." He held her stare a moment. "Let me show you. You may say no any time you like."

"I've heard that is not true," she said. "That once I say yes, there's never again a no allowed."

He recoiled as if that thought were an anathema to him. "Not with me. Let me be very clear, Thomasina. You may say no to me at *any* time. You said I would claim you, which implies some kind of ownership, but I have no interest in that. You are the only person who controls your body, your mind, your heart...I would never try to bend you or take that away. If at any point you don't want anything I do, you say no and that ends it. We may discuss it further, but I will never do anything, especially in our bed, that you don't enthusiastically agree to."

She pondered that a moment. She and her sisters had sometimes discussed the realities of marriages arranged by their father. Not the passionate part that Jasper was describing, for none of them had any better understanding of those mechanics than Thomasina did.

But they had spoken about the loss of freedom and autonomy over themselves. It was a shared fear.

And yet here Thomasina was, a few days from a forced marriage to a man who inspired a great deal of conflicted emotion in her... and he was offering her independence. Ownership over her own life.

And not for the first time, she silently thanked Anne for being so reckless and leaving her unwanted fiancé to Thomasina. Even though those thoughts were wrong. Even if she feared for her sister, she wanted this man.

So she nodded. "Show me then."

He let out a broken breath and then leaned in to kiss her once more. She felt his hands moving even as she lifted her own to rest against his hard chest. His fingers glided up her sides until she shivered, then around the back of her dress to unfasten her buttons.

She broke away from his mouth as he did so and stared up at him. "You're going to—to undress me?"

He nodded, though his hands stilled. "I want to see you, Thomasina."

She hesitated at that request. To see her undressed felt like a huge leap. Would he like what he saw? But then again, it would happen whether it was tonight or in a few days, and since he had claimed he would not take her tonight, that meant she would have more time to become accustomed to his eyes on her. His hands.

She nodded and slowly turned to grant him more access to the back of her gown. He finished flicking each button open and then his hands glided inside, between her dress and her chemise beneath.

They exhaled together, a matching breath, as he pushed the fabric forward until her gown dropped around her wrists. She pushed it away and he tugged, pooling the fabric at her feet.

She wore a chemise and flimsy little drawers, and beneath were her silk stockings, held up by ribbon that matched the color of her now-discarded dress. As if he had been meant to see her like this when she chose her clothing before supper that evening.

"Look at me," he whispered, his mouth close to her ear behind her.

She gripped her hands into fists on the mattress, her heart racing so fast she was certain he could hear it.

"Please," he added, and then he pressed his mouth to the place on her neck just behind her ear.

She gripped the coverlet tighter as a tiny cry escaped her lips. What was he doing to that exquisitely sensitive spot she hadn't ever known existed? It was like he'd found a place to touch her that lit her entire being on fire. Except she wanted to burn.

Slowly, she turned around and faced him. He stepped back, hands clenched at his sides as he looked her up and down.

"You are more beautiful than I ever dreamed," he said softly, and reached out to smooth his fingers along her bare upper arm.

He glided higher, hooking a finger beneath her chemise strap. He leaned in as he tugged it, drawing it down as he traced the path of the fabric with his lips. She couldn't hold back another gasp of pleasure and held tight to the mattress behind her with one hand as she drove the fingers of her other hand into his hair.

He chuckled against her skin and trailed his lips back up her shoulder, across her collarbone, drawing the other chemise strap down and tasting the trail of it.

Her chemise bunched around her waist, and they both looked down at her at the same time. She was bared from the waist up, and heat suffused her cheeks as he stared at her naked breasts with their dark nipples at full attention as she anticipated what would come next.

He cupped them, drawing his thumbs across the tips and eliciting yet another gasp she couldn't suppress. She felt like she'd never been awake before, not fully alive, and here was this man bringing her into the world with his hands and, dear God, his mouth. He bent his head and drew one nipple between his lips, sucking and swirling his tongue around her as he continued to massage and pluck the other breast with his thumb.

She found her hips rocking forward, meeting his as he touched her. Her legs shook, there was a deep ache growing between them. She needed him to ease it, but she had no idea how he could ever do that. How to ask for it.

Luckily he didn't seem to require that knowledge from her. He drew back from her breasts with a pop as her nipple left his lips. He pushed her chemise and drawers down in one smooth motion, leaving her fully exposed.

And fully at his mercy.

CHAPTER 9

Thomasina was naked. It had happened that fast and she stood before him, trembling with nervousness and pleasure mixed, and watched him watch her. He had a possessive, dark smirk on his face, and he let his hand trail across the soft swell of her stomach.

Then he looked into her eyes. "I am going to lie on the bed with you. And I'm going to do very wicked things to you. And you're going to come."

She blinked. "Come where?"

"I'm going to build such pleasure in you that you'll need to cry out and scream my name, and then it's going to overwhelm you. And you will never look at the world the same way again," he explained.

"I already don't," she murmured.

He caught her in his arms, kissing her again as he swept her up and placed her on the bed. He joined her, lying on his side next to her, kissing her as he lazily stroked his hand up and down her body. Each stroke brought his fingers lower, closer to the center of herself, the valley of her sex. And when he finally cupped her, she arched into his hand with a hiss.

He broke the kiss. "Yes?"

She nodded, unable to form coherent words as he stroked his hand over her, grinding his palm into the apex of her thighs and eliciting an electric shock of pleasure through her.

"Is that coming?" she gasped out.

He shook his head. "When it happens, you won't have to ask. Now relax if you can. Let me do this."

She nodded, though she felt anything but relaxed. Coiled and hot and achy, yes. Relaxed, most definitely not.

His fingers moved again between her legs, but this time he opened her, teasing her outer lips apart and then tracing her opening with his fingertip. She shut her eyes, resting back against her pillows, and sank into the sensation. Odd and wonderful, like someone was sparking flint over and over between her legs, and the heat grew with each passing second.

His finger pressed harder and she felt the muscles at her entrance give way, allowing him access. She braced around him, the oddness of being breached accompanied by just a little pain mixed with pleasure. She flexed around him and he groaned like she'd hurt him.

She opened her eyes. "Was that wrong?" she gasped.

He shook his head. "Very right. Do it again."

She did, squeezing hard around him and rocking her head back at the unexpected pleasure in that action. He pressed a thumb somewhere else, at the top of her sex, outside of her body, and swirled it there as she clamped around his finger. Slowly they moved together, her grinding against him as he plundered her.

"You're a natural," he whispered, leaning in for a kiss. "That's right. Ride it. *Feel* it. Don't reach for it, don't fight it. It will happen when it happens."

She wasn't sure what he meant, but something *was* happening, certainly. The pleasure of his touch seemed to mount as she arched against his hand, his fingers, his thumb. She reached out, gripping the lapel of his jacket, clinging to him as she rode higher, harder, and finally, just when it seemed like she'd reached the top of an insurmountable wall, her entire body began to shake. Waves of pleasure rolled through her, taking her control, stealing her breath. She began to cry out and he dropped his mouth to hers, silencing her keening with his lips as he drew the pleasure out longer and longer.

Only when she collapsed back, her hand dropping away from his body, did he gently withdraw his finger from her still trembling sheath. He curled his body around hers, resting his hand on her stomach.

And for the first time since Anne had requested her help and set this madness in motion, Thomasina's mind emptied and she found a modicum of peace.

Thomasina wasn't asleep. Even though her eyes were closed, Jasper could tell she was only deeply relaxed. It was a powerful thing, to be able to erase her troubles, even if that was only temporary. An unexpected benefit of watching and feeling her reach the heights of pleasure was that it had alleviated his own worries for a moment, too.

Touching her had been everything he'd hoped for when he staggered into her room that night, knowing he shouldn't and yet unable to deny himself.

Thomasina was a responsive lover. She liked his touch, she welcomed it, she had asked questions and given answers freely, though her upbringing had surely told her that ladies weren't interested in such things. He had no doubt that once they were married, she would become an enthusiastic bedmate.

Which was more than he had ever dared hope for when he realized that he would have to arrange a marriage for monetary gain.

Even now he leaned on his elbow, watching her in that blissful state of pleasure, and he wanted so much to push her legs wide, to fit his extremely hard cock into her and take her. To find release deep inside of her as she clung to him and called out his name.

What would be the harm in that when they were to be wed in days? Hours, almost. He could count the hours if he cleared his addled mind enough. Didn't that mean he could have her and find the same release as she had?

He looked at his hand on her stomach and clenched his fingers gently against her flesh. She made a soft sound of pleasure and the decision was made for him. He leaned in, kissing her gently as he let his hand move to his trousers. He was about to loosen the fall front when there was a light knock on the door across the room.

Thomasina's eyes flew open and she jerked her face toward Jasper. "Oh no!"

"Thomasina?" came Juliana Shelley's voice from behind the door. "May I come in?"

"The door isn't locked and she won't take no for an answer," Thomasina gasped, jumping up and tugging her tangled chemise over her head.

Jasper got up to move to the dressing room door where he could depart through the other adjoining chamber, but the door was already being opened. He had no choice and dove under the bed.

He lay there flat on his stomach with dust pluming up around him and watched as Thomasina's still-stockinged feet padded toward the entrance to the chamber her sister was so rudely breeching.

"Are you well?" Juliana's voice said, similar to Thomasina's, certainly, but not identical. Thomasina was more musical, perhaps a little more halting.

"Of course," Thomasina replied, breathless from both shock at being interrupted in such a state, but he thought also from the lingering pleasure. His poor cock, which was now pressed against the hard and dusty floor, twitched in painful response.

"Why are you in your chemise and stockings?" Juliana asked, confusion lacing her tone.

Thomasina gave a nervous giggle. "Oh, I-I just wanted to lie down after supper. This was as far as I got by myself."

"How did you manage to unfasten your dress?" Juliana asked. "I've worn that one before, I would *never* be able to unfasten it by myself."

Jasper squeezed his eyes shut. If Juliana pushed, if she pried until the truth came out, that would only be just another scandal, minor or major, for him to deal with. This one of his own making because he had so little self-control around the woman who would be his wife.

And then he made it worse as he drew in a breath, along with some of the dust particles beneath the bed. His nose tickled and he clasped a hand over his nose and mouth, trying to hold back the sneeze. He couldn't and it bubbled out, muffled by his hand.

"What was that sound?" Juliana's voice came again.

Thomasina made a sound that was in no way similar to his sneeze. "Just me." She repeated the little noise. "Bit of a scratchy throat, that's all. What was it you wanted, Juliana?"

"Thomasina—"

"Honestly, my dear—" He heard her frustration in every word. "—I am simply *so* tired with all the excitement. It has been such a long week. I would love to just go to bed and start over tomorrow."

Juliana let out a gasp that was clearly of displeasure. "Oh, I hate to think of you so upset at this terrible turn of events. But what can we do? How can I *save* you and fix all this?"

Jasper tensed at the question and the true fear and anguish that laced Juliana's voice. She feared her sister's future with him. But was that just because of the shocking circumstances of their engagement or because Thomasina had voiced similar concerns?

Would those worries change now that they were so intimately connected? He didn't want her to fear him, certainly. He wanted her to be...*happy*, he supposed. Though holding the happiness of another person in the palm of his hand was certainly not what he had ever sought to do in his life. It was a dangerous thing, after all. Something he could easily make a mess of and end up destroying such a gentle soul as Thomasina Shelley.

He rested his forehead against his hand on the floor and fought another sneeze that rose up in him. This was impossible. They were certainly going to be found out.

"You needn't fix anything," Thomasina said, and their voices were fading now, as if she were guiding Juliana from the room into her adjoining chamber. "I promise you I don't—"

She was gone then, he could no longer hear whatever she said to comfort her sister. No longer eavesdrop on her inner feelings about their impending marriage. He remained under the bed, twitching his nose. He had no idea if Thomasina had shut the connecting door or if the sisters would return. Until he was certain, he wasn't about to reveal himself.

After a few moments, the door to the chamber shut. "Jasper?" Thomasina whispered. "Are you still under there?"

He pushed himself from under the bed and rose to face her. She was standing with a hand clasped over her mouth and tears were lit in her eyes. His heart ached at the sight of it.

"I'm sorry," he began, and then let out the sneeze he had been fighting. It was followed by three more, and only then did Thomasina drop her hand away and he discovered she was...

She was *laughing*.

Tears of mirth, not humiliation, streamed down her face as she bent over, clutching her stomach with every bubbling giggle that rose up in her. He stared, not just at how changed she was when tied up with such humor, but because looking at her in such a state made him feel...lighter. Lighter than he had in a very long time.

"Oh God, when you started sneezing!" she giggled, wiping helplessly at the tears. "Oh Jasper, you should have seen my face! I *know* I was as red as a currant and poor Juliana must think my room is positively infested with some kind of squeaking animals."

"Squeak," he argued. "I'll have you know I never squeaked in my life."

Her laughter grew louder. "I beg to differ, my lord. Squeak you did!"

"Well, be that as it may, I'm glad *you* think it's funny," he said with a shake of his head and a small smile of his own. He motioned down at his dark clothing, which was now pale gray with dust. "Look at *me*."

She came a step closer and her laughter continued. "Oh, Jasper," she wheezed. "Your lovely vest."

He shot her a playfully dark look. "My valet will certainly have questions."

She moved around the bed now and his awareness of her ratcheted up as she began to brush the dust away from his clothes. She was giggling helplessly as she did it, completely unaware of him as he stared down at her, wanting her so much that it stunned him. And there she was, within arm's length, still in that flimsy chemise and it would be so easy to just…

But no. He had to regain some self-control. They had already almost been caught in a most compromising position. He had to remember that he was a gentleman and he had to wait for what he wanted, just as he should have from the start.

"I *am* sorry," he said softly.

She jerked her face up to look at him instead of his dusty waist-coat. "Why?" she asked, and her tone held genuine confusion.

He motioned his head toward the door. "We were almost caught. I ought to have been more mindful of the humiliation I could have caused you tonight. The scandal."

She wrinkled her brow, and instead of continuing to brush off his vest, she rested her hand gently on his chest. He felt the warmth and weight of each of her fingers and was keenly aware of both the desire they inspired and the peace that unexpectedly followed.

"What scandal is that?" she asked.

He motioned again to the door and rolled his eyes as he tried to keep focus. "Your sister."

She smiled and shook her head. "You mean if Juliana had realized you were under my bed? You mean if she had confronted me about having you in my room doing...well, some very naughty things."

The way she said *very naughty* made his stomach tingle and need spread through his veins.

"Yes," he said through clenched teeth.

"I might have been a bit embarrassed," she admitted with a small shrug. "But I promise you that my beloved and highly *protective* sister would *never* allow a scandal to follow such a discovery. She wouldn't have said anything to anyone."

"It was still imprudent of me," he muttered.

She tilted her head. "Perhaps we were *both* a little imprudent, but that doesn't mean what we did was *wrong*. Jasper, we are to be married in a few days. Doing this...what we did...it isn't such a terrible thing. Not scandal-worthy, at any rate. And I hope you are not truly sorry that it happened, because I'm not."

He stared down into her upturned face, still a little flushed from her laughter and excitement and the pleasure she had experienced at his hands. She certainly didn't *look* upset. A fact he was truly happy about.

"You aren't sorry?" he repeated.

She shook her head. "Not at all. I was nervous about our wedding night, about whatever would be expected of me when it came to...wifely duties. It is often described to ladies in rather dire terms. But now I am...I'm not afraid anymore of what will happen. In truth, I..." She trailed off as her cheeks brightened with high color again. "I-I look forward to it if it will be anything like what we did today."

He swallowed hard. "It will be better," he promised, his voice low and rough with the desire that coursed through him whenever he was near this woman.

Her lips parted and her breath shuddered out in a choppy exhale. "I trust you," she whispered.

He flinched at that sentence, so small and yet so powerful. So undeserved, considering he was already keeping things from her.

He turned away, for he was not yet willing to share those things. "I will endeavor to make you happy that you give me such a gift. Now I should go before anyone else bursts in on us and I end up under the bed again. I don't think my constitution can take the dust."

"Very well," she said, tracking him as he moved to the door to the hallway. He heard the concern in her voice. The worry that perhaps she had done something wrong. Of course, she hadn't. *He* had.

But until he knew more about the circumstances of Anne's disappearance, he couldn't say anything to her. He wouldn't.

"Goodnight," he said, turning to look at her one more time at the door.

She stood beside the bed where he had stolen her pleasure, hands clasped against her thighs, watching him intently. But her voice didn't tremble as she said, "Goodnight, Jasper."

He left her then because he had to. He left her because if he stayed he would never leave. And that was the kind of connection that could change everything, that could take his control. He couldn't allow for that. Not today. Perhaps not ever.

CHAPTER 10

Juliana adjusted the veil, pinning it into Thomasina's hair gently as she watched her work in the mirror. Thomasina shifted as she looked at the image of a woman she hardly recognized. Herself, after all.

And yet different.

She had *been* different since Jasper touched her a few days before. He hadn't made any effort to repeat that touching during the whirlwind that had at last taken her to this day, her wedding day. But she had certainly touched herself since, exploring the places where he had made her shake with pleasure.

It was an education to say the least, and now she looked forward to their wedding night all the more.

"At least we did not have to alter Anne's gown," Juliana mused.

"Yes, I have inherited a great deal from our wayward sister," Thomasina whispered as she pushed away the more sensual thoughts and replaced them with worries. She caught Juliana's eye in the mirror image and shrugged. "I thought she would have come back by now, dragging a husband behind her."

Juliana nodded. "I admit, so did I. Gretna Green is not so far. At least she could have written us."

They sat in silence for a moment, their shared fears hanging between them like a guillotine poised to slash their hopes and dreams.

"I miss her more than anything. Like a limb was cut from my body. I dream of her nightly," Juliana whispered.

Thomasina's lips parted. "I have dreamed of her too. I see her rowing away on a boat in the fog and I can't—"

"You can't reach her," Juliana breathed. "I have had the same dream."

"If we are dreaming the same worrisome thing, do you think she is well?" Thomasina asked.

Juliana let out a shuddering sigh. "I have no idea. I pray she is, but I fear the worst. What kind of man would—"

She cut herself off and walked away from Thomasina, but the unspoken words rang in her head. Poisoning everything else.

"There is nothing we can do," Juliana said softly, perhaps more for herself than for Thomasina.

"Isn't there?" Thomasina said.

"No. It's up to Father and perhaps Lord Harcourt to pursue her now." Juliana clenched her fists at her sides. "Not that either of them seems interested in doing so."

Thomasina bent her head. Juliana wasn't wrong. Their father was laissez-faire about the entire situation regarding Anne. Jasper also cut off the subject any time it came up.

"Then perhaps *we* should," Thomasina said. "We are limited in our resources, of course, but we don't have to sit around waiting to hear the worst, do we? We could interview the servants, we could search more closely in Anne's room."

Juliana lifted her gaze. "We could," she conceded. "Though I admit I fear what we might find. It's why I haven't brought up that exact suggestion myself."

Thomasina felt tears sting her eyes and blinked them away. "But we have to be brave, don't we? For Anne?"

Juliana's throat worked gently at that statement. She nodded.

"Yes. For Anne, we must. And we will do exactly that once this wedding is over." She lifted her chin, and there was the forced smile that didn't reach her eyes. "But we do have something else to discuss before I send you out into the day to wed this man."

Thomasina blinked in surprise at the change of subject, though she did feel better knowing Juliana wanted to pursue more information about their sister. "We do?"

"Yes, er—" Juliana flushed crimson and refused to meet her stare. "Er...the expectations of a wedding night. Since no one else is going to step up and offer any advice, I feel it falls to me as your older sister."

"By four minutes," Thomasina said with a smile. "And what advice can you give me, unless you have had lovers you never disclosed?"

Juliana's furious blush deepened in answer to that question. "Of course not. But before we left London for Harcourt Heights, we... Anne and I...we..."

Juliana shifted with discomfort and Thomasina shook her head. "What?"

"We found a book," Juliana said slowly. "Well, *I* found a book. And Anne found me with the book."

"A book? What kind of book? Why wasn't I invited to look at the book?" Thomasina asked, firing off one question after another.

Juliana shrugged. "You were at the museum with our cousins. And it was a very...a very naughty book. Anne was insistent about reading it from cover to cover. She said it might help her prepare for a wedding night."

Thomasina stared, her jaw dropped open. "Great God, Juliana! And what did the book say?"

"Show, actually." Juliana shifted. "There were illustrations. Very explicit. I should have brought it, as it is hidden in London, but Anne had already looked at it and I didn't think I would be forced to have this talk with you for some time yet. Father would have to be appeased for a while with his earl. We would have had more time before he turned his machinations on you or me."

"You are purple and you are rambling," Thomasina interrupted. "So it must have been quite a book."

She flashed to Jasper, his hand between her legs, his fingers doing magical things. Was *that* in the book?

"Yes. The women in the illustrations actually looked happier with their...*situation* than perhaps we were led to believe by our aunts and married cousins." Juliana huffed out a breath. "But I *can* explain to you if you'd like."

Thomasina bit her lip. "Er, no. I mean, I'd certainly be interested in seeing your book when we all go back to London, but I think I shall trust my husband to introduce me to...to the pleasures of our marital bed."

Juliana tilted her head in surprise. "Oh. So you believe there will be pleasures?"

"I do," Thomasina whispered with a smile. "He has...he has been nothing but gentle with me since our strange circumstances brought us to this day. And when he kisses me—"

"He kissed you?" Juliana gasped, leaning forward. "When, where?"

"A few times since Anne left," Thomasina said. "And I liked it. Very much."

Juliana seemed to ponder that a moment. "I'm surprised. Anne always talked about how cold Lord Harcourt was, how distant. I didn't think he could be passionate in any way."

A sudden desire to defend Jasper rose up in her, but Thomasina tamped it down. There was no reason to reveal her growing attachment to Juliana, who would surely only point out the foolishness of it all. Rightly so, perhaps.

"I think they were not a good match," she said instead. "And maybe he and I could be a better one. At any rate, this is happening almost right this moment and I am...I *must* be...content with the outcome."

Juliana stepped forward as Thomasina got to her feet, and together they looked in the mirror. They were parallel images of each other, but for Thomasina's pretty wedding dress. The only remnant of Anne. Anne, who she ached for on this most important of days.

"I worry about you as much as I do her," Juliana mused. "But if you claim you could be happy with this man, I will do anything in my power to ensure you will be."

"I know you will, you always fix things," Thomasina reassured her.

Juliana's smile faltered and she turned toward the door. "We should go down, I'm certain they are waiting for us. For you, really. It's time."

Thomasina's heart leapt at those two words, which held so much power. It *was* time. Time to surrender the name Shelley and take the title of Harcourt. Time to give herself over to a man who confused and confounded her. Time to become his wife and then his lover.

It was time to start the new chapter in her life.

Jasper held out a glass of champagne to his mother and tried not to contemplate the cost of such an extravagance. Shelley was paying for it, so he supposed he should just enjoy it, but he couldn't help trying to track it in the ledger that always ran in his mind.

"And so you are married," Lady Harcourt said. "Which makes me the dowager."

"It does," he said, focusing his attention back on her. His mother was dressed beautifully, not a hair out of place, looking the part of mother of the groom. Except she didn't smile. She never smiled. "I hope you are not unhappy with that outcome."

She shrugged and stared off into the crowd without any emotion on her face. Jasper frowned. He was doing all this partly for her, to make up for the shame she had been forced to carry both by her husband and by his firstborn son. And yet *nothing* Jasper did ever seemed to help her. Change her. Please her.

But somehow he still tried. And tried. And tried. It had always been that way, for as long as he remembered. His father had tried to talk to him about it once. Tried to steer him away from, as he had called it, dancing to her tune. They'd had a row, of course.

But Jasper always had those words in his mind when he looked at her. That his mother would never be satisfied.

He'd worried he might find the same in a wife once he had gotten to know Anne Shelley. Her hesitations about him and their future had become very clear over the weeks and months, even before she ran into the night with a villain to escape him.

Now it was different. Now he was married to Thomasina.

His gaze found her in the crowd. She was standing with her sister and another friend, smiling and laughing. She looked pleased and she was always pleasing. Her father had described her that way, and Jasper had felt it, her drive to make him happy and comfortable, even at the sacrifice of herself. But was that better than a lady who disregarded his comfort? He didn't feel like it was.

She must have felt his stare, for her gaze flitted toward him. Her smile broadened as she tilted her head in acknowledgment.

And for a moment, everything else fell away. His worries about her quieted and the world was...*right*. It was right even though there were whispers in the room about the scandalous switch in brides. About Anne not being here to wish her sister well.

About everything Jasper had fought to keep secret and private and failed at miserably. Even his own thoughts about the situation with Maitland and Anne faded a bit. He was able to forget the news he'd received from Reynolds earlier in the day.

He forgot everything but Thomasina.

"It looks as though some friends are coming to wish you well," his mother said. "I will leave you to them."

She walked away without a backward glance, and Jasper sighed and forced a smile as two of his acquaintances from neighboring shires reached him. Lord Barnaby and Thomas Walker had been friends of his in school and in London. They were wilder than he was, of course. Everyone was.

"Many felicitations," Barnaby said, his words just a touch slurred as he pounded Jasper's back a bit too hard. "You've landed a Shelley sister—that comes with a fine prize of a dowry."

Jasper pursed his lips, although the man was only speaking the truth. Still, it seemed uncouth and potentially hurtful to boil down his new marriage to such terms when it was hardly a few hours old. "And the bride is winsome, as well," he said softly.

Walker stared across the room at Thomasina and shrugged. "She is quite pretty, yes. Always were a bit of an oddity, those Shelley sisters. It's hardly natural for three women to be identical in every way." He shuddered. "Twins are bad enough."

Jasper glared at him, but before he could retort Barnaby was talking again. "Of course, it made switching one out for the other easier. They're interchangeable and so is that lovely pile of money that goes along with them, eh?" He laughed. "Makes the peculiarity of their birth a little more palatable."

Jasper set his drink down on the nearest surface and stepped up in Barnaby's face. "Listen here, you drunken lout," he began, just barely containing himself from grabbing for the man's lapels and shaking him. "I will not hear a bad word against my wife nor her sisters. Interchangeable they are certainly not. I will have you know—"

"Harcourt?"

He froze and so did the other two men, and they all turned to see Thomasina standing there, just at Jasper's elbow, her face lined with concern.

"My lady," Barnaby said, at least having the awareness to blush at the idea she might have heard his unkind words. "I did not realize you were so near."

She smiled, a tight little expression. "I would assume not—you three seemed engaged in intent conversation. But I require the company of my new husband, if you do not mind." She held out a hand, meeting Jasper's gaze and holding there evenly. Her eyes said everything, telling him to come away.

He looked around and found a few people watching. Although he hadn't touched Barnaby when he stepped up to him, he realized now just how loudly and sharply he had spoken. No one within a five-foot radius could have been confused about his displeasure. They were all waiting for what would happen next.

But what had happened was Thomasina. Who effortlessly inserted herself to keep him from his worst impulse, drawing him away from the new scandal he might have created. Being everything he needed in this moment and hadn't realized.

And so he took her hand and let her be that.

"Many felicitations, my lady," Walker called out weakly, and Barnaby muttered the same as she and Jasper walked away.

She guided him through the crowd, friendly and easy as she maneuvered him toward the terrace, smiling at their guests, responding with everything pleasing and light as they were acknowledged and congratulated.

But once they exited the ballroom and she shut the door behind them, he felt the weight of the effort in her every move. Her shoulders rolled forward a fraction and her smile faltered. She released his arm and motioned toward the terrace wall. They moved to it together and she faced him, exploring his expression carefully.

"How much did you hear?" he asked softly.

She shrugged one shoulder. "Enough to know that nothing was said that hasn't been said a dozen times over the years. A hundred times, probably. Why did it upset you so much? Neither of them meant any harm."

He drew back. "They didn't mean any harm? How can you say that? You and your sisters may look alike, but you are not identical, not truly."

"It means a great deal to me that you do not think we are, but the rest of the world has always seen us as an oddity."

"Don't say *oddity*," he grumbled.

She smiled, as if she were far older and wiser than he was. "Do you know how rare it is for triplets to survive birth? Even twins do not always make it. I have never met another trio like us and neither has anyone else in our acquaintance, I would wager. We *are* an anomaly, Jasper. To some we are like a traveling show with its attractions."

"Still, they shouldn't say it," he said.

"It's rude, I agree. But I have grown accustomed to their whispers, though I am sorry you are just realizing them now. Perhaps you would have chosen differently if you had known that simply linking yourself to us is yet another of your hated scandals."

He pursed his lips at her response, which she gave with such an attitude that their whispers didn't matter. And perhaps after hearing them all her life, they didn't to her. But he found it wasn't the scandal that bothered him about what had been said…it was that the words about his wife…his *wife*…were so cruel and untrue.

"You should not have been exposed to such falsehoods and slurs all your life," he said softly.

She sighed. "Perhaps not. But I have been, so it is not new to me. And if you are going to shout at everyone who says something unkind about me or my sisters, you will be hoarse by the time the leaves change. It is best to ignore them, and to focus on those who know the truth."

"That you're not the same person, copied over and over," he said.

She nodded. "Yes. Although I have never met a friend who could identify me immediately as you claim to do, I know many who can if I start talking."

"And aren't pretending to be your sister," he said, arching a teasing brow as his defensiveness and heightened emotion began to fade a little.

She laughed, for which he was grateful. Not so many days ago, she would have blushed or apologized for her deception. "Yes, *obviously* when I am being deceptive everyone falls under my spell but you."

He let his gaze flit over her face in the fading light of the sunset in the distance. "I am definitely more than capable of falling under your spell, Thomasina. I assure you of that. And very much look forward to proving it as soon as we can manage to get all these people out of our house."

Pink tinged her cheeks and she laughed again. "I am glad we are of a mind. Interlopers, all of them. Just here to drink our wine and eat our food. I would much rather be alone with you."

He could no longer deny himself, and with a broken sigh, he reached up to stroke his fingertips over her cheek. Her breath grew ragged and short with the action and her pupils dilated with a desire that made him rock hard in an instant. He leaned in, brushing his lips to hers.

She wrapped her arms around his neck, opening to him in that moment, and he let his mind empty as he kissed her. Lost himself in her. Drowned in her.

"We should go back inside before I do something imprudent on the terrace," he said as he broke the kiss but not the embrace.

She stared up at him with a smile. "Perhaps we'll save imprudent for another day. Come, let's go pretend we actually like all these people."

He took her hand again, threading his fingers through hers as they broke their embrace. And as they returned to the house together, he couldn't help but feel a bond between them. A connection he had always drawn away from.

But in this moment, it felt right. And that made him question everything he'd ever planned, everything he'd ever wanted. And everything he was keeping from her about her sister and his part in her disappearance.

CHAPTER 11

By the time they had managed to force the farewells of their guests, it was late. After midnight, in fact, and as she sat in the dressing room of her new chamber with Ruby brushing out her hair, Thomasina could not help but wonder if Jasper would want to consummate their union tonight. He had to be as tired as she was, after all the excitement of the past few days.

She stared at the door that connected the countess's chamber to the earl's and shivered at how close she was to him now. So close and yet it felt like miles away.

Not that she didn't know he wanted her. After the unpleasantness at their wedding gathering, he had remained by her side the rest of the evening, his hand finding the small of her back when she needed strength, his gaze holding hers with intention and a new connection that she had to hope was real.

She wanted it after all, more than anything. Enough that it frightened her, because Jasper had been very honest when he told her he hadn't intended to share his heart with his wife. But then again, he hadn't *intended* to marry *her* at all. So intentions could be thwarted, couldn't they?

She smiled up at her maid. "Thank you, Ruby," she said. "I think that will be all for tonight."

The maid cast a quick, nervous glance toward the adjoining door before she set the silver brush down on Thomasina's dressing table and bobbed out a curtsey. "Yes, my lady. Good luck."

Thomasina caught her breath as Ruby hurried from the room and left her alone in the chamber. *Good luck.* Great God, but it seemed everyone was determined to see her as going into a lion's den tonight. But she felt a sense of rightness as she thought of surrendering to Jasper.

Assuming, of course, he wasn't already snoring away in the chamber next door. Did he snore?

"I suppose I'll find out," she muttered to herself before she got up and moved to the full-length mirror across the dressing room.

She was wearing another of Anne's castoffs from her trousseau. A pretty, pale pink nightgown that was almost sheer, the fabric was so thin. It had elbow-length sleeves and tied with a perfectly formed bow right between her breasts. After brushing it until it gleamed, Ruby had bound her hair loosely with a ribbon that matched the nightgown, and Thomasina pinched her cheeks to give them the color her nervousness did not allow for.

With a long breath, she faced the door and marched to it. She lifted her hand to knock and then hesitated. She was Jasper's wife now. Did a wife knock? Did she just come in to show she was confident? It would be a lie, of course, but...

She cut off her thoughts by pushing the door open and caught her breath. It was a lovely chamber, with a large bed across the way. A fire burned on the back wall, brightening the room. And even if it hadn't, there were dozens of candles and lamps lit to make the room glow in a romantic way.

If she'd thought Jasper might be sleeping, she was very wrong. Instead he stood beside the fire, poker in hand as he stirred the coals. When she entered, he pivoted toward her, the poker going slack in his fingers as he stared at her.

She stared back. Jasper had always been so pulled together, almost perfect. Even the day he had stripped her naked and pleasured her, he had remained entirely clothed. Tonight, he was not. While she had readied, so had he. His jacket and cravat were gone, his boots too, so that he was barefoot.

But the place her eyes went, could not tear away from, was his bare chest. He was shirtless and she could no longer breathe. He was spectacular, with a body that rivaled that of any statue in any garden or museum in all of England. All the world. He seemed to be formed from granite. He had defined shoulders, a broad chest, and there were ripples of muscle on his stomach. Muscles that trailed tantalizingly into the waist of trousers, which slung dangerously low, indeed.

She felt a little dizzy at the idea that she would be allowed to touch him tonight. He would touch her. And then they would truly be wed in the eyes of any entity that might question the union.

"You are lovely," he said, and suddenly it felt like she could move again.

She smiled at him, trying to return focus to his face and not the shockingly bare chest displayed for what felt like her pleasure.

"Thank you," she said. "I-I wasn't certain if you would want me. I thought with it being so late you might wish to just sleep."

His brows lifted. "You think after three days of being unable to think of anything except touching you that I would want to stay away tonight?"

She bit her lip. "You thought of me?"

He nodded. "Very much. Perhaps more than I should. But there it is." He tilted his head. "Although if *you* are tired, I would never dream of making you—"

"I'm not tired," she interrupted, her voice lifting. She blushed at her own ardor, revealed in three tiny words. "I want to be here."

"Then come in," he said with a half-smile. "And shut the door."

She did so and caught her breath at what seemed like the exceedingly loud sound of the door clicking shut. Now they were alone in his chamber. And it was time for everything she both didn't fully understand and yet wanted.

"I won't know what to do," she blurted out.

He cocked his head. "You will once we start," he promised, and held out a hand to her.

She took it, her fingers shaking as they met his, and didn't resist as he drew her into his arms at last. She shivered at the feeling of his bare skin against her. So intimate and arousing without him even doing anything but holding her.

And then he did more and her world ceased to exist.

He kissed her and she opened to him, surrendering because she had longed to do so for what felt like forever, even though it had only been a few days. He took what she gave, gently, almost reverently, as he tasted her and teased her with his tongue. When she shivered with pleasure, he smiled against her lips.

"May I undress you?" she asked.

He chuckled. "You took the words out of my mouth—I was going to ask to undress you."

She shook her head. "You've already, er, seen me. I'm sure there is nothing new for you to find. But I've never seen—that is, I don't know, er..."

"Firstly, there will never be nothing to find when it comes to undressing you," he corrected. "But I understand why you would want to do the honors first. A man's body is new to you." He lifted his arms. "You may unfasten me or I could do it for you."

She stared at the fall front of his trousers, stared at how the thing underneath strained against it, just as it had a few days before. And her nerve vanished.

"You will be better at it," she said, covering her hot cheeks with freezing hands.

He chuckled and lowered his fingers to the buttons. He unfastened them slowly, watching her as he did so, and made what felt like quite a show in lowering the fall front and then pushing the entire contraption down around his ankles. As he kicked the trousers away, she gulped.

So there it was. His...his member? What did a man call it? She didn't know, but it was something to behold, far bigger than that of any statue she had ogled in her day. And it was hard too, curling up toward his stomach almost like a weapon to be wielded.

"And what do you think?" he asked, amusement in his tone, but not cruelty. "Now that you've seen what the fuss is about?"

"I don't know what to think," she admitted as she forced her gaze back to his. "I know you put that..." She motioned vaguely at it. "Into me. Which seems unlikely, but that is the story, so who am I to argue? I've heard it hurts. But your fingers didn't hurt. Still, it is bigger. And yet I don't think you would hurt me."

His expression softened a fraction. "I wouldn't hurt you on purpose," he corrected. "But your innocence will make you very..." He swallowed. "Er...tight. And it will hurt the first time I enter you. Though hopefully not too much since I intend to make you very ready for me."

"How?" she asked, truly curious.

"You are certainly direct," he said with another laugh. When she drew a breath to apologize, he held up a hand. "I like your directness, Thomasina. I'll touch you like I did before."

She smiled wider. "Oh good. I liked that. Though when I did it myself it wasn't quite as, er, intense as it was when you did it."

He stared a beat, two, and then cleared his throat. "You touched yourself since that night?"

"Every night since." She tilted her head. "Was that wrong?"

"Definitely not," he croaked, and sounded like he was having difficulty breathing. "But I would very much like to stop talking now and just—"

He interrupted himself by grasping her waist and tugging her against him. His mouth came down again, this time a little less gently, and he devoured her as she lifted into his naked body and opened herself to everything that was about to happen. He pushed her toward the bed, but when her backside hit the edge he stopped, drawing away, the only sound in the room their shared panting breaths.

He lifted his hands to the bow that held that scandalously sheer gown together and tugged one end. It fluttered open and the gown parted. He squeezed his eyes shut for a moment and then opened them before he reached out and slid a hand beneath the parted fabric. His fingers touched her skin, resting against her shoulder, and she whimpered shamelessly, for it was like he had shocked her with something electric and now she was alive in a way she'd never pictured before in her rather sheltered life.

She wanted more.

He gave it. He pushed the gown away, it fluttered to the floor, and now they were naked together and everything felt more... present. Urgent.

Did he feel it too? She thought he might by the way his gaze flickered to hers—there was a question in his stare. A moment where he almost looked as confused as she felt by the intensity of the desire between them.

He seemed to recover fast enough. He smiled, that little wicked half-smile that only seemed to be for her, and then he slid his hands down to her waist, his fingers skimming her skin until she dipped her head back with a hiss. Then he lifted her onto the high bed. Their faces were even now, and he took advantage by stepping into the space between her legs and kissing her once more.

She cupped his cheeks, tilting her head for better access and sighing as she relaxed with the rightness of this moment. There was no fear anymore, no concern. He would take care of her. She knew that as well as she knew her own name or her hair color or the flavor of her favorite biscuit.

She also knew something else in that moment as he laid her back against the pillows and took a spot beside her on the bed. She loved him.

Her eyes flew open as that wayward thought jolted through her mind. She loved Jasper. And it was true, as much a fact as the others she had noted a moment ago. She loved him and she had loved him from the first terrible moment her father had introduced the man to her and her sisters and declared he would be for Anne.

She had loved him then, secretly and furtively, filled with guilt and regret. She had loved him when she pretended to be Anne and fitted herself into the place as his bride first as a lie and then in truth. And she loved him now as he drew away and stared at her with concern on his face.

"You look frightened...shocked," he said softly.

She shook her head. As much as she knew the truth of her heart, this was not the time to share it. Not yet. Not if she wanted what would happen next to contain no awkwardness or pity. And she didn't. She just wanted the passion, the connection.

"I'm not afraid," she said. "I'm just ready."

He chuckled, the vibration of the sound seeming to pluck all her sensitive nerves as much as his touch did. "Not quite," he said. "But you will be."

He leaned in and pressed another kiss to her lips, but this time it was brief. He didn't linger but began to nibble his way lower, down her throat, across her collarbone, down the trail between her breasts. He paused there, drawing his mouth to her right breast and languidly licking her nipple. She shuddered at the sensation, one she had been dreaming of for days since he touched her last.

She lifted into him, dragging her fingers into his hair and holding him there as he licked and sucked until her entire body felt weightless with pleasure. He smiled against her skin and moved to the opposite breast. He repeated every action there, in the same order. She lolled her head against the pillows and whispered his name.

He lifted his eyes as he swirled his tongue over her. "Is that you begging, my lady?"

She found herself smiling at his teasing and the easy way he made her comfortable in this moment of highest tension. "Is that what you want? To make me beg?"

His pupils dilated, erasing the brown almost entirely, and that wickedness he tried to hide in good company flashed to the surface. "Most definitely."

"Then please, please," she said, ignoring the shock of her own wantonness that he had discovered. "Don't stop."

He lowered his head and sucked her one last time before he drew farther down, caressing the swell of her stomach, the curve of her hip. His lips traced the line where the two met and then he settled between her legs.

She stared down at him, perched between them, and drew in a shaky breath. There was something so infinitely sinful about seeing him there, inches from her most private of places. She didn't know his intentions, but she wanted to see them through.

He pushed her legs wider, exposing her in a new way. She blushed and fought the urge to shove him away. If he wanted to see her like this, she wouldn't stop him.

"When I touched you here, you liked it," he said, an arrogant statement, not a question.

"Yes," she agreed. "Very much. I think you know that, though."

"I also know you'll like…this…"

He leaned in and his mouth was on her sex before she could guess what he would do. She sat up partially in shock, staring at him as he kissed her outer lips. Then he spread those open, exposing her further, and drew his tongue along the wet length of her sex.

She fell against the pillows with a garbled moan. What was this feeling, so unlike even the other pleasures he had given her and she had found on her own since? *This* was something different. His tongue moving along her body was magic, and she gripped the coverlet in both fists as she lifted her hips to greet each stroke.

He gave fast and hard, teasing at first, then beginning to focus more and more on the bundle of nerves at the top of her sex. She twisted the coverlet, arching her back as sensation rolled over her.

And then, without warning, she came. Her sex twitched out of control, sending waves of pleasure outward through every part of her aching body. He dragged her through the release with his tongue, continuing to take and claim and tease until she flopped back.

"Please, please," she whimpered, this time truly begging.

His lifted his head from her with a smile and then crawled up the length of her body. He kissed her, and she tasted the salty sweetness of her release on his tongue. She wrapped her arms around him and took more as he groaned against her.

He drew back and looked down at her, his dark gaze holding hers. "It's time," he said softly.

She nodded without asking for clarification. She knew what he meant. Time to claim her at last. Time to make this marriage one of body. She opened her legs wider and he nudged himself tighter between them. He watched her as he fitted his body to hers. His member…she still didn't know what it was called…touched where he had licked her, and she dug her fingernails into his bare arms as he inched forward.

She stretched to fit him and there was pain, just as he had said there would be. But not terrible pain. Not something that made her want him to stop. It was a rather beautiful pain, of something new being made out of two separate parts. And when he was finally fully seated inside of her, she flexed around him to test this new sensation.

He grunted. "If you keep doing that, it will become much harder for me not to take you hard and fast."

She blinked up at him, for those words caused a ricochet of desire. "Why don't you?"

"Christ, Thomasina," he said, ducking his head into her neck with a laugh. "Because this is the first time and I'm trying not to hurt you. I promise you, you'll get hard and fast later. Tonight, slow and gentle."

She nodded. He knew best in this, of course. She would learn more as they went, it seemed.

He moved and her thoughts emptied at the slick slide of him through her tender body. He ground his hips as he took her, his pelvis meeting hers with every stroke and bringing her pleasure back to life. As he did so, she began to understand, and she lifted to him, matching his pace and rhythm with her own.

His embrace grew tighter, his hips pistoning a bit faster, and she reached to meet him, her vision blurring as new pleasure darted through her body. How could he make her feel so alive? How could every touch be better than the next?

She didn't know, but she didn't need to know as once again the pleasure crested and she keened beneath him. He quickened, moaning as he dragged his hands down to cup her hips and lifted her hard against him as he thrust and thrust, and then his neck tightened, the cords of tendons becoming outlined and she felt the heat of his release flood her.

He collapsed over her, his arms around her, his breath warm against her neck. For a moment they were quiet together, and she smiled against his skin because she was his now.

Nothing could change that fact.

J asper rolled over and looked at his wife in the dying light of the fire he was too lazy to get up to stoke. She was asleep and she had earned that rest, certainly. After all, he had made love to her for hours, over and over. He hadn't expected *that* to happen on their wedding night. But it was like the moment he claimed her, he never wanted to be parted from her again.

Which was a troublesome thought, in truth. A contingency he hadn't planned for, just as he hadn't planned for the situation with her sister or with Ellis Maitland. For a man who always focused on the plan, these deviations vexed, indeed.

He moved, sliding his arm from beneath her head. She made a little sound but rolled away from him and continued to sleep. He reached down and pulled the coverlet up over her naked body, then got up. He found a robe draped at the end of his bed and threw it on over his shoulders, then paced from the bedroom into his adjoining dressing room. He sat down at his desk and withdrew the letter he had received from Reynolds just that morning.

Thomasina had helped him forget his troubles for a while, but now he refocused as he should and reread the words on the page. Reynolds didn't wax poetic but wrote simply that he had discovered the name of the man Maitland had turned Anne over to: Rook Maitland.

"Rook." Jasper shook his head. "These names."

He had no idea if this second Maitland character was a brother to Ellis or a cousin or just someone who had adopted the name when he joined Ellis's gang. But there could be no good in the man if Ellis was his partner.

Reynolds had already declared he would try to find out more about the second Maitland person. Jasper rested the letter on his writing table with a sigh and rubbed his eyes.

"Jasper?"

He turned and found Thomasina standing in the entryway to his dressing chamber, just a sheet wrapped around her, and not very well either, for her skin peeked tantalizingly through the gaps.

"I woke up and you weren't there," she said, tugging the sheet higher.

He folded the letter and shoved it back into the desk before he got up and faced her. "Yes, I'm sorry. I couldn't sleep and thought I wouldn't keep you up."

She wrinkled her brow. "Something is troubling you? Can I help?"

He flinched at that question. So simple, so complicated. And for a moment, he longed to do exactly that: open up and tell her everything. Everything about Solomon and their complicated relationship, everything about loss and grief and hate all rolled up into one painful package. He longed to tell her about Maitland and his threats. But that would also mean telling Thomasina about what a dangerous person Anne had involved herself with.

What good would that do except to worry her? Make her question? He had no doubt she *would* question. And pry and wheedle. She would want to help, and she couldn't help because this was *his* problem.

So until he had more information there was nothing to say. His troubles were his own and that was exactly where they should stay. Even if that violated their agreement to be honest with each other as their marriage began.

"You *can* help," he said, and moved toward her, away from the evidence of his brother's failures. Away from the evidence of his own. When he reached her, all those things seemed to fade a little. He leaned in toward her and nuzzled the side of her neck. She was soft as silk. "Come back to bed with me," he whispered.

She seemed unhappy with that answer for a brief moment. It was obvious in the tension that swept across her body. As if she could sense there was more to be said or done, though he didn't know how she knew when they were barely acquainted in their young marriage.

But then she wiped her concerns away and smiled up at him. The Thomasina bound to please was back, hoping to make him happy without pushing him too far.

"Yes, Jasper," she said. She reached out to take his hand as she let the sheet fall away. He gaped as she leaned into him and made promises with her body. Promises that he could forget everything that had gone wrong in his life for just a little while longer.

CHAPTER 12

Thomasina forced a smile up at Ruby as her maid put the finishing touches on her hair. She had to force the smile, for she had too many troubling thoughts on her mind. First of which was that she had awoken alone in the chamber next door that morning. Jasper had left without waking her.

She supposed she could tell herself that he wanted to let her sleep after their extremely passionate and strenuous night. But she felt something else to the abandonment. Something that troubled her. It was the same feeling she'd had when she found him in his dressing room reading over a letter the night before.

It felt like he was hiding something from her. Keeping her at arm's length. Even lying to her. But he wouldn't do that, would he? They had promised not to lie and he seemed a man who honored his promises. So perhaps she was being silly?

She left Ruby to tidy up her chamber, not a huge feat considering she hadn't slept there, and headed out into the house. Although it was very late thanks to her equally late night, the house was quiet. Everyone else had probably already eaten their breakfast and gone on with their day. The fact that she and Jasper hadn't come down to join them would be whispered about with knowing looks.

Now she understood the meaning of those expressions far more.

She took her time as she moved through the estate, continuing the tour Jasper had begun a few days before and then stopped abruptly. That seemed to be the way between them, really. Starts and stops. Connection and withdrawal. All dictated by the man she had married.

She stepped into a hall and looked around with a smile, for here was the gallery of family portraits that seemed ubiquitous on every fine estate in the land. Still, one could learn a great deal from looking at man's family history, so she glanced up at the portraits and found little hints of Jasper in many a gentleman and lady who stood staring sternly down at her.

Toward the end of the hall hung three portraits that made her stop. One was a family with a tall man, a woman who was obviously the dowager countess, and two boys. The older looked a bit sullen, his gaze darted away from the rest of the family. And the younger was Jasper. She leaned in, looking at that little boy face with its slight smile.

Her children would share some of those features, she realized with a start. They would stand together for a painter and make a similar portrait in some faraway time and place.

Would they look so disconnected as Lord and Lady Harcourt did? There must have been a foot between them, and Lady Harcourt was turned slightly away from the earl, as if the very act of being near him was a trial.

Thomasina sincerely hoped her future would not be like that. It was far too common in Society.

The next portrait in the line was of Solomon Kinkaid, the last Earl of Harcourt, but this time he was an adult. His hair was too long for current fashion, his gaze a little bleary, as if the painter had caught him in a drunken moment. Based on all she knew about Jasper's late brother, that was probably true. Everyone knew the previous earl was a wastrel and a libertine. He had caused many a scandal in the short course of his life and ultimately by the mode of his death.

And *that* was what Jasper was fighting against now. But still, as she stared at the other man, she could see he and Jasper had a similar mouth. Solomon's hair was darker than his brother's, his eyes blue. They'd not shared a mother and it seemed they didn't have many like features.

She wondered what Jasper thought of him. He'd made a few vague mentions of the man. She had caught a glimpse of his deep sadness, but she had no idea if they had ever been close, either as children or as men. If he mourned Solomon still, a year after his untimely demise.

The last portrait in the line was the most important to her. Her husband, painted before he had taken the title, judging by the date on the brass label that was attached to the frame. Jasper looked younger than a mere handful of years before. There were fewer troubles in his countenance.

Who was this man? Was it only taking the title that had darkened him into a person who feared scandal to his very core? A man who only rarely smiled? One who was sometimes seen by others as hard or cold when neither of those things had proven true when she was alone with him?

She didn't know that any more than she knew anything else about the husband she loved. And she *wanted* to know. All of it. She wanted to hear his pains and be a balm to them. She wanted to know his triumphs and celebrate those, too.

She wanted it all.

"There you are, lazy bones."

She smiled as she turned to find Juliana entering the opposite end of the hallway. Her sister rushed through the gauntlet of painted eyes with a shudder. Juliana had always hated a portrait gallery, and she shook her head as she grabbed Thomasina's hand and dragged her away from it.

"Eh, their eyes are so horrifying," she said, and they linked arms and entered a pretty parlor just after the hallway.

"You always thought so," Thomasina laughed. "Anne and I used to giggle so much about it."

Juliana's expression darkened at the mention of their sister. "Yes. I hated how you two teased, but now...now I would do anything to hear her quips."

Thomasina squeezed Juliana tightly. "As would I. But we have each other, don't we?"

Juliana nodded, and then she seemed to wipe her darker emotions away. She turned to Thomasina and looked her up and down closely. "Well, you don't look any different."

"Why should I?" Thomasina said with a confused shake of her head.

"Because you have done the thing we were not supposed to speak of!" Juliana cried. "The first of us to do so." Her face fell. "I suppose *not* the first of us, after all. Perhaps Anne—"

Thomasina caught her hands. "Don't think of it. We must assume she is fine and doing only what she wants to do while we're parted. To think of any other possibility is too awful to bear."

Even more unbearable now that she understood what happened between a man and a woman. When it was desired, it was wonderful and perfect. If it wasn't...well, she could imagine how damaging it would be. She blinked at the sting of tears and tried to remain positive for Juliana's sake.

"What was it like?" Juliana pressed.

Thomasina felt the heat flood her cheeks and she darted her gaze from her sister's pointed one. "It was—it was..."

"Please don't start with the 'unmarried ladies shouldn't know' nonsense. We've always promised we would share this information." Juliana folded her arms in expectation.

"I don't want to hide it, I assure you," Thomasina said. "It is just that I'm not sure how to describe it. If you want the man, if he wants you, if he cares about your pleasure...it is more wonderful than anything I've ever thought could exist between two people. The entire endeavor makes you feel alive. Like you could fly, but also that you're grounded. And the pleasure is...intense."

"It didn't hurt like everyone always claims?" Juliana asked, leaning forward with gathering interest.

"Yes, a little. Though not after the first time."

Juliana's eyes boggled. "You did it more than once?"

Thomasina bent her head with a hot blush in response.

"Well, I suppose I will know soon enough. Unless Father decides to keep me a spinster so he won't lose his secretary, I will be the next to fall to his desire to marry his daughters well." Juliana twisted her mouth. "Until then I will only have to imagine."

"Well, there is a way to give *yourself* the pleasure," Thomasina said, her blush returning. "But I don't think we should speak about it in such a public room."

"No, perhaps not," Juliana agreed with a smile. "We will have to discuss it soon enough, though. After all, Father and I are still scheduled to return to London the day after tomorrow. He hasn't said anything different to me, despite Anne being missing."

Thomasina let out her breath in a long sigh. "Yes, if Jasper sticks to his original timeline that he created for his marriage to Anne, we will follow just a week afterward. I had hoped we would remain here and try to find her. Do you think Father is looking at all? I know we are commodities to him, but he *must* care that she is in danger, mustn't he?"

Juliana's dropped stare was the answer to the question that Thomasina feared she already knew. "He will *say* he cares," Juliana said carefully. "But now that Anne has done something so foolish, so scandal-worthy as running away, he knows he'll gain nothing through her. If she isn't a chip to be bargained with..."

Thomasina nodded. "Yes, I understand."

"I couldn't dare to hope that Lord Harcourt is looking. Would he, after our sister caused him so much trouble?" Juliana asked.

Thomasina twisted her mouth. "The subject of Anne is a tender one between us. He doesn't seem to like to discuss her."

"Now that you are married, perhaps that will change. Especially if things were as wonderful in your marital bed as you said. I've heard of ladies who manipulate that position with their husband for their own ends."

Thomasina frowned at the idea of using the physical connection between her and Jasper to get what she wanted. It felt like the only place he truly let her in thus far. But this was her sister they were talking about. Anne was in trouble, of that she had no doubt.

How could she deny any method of helping her?

"Well, since we don't know the intentions of the men in our lives," Thomasina said, "perhaps we should do what we discussed yesterday and do a little investigating of our own."

Juliana nodded. "I think we should, especially if I'm going to be forced to leave. What do you think of speaking to Nora?"

Thomasina grabbed her sister's hand. "I was just going to say that myself, but you probably know that already." They giggled, for they used to call that Triplet Magic, when their thoughts were so aligned. "You and Father spoke to our sister's maid just after Anne ran away."

"Father screeched at her," Juliana corrected. "It scared her half to death. Perhaps after a few days and with Anne not returning, it will give her reason to say more."

Thomasina nodded as she pulled the bell. Willard appeared and she asked him to fetch Nora. As they waited, she felt Juliana's stare on her. Appraising. All-seeing. She only hoped her sister wouldn't ask after her emotions with as much detail as she had pursued her experience in her marriage bed.

Talking about her heart felt even more intimate.

At last the door opened and Nora stepped in. The maid was a slight little thing, with pale blonde hair and wide blue eyes. Currently they were rimmed with dark circles. Her hands shook as she stepped into the space and glanced from Thomasina to Juliana.

"Good morning, my lady, Miss Juliana," she said, and her voice trembled even harder than her hands.

Thomasina stepped forward. "Good morning, Nora, please come in. I think you must know what we've asked you here to discuss."

To her shock, the maid lifted her hands to her face and began to weep loudly. Juliana's eyes were wide as she met Thomasina's and then she rushed to close the door and give this surprising moment some privacy.

Meanwhile, Thomasina rushed to put an arm around her as Nora hiccupped, "Y-You're g-going t-to s-sack me."

"No!" Thomasina burst out as she guided Nora to the settee and helped her sit. "Gracious, no, of course not."

Nora lifted her head from her hands and swiped at the tears that streaked across her cheeks. "You aren't?"

Juliana produced a handkerchief and handed it over as she took a place on the chair across from the settee. "No, most definitely not."

The young woman all but sagged in relief. "Mr. Shelley yelled so loudly the night Miss Anne ran away," she explained. "And no one's talked to me about anything since. I thought sure I would be on the street as soon as we reached London. Perhaps even left out here in the wilds where I'd never find a position."

Thomasina exchanged a guilty look with Juliana and squeezed the maid's hand. "I'm so sorry, of course we should have thought of your feelings. Everything has been such a whirlwind with the marriage and Anne's disappearance. I'm so sorry we didn't reassure you earlier."

"So Mr. Shelley won't put me out?" Nora asked, her tone filled with hope.

Thomasina worried her lip. "In truth, I'm not certain. Our father can be mercurial and he's angry at Anne. But I promise you that you won't be on the street. I'll find a way to help you, and so will Juliana."

Juliana leaned forward. "And if Anne were to return, she would certainly be our ally in protecting you."

Thomasina could see where her sister was steering the conversation. She didn't like the manipulation, but she could see it worked for Nora shifted on the settee gently. She smiled at Nora.

"Juliana is correct, of course. Your best advocate is Anne." She tilted her head to meet Nora's gaze. "What can you tell us about her disappearance?"

Nora swallowed and cast her eyes toward Juliana. "Miss Juliana was there when Mr. Shelley asked me. I didn't know she was going to run away."

"Of course you didn't," Juliana said. "I believed you that night when you told us that. But you and Anne were very close. I know she considered you a friend and perhaps confided in you when she felt she couldn't in us. Did she tell you *anything* about this Ellis person?"

Thomasina could see the answer to that question before Nora even answered. The guilty twitch of her gaze, the tensing of her hands. The maid knew something.

"Do you remember the country dance the family went to at the assembly hall the first week we got here?" Nora asked.

Thomasina nodded. "Was that where she met him?"

Nora sighed. "Miss Anne had been so…sad…since her engagement. I knew she wasn't happy. But that night she came home light as air and couldn't wait to tell me about this man she met on the terrace."

Thomasina shifted and she saw Juliana do the same. Their sister had said nothing to either of them about her sadness…or her connection to this new man.

"Did she say his name? His full name?" Thomasina pressed.

Nora shook her head. "Just Ellis. I tried to remind her that she was about to be a married lady, but you know Miss Anne."

"She can't be stopped once she wants something," Juliana mused.

"They met a few times during the weeks leading up to the wedding, but I never saw him." Nora's discomfort was clear. "Miss Anne kept telling me that she had no way out of the marriage, so there was no worrying about what she would do. But I swear she never told me she would run away."

Thomasina let out her breath in a long sigh. "I believe you. We should look through her things."

"I already did." Juliana scrubbed a hand over her face. "That first night. I found nothing."

Thomasina tilted her head at that revelation. Why had her sister done such a thing alone? Was it just her sense of responsibility that drove her?

"Well, perhaps you know of some secret place where she might have put letters or a journal she hid that might tell us more," Thomasina said to Nora.

"I'll look today," Nora assured them.

"Good." Thomasina got up, and Nora and Juliana did the same. "Thank you for your honesty and for your help."

Nora clasped her hands before her chest. "Of course. I adore Miss Anne. I'm so afraid for her. I hoped she'd come home by now."

"We all hoped that," Juliana croaked. "And we must still hope. It's all we have to cling to."

Nora nodded. "I'll go search now." She bobbed out a quick curtsey and left them alone again.

Thomasina let out a long sigh. "I hoped she would know more."

"So did I," Juliana agreed as she came to put an arm around Thomasina's waist. They stood that way for a long moment before Juliana continued, "Why didn't Anne talk to us about how unhappy she was? I knew she was restless, but not *sad*."

Guilt swelled in Thomasina. "I don't know. I *wish* I knew, but she never said anything. We might have failed her if she felt she couldn't speak to us. But we can't fail her now. We must do more. As much as we can to...to save her if she needs to be saved. You work on Father," she said. "Try to convince him to stay a while longer. And I will talk to Jasper about the search for Anne."

"That sounds the best option to me." Her sister leaned forward and hugged her. "I'm glad last night wasn't terrible. I worried for you. And I hope that once this situation with Anne is resolved that you will be truly happy in your new life."

Thomasina squeezed her sister hard. "I'm going to try everything in my power to ensure it. Now I will go find my husband and work on my side of this equation. I'll see you at luncheon in a few hours, will I not?"

Juliana nodded. "You will."

They moved into the hall together. Juliana turned one way to go look for their father and Thomasina retraced her steps back to Jasper's office on the other side of the estate. She thought about her duty as she went, about what she would say to him. About what he would say to her.

After last night, would things be different between them? For better or worse? She reached his study door and drew a long breath.

There was only one way to find out. She knocked on his door and then pressed it open slowly. He was seated as his desk, a quill clenched tightly in his fingers, his forehead lined with worry as he pored over a letter before him.

"What do you want?" he snapped without looking up.

CHAPTER 13

Thomasina started at the cold, dismissive tone. Did he know it was her at his door?

"I'm sorry to disturb you, Jasper."

He jerked his head up and looked at her. For a moment his irritation remained, but then his gaze flicked over her from head to toe and she saw some of the tension leave his mouth and eyes.

"My apologies, Thomasina," he said as he set the quill aside, shoved the letter under a pile of papers and got to his feet. "Did you need something?"

She stared at him, his hands clenching and opening at his sides, his posture stiff and uncomfortable. He was nothing like the wicked man who had claimed her the prior night. Held her and kissed her and shattered her over and over.

"Do *you*?" she retorted with an arch of her brow as she entered the study fully and shut the door behind her.

The action changed his countenance entirely. Now he tracked her movements. His pupils dilated a fraction when they were alone together. He wanted her, instantly and powerfully. That was something. "Do I what?" he asked.

"Need something," she repeated. "You seem out of sorts."

His lips thinned and the desire fled his face. "No, of course not. I was just in the middle of some—" His gaze ceased to hold hers. "Some business."

She kept moving forward, even though everything in her screamed to stop. To avoid any potential rejection. To keep from upsetting him if he truly wished her gone.

And yet the drive to support and help and comfort was so much greater than the fear.

She moved around the opposite side of his desk and leaned back against the edge so she was just next to him. He stared down at her, swallowing hard enough that she saw his Adam's apple work with the force.

"Shared troubles, remember?" she whispered as she reached out to catch his hand. She threaded her fingers through his, stroking the rougher skin, tracing the lines of his knuckles as their hands folded together gently.

He cleared his throat, and for a moment she felt him lean into her. Want to give to her, not just in pleasure, but something for her to hold and to support. That longing was written all over his handsome face, as was an intense loneliness she had never seen in him before.

But then he shook his head, clearing the vulnerability, and instead bent to kiss her. She let him, for what other choice was there? Her desire for him hadn't been tamped down the night before. If anything, it increased with every moment. And if that was what he needed, to drown in pleasure, she wouldn't deny him.

He did that for a brief moment, tracing the fingers of his free hand along her jawline as he deepened the kiss, tasting her and teasing her and setting her on fire.

But he pulled away at last, shaking off her hand and pacing to the sideboard where he rested both his hands as he calmed his panting breaths. "You are temptation embodied, my lady," he said, and cast a glance over his shoulder. "But I cannot give in this morning, as much as I'd like to do so. I've too much to do and am waiting for the return of Reynolds for—" He shook his head. "I simply cannot."

She nodded slowly. "Then perhaps we can discuss something else."

"What is it?" He turned and folded his arms, a shield. Against her, she supposed. Against her demands. That didn't bode well.

"Anne," she said softly. "I'm very concerned about her welfare, Jasper."

His jaw tightened. "If you wished to discuss your sister with me, you didn't have to play at the game of desire to do it. I don't need manipulation to consider your thoughts or feelings."

She drew back. "That isn't what my intention was at all."

He arched a brow. "Wasn't it? You didn't come in here and glide across my room and look at me just so in order to seduce me into your way of thinking?"

She would have laughed if this sudden turn of his mind were not so seriously taken. "I assure you, Jasper, I have no idea how to *seduce* anyone to my way of thinking or to anything else."

"*That* isn't true," he muttered, and shook his head almost as if that thought wasn't meant to be stated out loud.

She swallowed. "I came here to see you because it is the first full day of our marriage and you slipped out of our bed this morning like you weren't supposed to be there."

He caught his breath and then bent his head as though he felt some level of shame at that action.

She continued, "I came to see you because I wanted to make sure I hadn't displeased you—" He opened his mouth as if to speak, but she plowed forward because if she didn't, she would never be brave enough again. "I came to see you because I...I..." She stopped. There was no place for confession here. Not yet. "I *care* about you. And when I saw your expression I thought you might need...need a friend. Or comfort, in whatever form you would allow. *Those* were my first thoughts. Nothing so mercenary as you seem to believe."

He held her gaze for what felt like an eternity. "I was short with you, I was rude. I assumed. You did not deserve that. I'm sorry."

Those words were clearly not easy for him to say judging from his clipped tone and shifting posture. But she believed them to be honestly given. And she was shocked by that. Her father had never apologized for anything in his life. She didn't know many men who did.

"Thank you," she said softly.

"But you *are* worried about Anne," he said with a resigned sigh.

"I am." She moved toward him carefully, uncertain as to how to proceed. "With everything going on since she ran away, I hadn't been able to pursue the topic, or perhaps I was too afraid to. Perhaps I hoped she would simply reappear and I wouldn't be forced to seek answers. Whatever the reason, today I realized I had to press the subject, and what I discovered leaves me more nervous than ever."

His eyes widened. "What you discovered? What does that mean?"

She wrinkled her brow at his sharper tone. "Juliana and I spoke to her maid, that is all. We thought Nora might know something about this man Anne has linked herself to."

He took a long step toward her, his eyes wild for a moment. "And what did she say? What do you know about him and his motives?"

She caught her breath. This reaction was not what she had expected, given how little he had seemed to care for Anne. He'd made no attempt to find her that Thomasina knew about. And yet this topic was obviously upsetting to him.

"Nothing," she said slowly. "Nora said he met her at the assembly we all attended at the beginning of our time in Harcourt, but little else."

His jaw relaxed a fraction and he nodded. "I see. Don't you think, though, that it would have been better to leave talking to the maid to your father? Or even me?"

"Why?" she asked. "Nora is terrified of my father, and for good reason since he would sack her without reference. And she doesn't know you. Nora knows Juliana and me. We were the best ones to open the door."

Jasper was silent for what felt like forever. "I suppose you're right. And I shouldn't have expected that you would simply forget Anne's troubles. You couldn't. I know how deeply you care for her."

"But it was for naught anyway. There seems to be nothing to tell." She shook her head. "And I cannot stop thinking that my sister could be in true danger. I-I *feel* it."

He was frustrated by this subject, that was clear. But he also seemed less angry than he had when she first entered the room.

"I *think* I understand that," he said slowly. "I was not as close to my brother as you are to your sisters. Perhaps because we did not share a mother, perhaps because our temperaments were so diametrically opposed. Perhaps a dozen other hurts and reasons over the decades kept us from such a strong relationship."

He sighed and her lips parted. This was a glimpse of answers to the questions she'd had in the gallery not half an hour before.

"I'm sorry you weren't close. It is one of the great joys of my life to be so bonded with Anne and Juliana," she said.

"I can see that. *Feel* it." He shrugged. "Either way, I still worried about Solomon even though we weren't always brotherly. Your attachment to Anne is far greater, so I must think your emotions about her disappearance are also more intense."

She nodded. "We're triplets and the whispers about a stronger connection are, I think, true. Once when she fell off the rail of a roof and badly hurt her ankle, my own ankle hurt for days."

His eyes widened. "I have many questions about that, including why your sister was walking the rail of a roof."

"Our reckless Anne," she answered with a smile. "Your scandal was not her first, I assure you."

There was a ghost of a smile on his face, but then he waved his hand. "Do you think you feel this physical connection to her still?"

"Not as strongly since we've gotten older," she admitted, trying to ignore the sadness that came along with that loss. "I know she is alive, though."

He drew back with a sharp intake of breath. "Of course she is alive, Thomasina!"

She bent her head. "You could not be sure of that. We don't know anything about the kind of man who would take her when her engagement was so public. I wish I could understand what kind of villain wouldn't press his case in a more gentlemanly way. But I cannot fathom his motives or what she is enduring. Neither of us can because neither of us have laid eyes on the man to see what kind of person he is."

Jasper's lips tightened. "I suppose that is correct."

She shivered. "I may be naïve, but the fact that my sister is in danger is no mystery. But I would know if she were dead. I *know* I would."

Her voice broke, and she reached back to support herself on the arm of the nearest chair as all her fear mobbed her for the first time. She bent her head, trying to control her breath, trying to tame that terror once more.

He stepped forward and his arms folded around her. The fear dissipated with his touch and she sank into him, taking the strength he silently offered. The connection and the bond that she desired so greatly. She needed those things now, perhaps more than was prudent given the circumstances of their marriage.

But that didn't change the facts. Nor her feelings.

"I'm sorry," he whispered into her hair as he stroked his hands along her back. "I'm so sorry."

She lifted her gaze to his. "You needn't be sorry. Anne's foolish decisions have nothing to do with you. You were their victim, more even than me. It could make you unkind, but here you are...and you are more than generous to me."

His body tensed and he released her, pacing away as he ran a hand through his hair. "I doubt many others would accuse me of generosity."

There was a harshness to his tone now. Not directed at her, but himself. As if he needed punishment for something.

"Well, perhaps they do not know you," she said. "If they did, they couldn't say anything less."

"You ought not see me so highly, Thomasina," he muttered.

She felt him pulling away, easing back toward his desk. If he reached it, she believed he would put her off and the conversation would end. She couldn't let it happen. Not yet. "I must say that I fear what will happen when we go to London. It will be harder to track Anne from so far away."

He shook his head. "We are not going to London."

Relief flooded her, along with confusion. "No? But that was your plan when you were to marry my sister. You had not told me it changed."

He blinked. "I-I suppose I should have. Again, I apologize, I am not accustomed to another person's life being so entangled with my own. My decisions impact more than just myself. I'm certain I will remember it eventually."

"What made you change your mind?" she asked. "My sister?"

His lips thinned. "I won't tell you that Anne's disappearance doesn't have something to do with it. As does some other unexpected business I discovered waiting for me here."

She wrinkled her brow. Although Jasper hadn't written her sister off as their father had, he also didn't seem driven to find Anne. But at least if they were here, she could continue to press her case.

"My mother will return to London tomorrow as planned, though," he said.

She sucked in a breath. She would not be sorry to see the dowager go, though she wouldn't say that to this man. "Apparently my father also intends to leave on the original schedule."

He jerked his face toward her. "What? He isn't staying here to seek information on his daughter?"

His shock was comforting at least. And humiliating since the answer wasn't one she could pretend away. "No. I suppose he could do so in London."

"But you don't think he will."

"No," she admitted after a pause that seemed to last forever. "My sister has lost her value to him after this fiasco. If she has married this man, this stranger, he won't gain anything until he knows the worth of him at some future point. And if she hasn't—"

She broke off with a shudder.

He nodded. "Then she is ruined."

The words hung in the air between them.

"Yes," she whispered. "She is ruined whether by act or by implication. He won't be able to match her well. That is all that matters to him. He may be forced to settle with his earl and call it a day."

His lips parted. "His lack of concern is sickening." He pushed to his feet and paced the length of the room. "Have you spoken to him about staying?"

She shook her head. "Juliana is doing that today. She has always been the one to manage him. Manage everyone, really."

"I will add my voice to that chorus," he said. "At least he should be here, close by in case—"

He cut himself off and she flinched, for the potential outcomes were clear. Painfully so.

"In case she is found or returns of her own volition," she said, filling in the space with the scenario that pained her least.

"Of course," he said. "But I cannot guarantee I will be able to keep him here. At any rate, *we* will remain in Harcourt Heights. Unless..."

He trailed off and his dark gaze held hers a moment, seeking and analyzing in a way that made her feel utterly vulnerable to him.

"Unless?" she whispered.

"Unless you don't want to stay," he said softly. "Unless you want to return to London with your family. *Do* you want that?"

CHAPTER 14

J asper held his breath as his question made its impact on his new bride. If Thomasina left, in some ways it would be easier. Her questions about Anne only caused him guilt. He had directly lied to her more than once. Every time, it felt like a weight in his chest, though he had his reasons. Protecting her was paramount. But he hated to see her utter terror about her sister's safety. Terror he could not assuage, for she was right about the facts of the situation.

But the idea of not having her here with him...it was physically *painful*. He wanted her at his side. He wanted to be at her side, just in case. Just in case the worst happened. She would need someone then. He knew what it was like not to have anyone in that horrible moment.

She moved toward him, her hands shaking at her sides. "Whatever the past, Jasper, whatever the future, I am your wife now. I'm not leaving here until you do."

He stared at her, taken in and taken aback by her enormous strength. And by the support and connection she offered so effortlessly. She was suggesting she would be his partner. He hadn't had one of those in...ever.

He'd never had a partner, not truly.

She drew in a long breath and reached for him. Her fingers threaded into his own and she lifted his hand to her chest as she gazed up at him. "I would share your troubles, my lord. If you let me."

In that moment he wanted just that. To share his troubles. To take hers. And if he did that, everything would change. Nothing could ever be the same after that. Would it be worth it? To dive headlong from this cliff and hope he would find wings before he dashed himself on dangerous rocks below?

"Or ease them, at least," she whispered, and lifted up on her tiptoes.

He bent his head and met her halfway, their lips touching. He cupped her chin, tilting her face slightly to grant better access. She opened then, sighing into his mouth as he claimed her with his tongue.

He knew what would happen next. It was obvious what would happen next, right here in his study, on his desk. But before he could have her in such a wanton, wicked way, there was a knock on the door.

He blinked as he pulled away from her and stared toward the entrance. For a moment, his mind could not completely register what he should do next. Right now crossing to the door and locking it seemed the best course.

But she didn't allow that. With a smile up at him, she backed away, smoothing her skirts.

"Come in," she called out, with an almost wicked tone.

The door opened and Reynolds stepped inside. Jasper jolted, for he had been expecting his man after the letter he received the prior night—and another very early that morning, but he'd somehow forgotten.

Thomasina made him forget.

Reynolds came to a halt at the entryway. "My lady, I didn't know you were here. Many felicitations on your wedding."

Thomasina was blushing, but Jasper watched as she wiped from her face any embarrassment she might have felt at the interruption. She moved toward Reynolds with a pleasing smile and an outstretched hand.

"Thank you, Mr. Reynolds. We were sorry you missed the ceremony, but I have it on good authority that Mrs. Jennings has saved a piece of the cake for you. Now it seems as though you may have some business with the earl, so I will leave you. Welcome home." She turned toward Jasper. "And I hope you and I may...may continue with our conversation later today."

His eyes went wide at the implications in that statement, given so casually in front of his friend. "Yes, I would like that," he managed to choke out past a very dry throat.

She exited the room, closing the door behind herself and leaving him alone with Reynolds. Reynolds, who stared at him with a knowing gaze that made Jasper shuffle as he retook his place behind the desk.

"What do you look so smug about?" he muttered. "Sit down, won't you, and stop giving me that look."

"I'm not giving you a look," Reynolds said, and continued to do just that as he sat down on the other side of the desk. "I will just say that you and your bride seem happy enough. Perhaps you ought to lock your door a bit more often, but I suppose you'll learn that with time."

"Do shut up," Jasper said with a shake of his head. He straightened his shoulders and shoved teasing aside as he asked, "Any further news on Anne?"

Reynolds' expression grew serious. "No more than I what I wrote last night and this morning. She was in the company of Rook Maitland, no given name yet since I'm guessing the first is a nickname. No one in the area was completely clear, but he may be a cousin or a brother of Ellis Maitland."

"That is little comfort," Jasper muttered.

"This might be, though: when I spoke to the villagers about this

Rook person, there was nothing negative said about him." Reynolds leaned back. "He seems to have been unmemorable."

Jasper nodded slowly. "I suppose that *is* some comfort. Though I cannot imagine someone linked to Ellis Maitland isn't a villain." He drew a hand through his hair. "But Anne went with him of her own volition."

"Seemingly. They were seen getting onto a small craft—no one knew the captain—and sailing off toward Scotland. But my sources in any town they could have made landfall in have not reported their arrival."

Jasper jerked in dismay, and Reynolds held up a steadying hand. "It is likely they did not come to a town. There are dozens of small islands along that part of the coast and places along the mainland where they could have come in without notice."

Jasper let out his breath. "Still, to lose her…I cannot help but be concerned."

"I know."

"Were you able to find Ellis Maitland, or did he head after them to further claim his prize?" He shook his head. "I have to assume he has no real desire to marry her."

"I don't think so, especially since I'm not certain he was headed to Scotland." Reynolds got up and began to pace. "I lost him after your unpleasant encounter, but there has been no report of him since. Not along the roads north and not leaving out the port in Beckfoot. He has simply vanished."

Jasper clenched his fist on the desktop. "Then we are in no better position than we were to start with."

Reynolds shrugged. "Perhaps a bit better. We know Miss Anne is not with the worst villain of the two. We also know that Maitland wants something he believes you have. Enough that he would risk stealing your bride to get it."

"His damned treasure," Jasper spat, "if there ever was such a thing. Honestly, Reynolds, I have been combing through my brother's records for the year since his death, trying to detangle all his bad dealings, and I've never found *anything* about a treasure. Is there even such a thing or is Maitland crazy? Or did my brother double cross him?"

"I have no idea. But the truth is, I doubt your brother would have thought to record such a thing in his ledgers." Reynolds faced him. "Didn't he have a diary of some kind?"

Jasper nodded. "Really just a date book of sorts, to record his activities. There is little detail. I can find the old ones—I think they're in the library. I know the names to look for, at least."

"You do that. I'm going to continue to pursue any information on Rook Maitland, including what his real name might be and his connections." Reynolds arched a brow. "I assume your real goal is to find Miss Anne, after all. For both the sake of your new wife and your former fiancée?"

Jasper stiffened. Once he might have only been focused on Ellis Maitland. On protecting himself. But Reynolds was correct that his priorities had changed. Until he could bring Anne back to Thomasina and her sister, he would have to focus on that. Then he'd deal with the bastard who had orchestrated this.

"Yes," he said softly. "Thomasina is troubled beyond measure. She even tried to investigate herself, apparently. She and Juliana spoke again to Anne's maid."

Reynolds drew back in surprise. "Enterprising of them. Any information of use?"

"Only confirmation that this was a long plan of Maitland's. Apparently he approached Anne weeks ago for his wooing." He gritted his teeth at the thought. "But the maid didn't seem to know about Maitland's connection to my brother. So at least Thomasina doesn't know my family's part in her loss."

"And that concerns you?"

"All of it concerns me." Jasper sighed. "I'm hoping Thomasina will see this as a dead end and won't try to continue her search. I don't want her to make herself sick picturing Anne's situation with not one villain, but potentially two. Especially when we have nothing real to tell her." He shuddered. "So whatever you do, whatever you find, let's be very careful it doesn't get back to the family. Leave the telling to me when I feel it's right."

"Of course." Reynolds watched him closely, too closely. "You and I have known each other a long time, haven't we?"

"A decade, I suppose," Jasper said with a nod. "Since just after you left the navy."

"And we were friends, I think, before you took the title and asked me to take over as man of affairs," Reynolds continued.

Jasper wrinkled his brow. "We are still friends."

Reynolds chuckled. "Well, we may be that, but you know as well as I do that everything changes once you work for a man. The dynamic certainly isn't the same, nor should it be."

"What are you getting at?" Jasper asked, shifting the papers in front of him so Reynolds wouldn't see how this exploration made him uncomfortable. Any vulnerability always did, because it felt like danger.

"I saw you with your wife, Jasper," Reynolds said, reverting to a comfortable address he hadn't used in a year. "I saw your face when I came into the room, and I haven't seen that expression since before Solomon's death. A moment where my old friend, the one with far fewer burdens, still existed."

Jasper shook his head. "You saw a ghost then, because that man died alongside my brother, as surely as if he were shot in that duel."

"I thought that too, and mourned him when you took the title," Reynolds pressed. "But it seems he was only maimed, not killed that day. He was with her at that very desk not half an hour ago."

Jasper stared blankly at the papers before him. Sometimes he did feel like that old self when he was with Thomasina. The heavy weight of all he carried slipped away when he touched her, forgotten even if only for a moment and that made him...lighter somehow.

"Isn't it dangerous to forget one's duties like that, though?" he asked, to himself as much as his friend.

Reynolds' smile was a little sad. "I know you. You'd never forget permanently. But you deserve the break, I think, if you can find it with her."

"That wasn't the purpose of the marriage," Jasper mused.

Reynolds was quiet a moment. "It doesn't mean it isn't a fine side effect, though."

"She is unexpected," Jasper admitted slowly. "In a great many ways. I never thought to be surprised but I have been so far. And I don't...dislike the sensation. But it is not a love match."

He said it out loud and shifted beneath the cruelty of the words. The finality he had put on them, as if nothing could ever shift or change. Change hadn't been his friend of late, but now he felt an odd longing for it.

"It doesn't have to be a love match to be good or happy," Reynolds said with a shrug. "And I would suggest, in my last moments here as your friend and not your man of affairs who could be fired for such impertinence, that you ought not dismiss any person who can give you peace in a world of chaos." He nodded and his face went impassive. "Now, is there anything else you require before I continue my investigation, my lord?"

Jasper looked up at him. "No. Thank you, Reynolds. Thank you...*Benedict*."

His friend smiled slightly at the return to informality, then he saluted playfully and headed from the study, leaving Jasper alone. Except for the words that kept bouncing around in his head. About Anne, about both the Maitlands who had a hand in her disappearance, about Thomasina and whatever future he might build with her.

In that moment, he had a strong urge to go to his wife. An urge he didn't resist as he set his work aside for the moment and gave in to the peace Reynolds had seen. The peace Jasper had denied even though it was absolutely true and felt completely dangerous.

Thomasina sat in the parlor on a settee, her feet tucked beneath her and a book perched in her fingers. She was not, however, reading. She couldn't, for the words swam on the page every time she made the attempt, and she ended up reading the same sentence over and over without any understanding of its meaning.

She was distracted. That was no surprise, after all. Distracted by Anne, by the strange turn of events that had brought her here…and by Jasper. Their interaction in the study had been both unsatisfying in how she had learned nothing about her sister and only a tantalizing taste of Jasper's true character and history.

She was, as far as investigations went, a failure. But she couldn't stop thinking of her husband's face when he'd mentioned his strained relationship with his brother. Or when he'd asked her if she intended to stay with him or go to London if her father and sister left.

Both times he had seemed…pained. Almost younger, like those questions drew him back to a more vulnerable and sorrowful time. And yet he kept her from the heart of it. The truth of it. The truth of him.

Would it always be this way?

"I'm sorry to interrupt."

She started at the voice that came from the doorway. That of the very man she had been pondering endlessly since she saw him less than an hour before.

She stood and faced him with a blush. "You weren't interrupting," she said as she took him in from head to toe. Great God, but he was handsome. Looking at him was always a pleasure, *her* pleasure.

"The book in your hand tells me otherwise," he said, motioning to it. "I can leave you to it."

She set the book down with a dismissive wave. "I can tell you I was not attending the story at all."

"No?" He arched a brow. "You were preoccupied then? By what, if you don't mind my asking?"

She blushed, for she'd been caught. She shrugged and broke her stare from his. "By...*everything*, I suppose. You could name anything that happened during the upheaval of the last few weeks and I was distracted by it. The good and the bad."

He nodded. "I felt much the same after Reynolds left me. Perhaps we could..."

He trailed off and she wrinkled her brow at what was his obvious discomfort. That felt so different from the confidence he normally exhibited in front of her. It felt like an opportunity.

"What would you like to do?" she asked as she took a long step toward him.

His gaze flowed over her again, this time more charged with sexual energy. Her body reacted of its own accord, brought to life by him as was always true, it seemed.

"Walk with me around the estate," he said.

She drew back in surprise, for that didn't seem to be the message his look was sending. But she didn't mind. Walking and talking together felt as intimate as making love to him. And there would be plenty of time for that later.

"Yes," she said, holding out her hand and taking what she hoped would be the next step toward the relationship she wanted.

CHAPTER 15

J asper watched her hand for a moment, almost as if he didn't
know what to do with it. Or that taking it meant something he
wasn't ready to share. Thomasina held her breath, feeling the
importance of the moment, even though it seemed so casual on the
surface.

But at last he drew her closer as their fingers folded against each
other. When he smiled, it lit up his face, and she nearly staggered at
the way it changed him. Made him lighter and younger and even
more attractive. He so rarely shared that expression, and yet he
gifted it to her more than anyone else.

Like his pleasure was hers and hers alone.

A foolish feeling, but one she would cling to in the fog of her
love for him and her desire for something more than just a surface
relationship.

He guided her down the long hallway and to a back parlor. They
exited the house through a pair of French doors and out onto the
terrace that wrapped around the back of the home. The same
terrace where he'd almost kissed her when she'd been pretending to
be Anne what felt like a lifetime ago, though it was just a week.

There was a set of stone stairs in the far corner of the terrace, and he took her down their length and into the pretty garden behind the house. A maze of flowers and trees and perfectly trimmed hedges greeted them, and she smiled at the beauty of her surroundings.

"You approve?" he asked, and sounded as if he truly wished for the affirmative.

She nodded. "How could I not? It's beautiful. I do love a garden and this one is very fine. I've walked in it a dozen times or more since we arrived and always find something new and lovely. Did you mother oversee it during her time as countess?"

He frowned at this question, and she felt the wall going up between them immediately. "The dowager does not garden," he said at last. "I don't think she would want to be bothered by such a mundane thing."

She cleared her throat at the sudden discomfort between them. Whenever she asked him about his past, this was what happened. It severed the tenuous connection she was trying to build. But perhaps she was going about it wrong. Perhaps she needed to give before she would receive.

"Not everyone has the green fingers, as my mother used to say," she said. "She loved to garden and oversaw every bush and flower at my father's country estate. It is one of the few things I remember about her, but I learned to garden because of those lovely memories of her tending, cutting and arranging flowers. She used to make us these little bouquets, one for each, with our favorite flowers in them."

"Different favorites?" he asked.

She smiled. "Yes. She, like you, recognized the three of us were individual people, even if we did share a face."

"She died when you were very young, didn't she?"

She was a little surprised he knew that, since he had obviously cared little for the bride he'd chosen for purely monetary reasons. She nodded. "We were just five when we...we lost her," she said with a sad shake of her head.

"How, if you don't mind my asking?"

She hesitated and then said, "In childbirth. My father wanted sons, even though the difficulty of *our* birth made that even more dangerous, I think."

"He pushed on anyway," Jasper said. "I suppose that doesn't surprise me."

"No, he is a bulldog in all things," Thomasina said with a sigh as she looked off into the distance with unseeing eyes.

"There is a lake just over that little hill," he said, following her line of sight. "Would you like to walk to it? It's private and very pretty. I liked to fish there as a boy."

"With your brother?" she asked.

He stiffened, though he didn't release her as they walked along the path out of the garden, through a long, flat section of grass. "Yes," he said at last. "Solomon and I *did* fish together there when we were young. He taught me to fish, actually."

"Then you were close once," she said softly.

He cast a glance her way. "I sometimes don't remember it after everything that happened in more recent years. But…yes. There was a time that we were close, when I was very young. He was six years older than I was, so we were leagues apart, but he could be…kind. He could also be awful, but I suppose all brothers are from time to time."

"I never had brothers, so I don't know about that," she said, freeing him again from having to speak more than he wished by turning the lens of their conversation on her. "My father was obsessed with having heirs for a while but never got his wish, so I can only speak to the bond of sisters."

"Why didn't he marry again, after the loss of your mother, if sons who could inherit and increase the family fortune were of such importance to his grand plans?" he asked.

She shrugged. "I've often wondered that myself. I think he *must* have gone out onto the marriage mart as soon as it was seemly, I cannot imagine him doing otherwise. But no one was ever good enough for his standards, I think. He's always thought he deserved the best. I suppose he didn't like the pedigree of whoever was willing to settle herself with him."

"A blunt view of your father," he said.

She stopped as they crested the hill and looked down onto the vast, blue expanse of a gorgeous lake. "Oh, you are lucky to have water on both sides of your home. The lake here and the sea to the opposite. I adore it. I shall be very happy with both vistas."

He caught her elbow and drew her a fraction closer. "I didn't mean what I said as a slur," he explained. "In fact, I think your father deserves the censure. He hasn't proven himself very high in my estimation."

She flinched, for many would judge the child with the same harshness as they did the parent. But Jasper's gentle expression didn't show that. She sighed. "I think he might blame…blame us for his troubles as much as himself. Ladies were fearful that if his first wife bore multiple children like us, they might face the same fate if they married him. Childbirth is terrifying enough a prospect, but since most would not survive such an ordeal…"

He shook his head. "So he both blamed you for the reality and then planned to use you to change it. Again, I do not think that speaks highly of him."

"He is a man of his time," she said with a shrug that didn't show the pain she had gone through to get to that conclusion. "And he isn't *all* bad."

He arched a brow but said nothing, as if to grant her an opinion he didn't share. They moved to the edge of the lake and stared for a moment. He bent to pick up a rock, then tossed it. She watched as it skimmed along the surface. "Oh, how did you do that?" she asked.

He glanced at her from the corner of his eye. "You've never skipped a rock? No cousin ever taught you?"

"No, our male cousins were older and thought us odd for being triplets," she said. "I've never done it. I don't think I've ever *seen* it."

"It's all in the wrist movement," he explained, and picked up another rock. He flicked his hand and the rock skipped along the water's surface, farther than the last had done. "Do you want me to show you?"

She nodded and moved closer. He picked another rock from the shoreline and stepped behind her, folding her fingers around the smooth surface. She caught her breath as his body heat curled around her back, his fingers gentle on her bare wrist as he showed her the flicking action.

She tried it and the rock sank immediately. They both laughed and he searched around for another rock to try. "Sometimes it helps if they're flatter," he explained, tossing a few aside before he found the right one. He handed it over, and this time just watched as she tested it and failed once again.

While he looked for a third rock, he said, "So your cousins joined the chorus against you three sisters. No wonder you are so close."

She shrugged as she took the next rock she was to try. She rolled it in her fingers. "They were always accusing us of trading places and playing tricks on them. They hated that they couldn't tell us apart."

"*Were* you trading places and playing tricks?" he asked.

She tossed the newest rock and it skidded just barely before it sank. "Oh, so close!" she cried out in pleasure, holding out her hand for another rock. "Er, *sometimes* we traded places, and it was hard not to play tricks on people who were so cruel."

He grinned. "I must admit, I *did* approve that answer."

"Even though you've been on the receiving end of the trick?" she asked, and hoped her voice sounded light. That night when she'd pretended to be Anne was still a tender spot between them. One she feared he didn't fully forgive.

"I hope you didn't do it because I was cruel," he said.

She shook her head. "No."

"To be fair, I *did* know it was you right away, so you didn't trick me," he said, and handed out another rock. He let his fingers glide along her palm gently before he released it.

She shivered at the contact of his skin on hers and blinked as she tried to focus.

"Try turning your body a little," he said, leaning to one side to show her. "And move your thumb along the top there..." She adjusted and he nodded. "Just so. Perfect."

She smiled and flicked the rock. It skipped along the surface of the water, bouncing out into the waves before it finally sank.

She jumped in place, clapping her hands with the pure joy of success. Jasper whooped and caught her waist, spinning her around before he dropped a kiss firmly on her mouth. She opened to him, and for a moment rocks were forgotten, problems were forgotten, everything was forgotten except the bond they were forging. She lifted into him with a shiver and sank into that connection with a sigh.

He parted from her after what felt like far too short a time and smiled as he steadied her. "Good show, Thomasina, that was wonderful."

She laughed and smoothed her skirts as she stepped away from him. "I admit, I'm very proud of myself. I may not have a higher accomplishment than that in my life thus far."

"I doubt that is true. Would you like to try again?"

"Yes!" she said, bending to help him find a flat rock to toss next. "This is my main duty as countess now, I'm afraid. Everything else will be secondary to skipping rocks on the lake."

"Fair enough," he said with a chuckle, and picked up a handful of perfect rocks.

As he handed the next over, she glanced at him from the side of her eye. "You mentioned again that you knew me that night at the ball. And I know I've asked you this before, but I'm not sure you ever answered me. How *did* you know? You said it wasn't a trick to tell us apart, then what is it?"

She skipped the rock, just a bit farther than she had the last. He smiled at her triumph, but she could feel his hesitation at her question. She held her breath as she waited, expecting him to distract her or put her off directly. Then he sighed and faced her.

"There is a light in you that I don't see in Juliana or Anne," he said at last. "Something that draws my eyes to you across the room. Makes me move toward you, even before I should have. Even when I knew it was wrong. That probably sounds silly to you."

She faced him with a shake of her head. "No, not at all. That is lovely to think I have a light in me. It is…it's very special, and I hope it's true." She swallowed and dropped the rocks that remained in her hand back on the shore with a clatter. Garnering up her nerve, she moved toward him. When she reached him, she leaned up into him, pressing a hand to his chest. "My light, if it exists, is yours, you know. To help you find your way in times of trouble."

His body tensed and his face became serious. His pupils dilated as he stared down at her. Then he lifted his hand to her forearm, sliding his fingers up and up slowly. Her flesh dimpled with goose bumps and she couldn't stop the gasp of pleasure that exited her lips.

He leaned down, this time more purpose in his gaze, as he brushed his lips to hers. "You want to help me?" he whispered.

She nodded. "Very much," she said on what was hardly any breath left.

He drew her closer, flat against him, and his mouth found hers. He kissed her, but this time there was far more purpose to it. Far more drive. Her body sparked, the fire starting between her legs, shooting through her veins until every part of her felt the heat of longing.

"The best way to help doesn't have words," he growled against her lips. "And it is far more wicked than I know I should be."

With that, he wrapped an arm around her back and slowly lowered her against the grass next to the lake. She gasped as she stared up at him, realizing in that moment what his intentions were. To have her, right here, out in the open where, in theory, anyone could see.

But she wasn't afraid of that outcome, somehow. It excited her to know that he wanted her so much. To know that this man of strict propriety was willing to toss it aside for the chance to touch and pleasure her.

"Yes," she whispered in answer to the question he asked with his eyes and his hands rather than his tongue. "Yes," she repeated, and he caught the word with his mouth and there was nothing left to say.

~

Jasper had never been a libertine. He'd grown up around two and watched how their utter lack of control damaged and destroyed everything good around them. He'd been with women over the years, of course—he wasn't a monk either. But he'd never been the kind of man who would put a lady on her back next to a lake and ravish her.

Until now, it seemed. Now there was nothing he wanted more as he ground his mouth to Thomasina's and felt her answering desire in the desperate moans muffled on his tongue. She was lifting to him, already flush with erotic power.

He was helpless to it and to her. And in that moment, he didn't care about prudence or scandal or anything else but burying himself deep in her body and making them both forget everything but the rush of pleasure they would find together.

He pushed at her skirts as he kissed her, gliding his fingertips along the smoothness of her calf, the gentle curve of her knee. He flattened his palm against the garter on her thigh and she hissed in pleasure as her pelvis lifted to bump his.

"We don't have much time," he grumbled, reaching between them to unfasten the fall front of his trousers.

She nodded and shoved her skirts up, bunching them between them. He positioned himself at her entrance, finding her already slick for him. With a shudder, he slid inside in one long stroke.

She gasped, her eyes wide with surprise.

He laughed as he ground his hips against her. "You must have known that was my intention."

She nodded. "Yes, I just thought it would...hurt."

He stilled his thrusts and stared at her. "Hurt? Why would it hurt?" He shook his head. "Did it hurt after the first time last night?"

"No," she said, smoothing her hands along his back to comfort him. "I just knew we hadn't taken much time and you said that was how you readied me."

He wrinkled his brow, need still pulsing through the length of his cock as her body clenched around him. And yet her words still troubled him. "You thought it would hurt and you didn't protest?" he asked.

She swallowed. "I wanted you. Wanted this. And I knew you needed it."

He pursed his lips. "You wanted to please me."

She tilted her head. "You always say that like it's a curse. What is wrong with pleasing?"

"Nothing," he said, bending to kiss the tip of her nose. "So long as it doesn't trade your pleasure away in order to give me mine. That is not fair and not expected. Please don't do it again."

She stared up at him, as if this was a foreign concept. He hated that she'd lived a life where it was. "Yes, Jasper. I won't."

"Good." He pushed aside his hesitations and rolled his hips again, jolting at the electric heat that shot up his shaft and made his balls tingle. "And now I want to show you how good fast and hard can be, my lady. Just as good as slow and gentle."

She nodded, reaching up to draw his mouth to hers. He drove his hips forward, grinding against her as he took her. She lifted to meet him, moaning and crying into his mouth as she sucked his tongue. The little thrill of pain made his eyes go wide as he stared down at her face. It was lined with concentration as she arched her neck back against the grass and cried out his name.

Her sex milked him with ripples of release, massaging him until he could take no more of the pleasure. He slammed forward one last reckless time and then poured himself into her as he dropped his head into the crook of her neck and tried to find some purchase in a world that was now spinning with pleasure, spinning with her, spinning with possibilities he'd never considered.

And a future that was suddenly seeming more possible when he held her in his arms.

CHAPTER 16

Two days into her young marriage and Thomasina had discovered one very plain thing: her husband was a man of many faces and many moods. From the laughing friend who had taught her to skip stones, to the passionate lover who claimed her by a lakeside - and countless times in their marriage bed - to the man who stood in the foyer now.

A man who was almost unrecognizable when compared to the other two. His face was lined with dark emotion, his brow furrowed and his mouth turned down into a serious scowl as they watched his mother's carriage pull onto the drive.

In comparison to his dark expression, the dowager's face was passive, emotionless. And she barely glanced at her only son and the rest as she said, "Well, the time has come. You were under no obligation to gather say goodbye, but here we are."

"Travel well, Mother," Jasper said, stepping forward as if to kiss her cheek.

Thomasina flinched as the older woman stepped aside and nodded coolly. "Goodbye, my lord. I will send word when I reach London. I think you will do the same and I will arrange for a ball to mark my approval of your bride. Some will talk of the switch, but certainly if we ignore them long enough, the scandal will fade." She moved toward the door. "Goodbye."

She didn't look back but swept from the foyer and into her carriage, as if it were nothing, even though the trip was long. Even though she might not see her only child for weeks or more.

Thomasina watched Jasper as he waved to her. His jaw was set and some might see him as just as cold as his mother was, but Thomasina saw the truth. There was a flicker of regret in his countenance. A flash of pain that he buried deep under propriety and pride.

The dowager's disregard hurt him. Thomasina wanted to know more about that. She wanted to dig deeper so that maybe one day she could soothe that ache in him.

"Well, that is that," her father said, breaking the mood with a shake of his head. "I suppose we will follow soon enough."

Thomasina turned toward Mr. Shelley and then to Juliana. Her sister looked exhausted, and why wouldn't she? When Nora hadn't been able to find further evidence in Anne's room, Juliana had begun work to convince him to stay. That had gone on for days and he still persisted in his plans.

Thomasina gave Juliana a brief look filled with meaning and then took her father's arm. "Let us take a walk, Papa," she said, reverting to a more familiar address than she normally used. "That will do you good. Juliana wanted to read, I think."

Her father jerked his head between her and her sister. "Ah, I thought you were Juliana. Thomasina then. You wish to walk?"

She bit back the painful reaction to his continued lack of differentiation between her and her sisters and forced a smile. "I do. And Jasper—"

Her husband looked at her as if he had all but forgotten she and her family were there. "Yes, good. I have some work to do in the library. I've been putting it off too long. I'll see you all later."

Thomasina flinched as he departed the foyer with very little further interaction. But she was driven to the course of turning her father's mind. She had to focus on that, not Jasper's dismissal.

She edged her father out the door and down the path that led to the stable and beyond toward the beach below. As they walked, he drew in a breath and made a face. "I've never liked the sea air," he said. "Sour, I think."

She tilted her head. "No? I find it bracing."

"Then you will be happy here," he said. "And you should thank me for my quick agreement to give you over as replacement for Anne."

"That is what I hoped to speak to you about today," she said softly. "You cannot truly think to leave before we know Anne is safe, can you?"

Her father stared off toward the sea as they crested the bluff and picked their way down the narrow path to the beach. "Juliana has been haranguing me enough on this subject, and now you start. I thought you were the quiet one."

Thomasina sighed. "I am not *only* that, Papa. I have other parts of my personality, you know."

"Well, I like the one," he grunted. "But I suppose you think, like your sister, that I owe it to Anne to stay."

"Don't you care what is happening to her?" Thomasina asked. "Does it not wake you at night to picture it?"

He seemed to consider that question, and then he sighed. "Anne was always wild. If she made bad decisions and does not like the consequences, then I suppose she will learn a lesson."

She drew back in horror at that dismissive response. She felt a sudden desire to rail at him, tell him what his disregard had meant to her, to her sisters, over the years. To demand the respect and care he ought to have given since their mother's death.

But she didn't. Not only did she not have the strength to confront him on the subject, she knew it would do no good. Her father wouldn't change. He didn't care to change.

He didn't care at all, and now that fact slapped her harder than it ever had.

If she wanted him to give in to her desires, she had to use a different tactic than the mere fear for Anne's safety. That wasn't enough to tempt him.

"Don't you worry that if you return without Anne, it will reflect badly on you?"

"How could it? No one knows anything but that your sister was replaced as Harcourt's bride."

"But that explanation won't hold up if she isn't with you when you return to London. You must worry that it will be said that you abandoned your daughter to some unknown fate? Versus if you stay here—if we are able to find her, you can either pretend that her potential marriage to this...this Ellis monster...was part of a greater plan. Or you can play on the sympathy of your friends for her terrible position."

He stared at her and she could see her words had sunk in. "I suppose that is true," he said slowly. "I can play the grieved father, clucking my tongue at how poorly my motherless daughter turned out."

She flinched once more at his coldness and barely held her rage in check. She would get what she wanted if she could maintain control.

He nodded. "You have convinced me," he said. "I will stay here at least another two weeks and we will wait for your sister. I'm certain some word of her will come back to us by then."

"Yes," Thomasina said, and didn't have to pretend her utter relief. "Especially if you put some money into the proposition."

He wrinkled his nose as if the prospect were distasteful. "Seems like throwing good money after bad, but I suppose you're right. Fine, I will discuss it with Harcourt after supper. Now I want to go examine this piece of flotsam that might be from a ship. You wait here."

He strode off down the sand, leaving her to wait for him in all his selfish glory. And yet she had obtained what she wanted, even though it didn't feel like much of a prize.

And it made her long all the more for Jasper, and the comfort she now felt in his arms as they settled into the life that would be theirs for many years to come. She only hoped he would open those arms to her. She needed it.

~

Jasper cursed as he tossed aside yet another of his brother's frivolous date books, marked with long lines of parties and games and meetings that couldn't help him determine anything about Maitland's claim of a treasure. They only proved how foolish his brother had been as he dragged centuries of their family name behind him through the mud.

"I fear I'm interrupting you." He jerked his head up and found Juliana Shelley standing at the library door, leaning on the jamb as she watched him through a hooded gaze.

"What is it, Miss Juliana?" he asked as he shuffled the disorganized books on the shelf around and found the next journal in his brother's collection.

Her eyes went wide. "You really *can* tell us apart," she breathed.

"No," he snapped, his frustration getting the better of him when it shouldn't. "I can recognize Thomasina. Since Anne has taken off to God knows where…"

He trailed off at how her expression fell, but she nodded slowly. "Ah, so a process of elimination," she said.

He stretched his back and tried to find some level of gentlemanliness in his ill humor. "Yes." He sighed and softened his tone. "Were you in need of some assistance?"

"I'd like to talk about my sister," she said softly.

Jasper squeezed his eyes shut. He had enough guilt about this subject when it came to Thomasina, he didn't need Juliana's worries on top of all that. "As I have told Thomasina numerous times, Anne is—"

She moved a step closer. "I wasn't asking about Anne."

His jaw tightened, and for a long moment, they just stared at each other across the room. Then he nodded. "I see."

Her expression collapsed a fraction and she worried her hands before herself gently. "It isn't that I'm not worried about Anne. But she is resourceful." She arched a brow. "And I somehow don't believe you are as cold as you pretend to be when it comes to her safety. So I must believe that she will be found or return on her own."

"Then your concern is Thomasina," he said.

She nodded. "Yes. She is...gentle, my lord. She is kind, sometimes even to her own detriment. If her heart were broken..."

"You think I would break her heart?" he asked, and was surprised how much that idea stung him.

"Perhaps not on purpose," she said.

"Because I'm not so cold as I seem."

She pursed her lips. "Nor are you immune to her. I've seen you look at her. But that is the trouble in the end. She'll see it too. She'll want some kind of...some type of fairytale that people like Anne or you or—or *me* know doesn't truly exist. But when Thomasina discovers it doesn't, it will crush her."

Jasper bent his head. And there it was, the fear he felt spoken out loud by a woman who shared his wife's face.

"If she loves you, my lord, she will do anything in the world to please you. Anything to find some tiny hope that you might feel the same about her."

He nodded slowly. He could see that about Thomasina. He had felt it. "I've noticed how desperately she wants to please," he said.

Juliana flinched as if that observation were a pain to her. A heartbreak. "Yes. We all had our way of coping, I suppose."

He cocked his head as he examined Juliana. He had thought very little of her during his engagement, focusing instead on Anne because he felt he had to and then Thomasina because he couldn't help himself. Now he found himself curious about this third Shelley sister.

"And what was your way?" he asked.

"I fix things," she said softly. "But I might not be able to fix this if it goes too far."

"So you're doing it now," he said.

She shrugged. "I'm trying. I couldn't protect Anne. I don't want to see Thomasina hurt."

Jasper opened his mouth to respond, but before he could there was the sound of a clearing throat at the door, and then Thomasina's voice said, "Juliana?"

All the color bled from Juliana's cheeks and she pivoted to face her sister in the entryway. "Thomasina," she gasped, her breath short.

Thomasina entered the room, her gaze focused on Jasper and Juliana. Normally he could read his wife's expression, he had become adept at parsing out the fine movements that told him her desire or her happiness or her fear. But in that moment she was emotionless. It was only the paleness of her cheeks and the tightness of her smile that made him realize she had likely heard some of their conversation.

It was evident from how Juliana's hands shook that she knew it too.

"I didn't see you there," Juliana said, coming closer to her sister.

"No, I think you didn't," Thomasina said softly, and her stare held Juliana's for a long moment. "Do you mind if I have a moment with my husband?"

Juliana nodded, but as she moved toward the door, Thomasina caught her hand. They stood, eyes locked, and then Thomasina squeezed gently. Juliana seemed to relax and then exited the room.

Thomasina sighed before she shut the door behind herself. Jasper smoothed his hands against his jacket as he watched her begin a slow stroll around the perimeter of the room, looking at all the books on the shelves. "Did you and your father enjoy your walk?" he asked.

She jerked her face toward him and gave a wan smile. "You know he is *always* a pleasure. I did convince him to stay two more weeks, to at least look like he gave a damn about his missing daughter once the truth comes out." She shook her head. "So it was not for nothing."

"Good," he said.

"Do you want to speak to me about what you and my sister were talking about when I came in the room?"

He pressed his lips together. "About you."

"Yes." She moved toward him. "She ought not have come to you to speak about me. I am an adult, after all. My marriage is not her business."

"She worries about you," he said softly. "Don't be too hard on her, it is a kindness not every person has from a sibling."

Her gaze relaxed a fraction and she sighed heavily. "I *know* she worries. It is her nature to look at each situation, find the problems and then try to fix them. I still object to her involving herself in my marriage."

He tilted his head, for this was a rare glimpse at a Thomasina who *didn't* want to please. She was angry, though she barely showed it. But there was a fire in her eyes that drew him in.

"Will you tell me what was said?" she pressed.

He let his breath out in a long sigh. "She only reminded me that I must be very clear in my intentions. And she isn't wrong. You and I have an intense physical connection. That is something more powerful than I thought could be."

"Yes," she agreed with a tiny shiver that made his cock twitch. "I couldn't have pictured that I would...I would want you so much. I *like* the wanting."

He fought for focus when she was so innocently seducing him. "But a deep connection that comes from physical pleasure can easily be misconstrued. It can be misleading."

"How so?"

God's teeth, how he hated this conversation. Hated how she watched him so carefully, read him so thoroughly. He saw the glimmer of something he could not desire, couldn't take, in her eyes. He wanted it more than he should.

He cleared his throat. "You and I discussed what the limits of our marriage would likely be before we said our vows. Those have not changed, Thomasina. If you want something else, I may not be able to give it to you. And I don't want you confused by the passion between us."

She folded her arms and that spark in her stare grew hotter. "You don't know what I want, Jasper. Neither does my sister. Neither does anyone, truth be told, because no one *ever* asks me. She assumes I am a fool and will mistake what happens in our bed for a deeper connection. So do you, even though you have lectured me more than once on the fact that you could not love me."

He caught his breath, for that wasn't what he'd said or even meant. "It is a general—"

She spun away from him with a huff of breath. "Please do not start this tedious conversation over again, husband. I shall go mad from it and run screaming from the room. You do not love me. I…" She trailed off and her shoulders rolled forward just a fraction. "I accept that," she finished, softer now. "What we have is enough. It will be enough. And I would appreciate it if we did not have to rehash this argument again. I will tell my sister the same thing."

He caught his breath as he stared at her, a goddess of fire in that brief moment. But perhaps a goddess who lied. Because even though she demanded what she wanted and he liked that, he feared that it wasn't truly enough for her. That he would hurt her.

And he didn't want to do that.

But for now, he would not press the subject. For now, he had other matters to attend to, and his wife was making demands he would respect.

"Very well," he said. "You know, you are very pretty when you are telling me what to do without apology. You ought to do it more often."

The heat in her stare faded a fraction and she bent her head with a shy smile. "I do not have much practice in doing anything but whatever is asked of me. Did I go too far?"

He moved toward her and caught her waist, drawing her against him with a smile. "No, my dear. Any time you want to put me in my place, you feel free to do so."

"Any time?" she whispered, her green eyes darkening with an unmistakable desire.

"Any time at all," he drawled before he brushed his lips to hers. She lifted against him, clutching his lapels with both hands as she molded her mouth and her body to his. He stood with her like that for a moment, then drew away. "Perhaps we will finish this conversation later."

She stepped back, her cheeks filled with high color, and then she gave him a little curtsey. "I look forward to it, my lord. Good day."

She tossed him a brief glance, then left him to the library, to his desire and to the duty he'd been fulfilling before he was interrupted. One that seemed a little less painful after a few moments with her.

He only hoped he wouldn't end up trading his own comfort for her heartbreak. He would have to be careful he did not.

CHAPTER 17

Thomasina left her conversation with Juliana until right before supper, mostly because she didn't trust herself not to let her anger be too sharp, too focused. So she had gone to her chamber and simply stewed a few hours. Now, though, she stood before Juliana's chamber door, pushed her shoulders back, and knocked lightly.

"Come in," her sister's voice responded, perhaps with a bit of hesitation. After all, who else would it be but Thomasina? She was certain Juliana knew she was not happy with her. That didn't even come from their bond of being triplets.

She entered the chamber. Juliana stood before her mirror, her maid Mary smoothing the last wrinkles from her gown. She looked lovely. Juliana always had an air of confidence about her. Not as showy as Anne's, of course, but something of strength that flowed through her easily.

But as Thomasina stepped inside, Juliana's expression wavered. Thomasina saw the fear in her sister's eyes, the terror that they would quarrel and their relationship would be damaged. They had so little left without Anne there. Just each other now and she didn't want to lose that any more than Juliana did.

She glanced at Mary and said, "I'd like a moment with Juliana. Thank you."

Mary nodded. "Yes, my lady."

As the maid left, Thomasina shook her head. "I hardly know what to think any time anyone addresses me as such. *My lady*. It feels so foreign."

"Over time you'll grow accustomed to it," Juliana said as she watched Thomasina move across the room and fiddle with the bottles on her dressing table. She shifted. "I'm sorry."

Thomasina faced her, keeping her upset in check as best she could. "If you want to speak to someone about my marriage, I would appreciate it if you came to *me*. It is tenuous enough a bond in these early days, after so much upheaval. The last thing I need is for you to create a situation where there doesn't need to be one."

"I was only thinking of your happiness," Juliana explained, though she ducked her head as if chagrined.

Thomasina nodded. "I realize that. Apparently you do not think I am intelligent or wise enough to protect that happiness on my own."

"I think you are good and lovely and kind and exactly the sort of woman who *wants* to love her husband," Juliana said. She shifted a little and her gaze held Thomasina's evenly. "Or perhaps already does. Already has for weeks, long before Anne ran away and left this mess to clean up."

Thomasina felt the color exit her cheeks as she stared at Juliana, her mouth dropped open. "You—you think I coveted Jasper?"

"I know you," Juliana whispered. "I *feel* you sometimes. The moment Father brought him into the room and announced he would be husband to one of us, it was as if your world had a new... light. I saw it pass over your face in an instant and then everything was crushed when he announced *Anne* was to marry the earl."

Thomasina took a long step back and found her hip bumping the back of a chair. "I would be a terrible sister to feel such a thing."

Juliana sighed. "No, not horrible. You would be human. It isn't as if Anne was in love with Lord Harcourt...quite the opposite."

"No, she didn't care for him," Thomasina agreed, though that fact still confused her. If Anne had only tried, certainly she would have come to care for him. It was good, then, that she hadn't.

Juliana continued, "But you wanted him, I think, and then you suddenly had him. And I know you have told yourself that you couldn't or shouldn't or wouldn't want more than the arranged marriage Father threw at you, but I...I worry. And I *should* have discussed that with you, not him. Once again, I tell you that I'm sorry."

Thomasina bent her head as the full power of her sister's words hit her like a slap across her face. The truth of them.

"Did..." She cleared her throat. "Do you think anyone else saw what you believed you did?"

Juliana took a moment to ponder the question before she shook her head. "No one knows you better than I do or Anne does. We are bound in such a powerful way. No one else could see your heart."

"But Anne might have?" she whispered, hating herself if that were true.

"Anne was wrapped up in her own dramas. If she could not desire Lord Harcourt, she would have assumed *no one* did." Juliana smiled, soft and a little pained. "But it *is* true, isn't it?"

"Yes," Thomasina said, and leaned forward on the dressing table with both hands. "God help me, it is true. I wanted him from the very beginning, just as you said. When I realized I could marry him in Anne's stead, I wasn't upset. I was afraid, I was uncertain, but I was happy. Worse, I want him even more now that I truly know what wanting means."

"Then you *are* in danger of loving him and you must be careful," Juliana said, rushing forward to squeeze her arm gently.

Thomasina dipped her head back with a gasp of breath. "I-I *do* love him."

She had said it out loud, and there the words hung between them. A wall and a curse and a glorious light. Something and everything and nothing all at once.

All the color drained from Juliana's face, and for a long moment she was utterly silent. Then she nodded at last. Her tone was carefully neutral as she said, "I see."

"And now you will scold me." Thomasina shook away her arm and paced the length of the room. "You will tell me I have no right to tell you not to speak to him when you are correct at what a fool I am."

"I would *never* scold you for loving someone." Juliana looked truly pained that Thomasina would believe otherwise. "It is only that I worry. Does he share these feelings?"

"Of course not," Thomasina said, throwing up her hands. "He hasn't pined after *me* for months, feeling his heart swell with every moment he spent with me. Learning my every quirk and habit until he could identify them without even looking."

"Oh dear," Juliana said softly. "That sounds very intense."

"It is." Thomasina sighed heavily and then shrugged, dismissing her heart though it wasn't as easy as the action implied. "Jasper *does* want me. He makes that abundantly clear."

"Yes, one would have to be blind not to see your physical connection." Juliana's cheeks were pink. "It practically makes the air around you hum."

Thomasina shivered at the thought. "Beyond that, I think he *likes* me, sometimes despite himself." She sighed again. "But he has been nothing but honest in his intentions. He did not seek out love when he arranged this union with our sister. In fact, he chose as he did because love was most definitely not in his plans."

Juliana worried her lip slightly. "And a man like Jasper follows through on his plans."

"He does do that," Thomasina agreed. "Which is a wonderful quality. He will be a dependable partner. And yet I want more than that. And sometimes I think…"

She trailed off, for she couldn't bear to say what she hoped for, despite all of Jasper's denials of her desires. But Juliana, of course, was too wise a sister not to see what she meant. "You sometimes think he might be able to care for you more deeply?" she asked.

"Sometimes I think it is only a breath away." Thomasina ran a hand over her face with the frustration of the situation.

"Perhaps it is," Juliana said with uncertainty. "After all, not one person since Mother has ever been able to tell us apart. Yet he knows you!"

"Yes, and that gives me some hope. When we talk, I feel like we are forging a path between us. And when he touches me..."

Juliana's brows lifted. "Is it really so very *good*? After all the fearful things we heard?"

"Better than anything," Thomasina said with a blush.

"Then perhaps he can be convinced," Juliana said. But it was clear she was worried. "Perhaps together—"

Thomasina stepped forward with a snort of laughter. "Oh no, my dearest sister, this is the one place where *together* we can do nothing. This is my marriage, my problem. You *cannot* fix it. You must trust me to handle it myself."

She could see how difficult an idea that was to Juliana. Juliana, who had fought to protect and support her sisters at every turn. Juliana, who solved all the problems of their family and friends. It was her role. Thomasina knew she was taking that away from her.

At last, though, Juliana bent her head in acquiescence. "Very well. I won't interfere again, though you know I'm always here to talk to if you need me. I suppose we are better served if I put my energy into Anne. Though without word from her or any other information from her things, I don't know how in the world to proceed."

Thomasina's face fell. Her sister was correct on that score. *Anne* had to be their focus now, not some silly future she desired but would likely never be. She couldn't spend her time on that right now at any rate. Jasper had been clear about his desires.

So she had to put her energy into something that mattered.

"We'll figure something out," she promised as she tugged Juliana into a hug and tried to forget everything else.

CHAPTER 18

Jasper stood with his father-in-law, but he wasn't attending to Mr. Shelley's nasal voice as he droned on and on. His gaze kept returning to Thomasina as she stood at the fireplace with her sister, their heads close together.

It had been almost a week since he had told his wife that he didn't want confusion in their marriage. He'd braced himself for her to argue and make her case and try to wear him down. And yet...

She hadn't.

Instead, she had pulled away, distancing herself from him during the day. She was polite, of course. She smiled and asked after his needs, she was kind to his staff and she took on the duties of a countess as if she had been born for the job.

But she no longer made efforts to connect with him on a deeper level. She no longer pressed him about his brother or his past or their future.

It was exactly what he had told her he desired. It should have made him relieved and happy to see her put away those foolish ideas of a love match. Better for both of them, he tried to tell himself.

And yet he felt no joy about it. He was annoyed when she pulled away, he was troubled when she gave him a false smile. It was very confusing.

It was only in their bed that he felt the connection that had started those first few days of their marriage. When she came to his bed, she was *his* Thomasina again. Passionate and sweet, enthusiastic and responsive. She was learning how to give him pleasure, she was adept at receiving it. He wanted to drown in her. He wanted to stay in their bed for a week or a month or a year and never return to his duties except for making her sigh out his name in release.

He wanted that despite all his other responsibilities. To her sister, for one. To his own estate. His search of his brother's diaries had yielded nothing even after days of tracking patterns and comparing dates. And Reynolds, who had sent a detailed report about Anne and Maitland and this other fellow, Rook. There was still very little about him in any record, but it was believed he *might* be on one of dozens of uninhabited islands that dotted the channel between England and Scotland.

Not much help on the whole. So he was feeling like a failure and a liar and like he'd lost something he didn't even know he wanted.

"...perhaps we should leave tomorrow then."

Jasper jerked his attention back to his companion and stared at Mr. Shelley in shock. "You're leaving despite your promise you would wait? I certainly hope it is to go looking for your daughter in Scotland, as I have asked you to do three times in the last week. As you have *agreed* to do multiple times and then not done."

Shelley shook his head. "Look for her there? Why? We both know the girl didn't go to Gretna Green or we would have heard something from her by now. She might have even returned, a new husband in tow, to crow that she thwarted our plans and followed her utterly foolish heart."

Jasper blinked. Shelley was constantly proving he was a bastard of the worst order, and yet it always shocked Jasper somehow. "And *that* doesn't make you want to chase her even more? The knowledge that she was taken in by a villain who had no intention to wed her?

Who has certainly taken advantage of that so-called foolish heart in the most ungentlemanly way?"

Shelley seemed to ponder the question a moment, then shrugged. "Some people must learn from their own mistakes. Anne is one of those people. If she suffers, it is only the consequences of her own actions."

The thin wire of control Jasper had been exercising with this man broke at last. He took a long step toward Shelley, catching his lapels in both fists and yanking him closer. Across the room, he heard Thomasina and Juliana both gasp, but he ignored them.

"Listen here, you pompous ass, I have kept my patience in the face of your utter disregard for not only your missing daughter, but for the ones that have been left behind. I will bear it no longer." He shook Shelley and the other man squeaked his fear as he clawed at Jasper's hands. "You will go to Gretna Green tomorrow morning, with a man or two of mine in tow, and you will do some bloody searching for your daughter. I swear on everything holy that if you run off to London, I will destroy you with a smile on my face. Am I understood?"

Shelley grunted as he wrenched himself from Jasper's grip and nearly deposited himself on the carpet at his feet. He smoothed his wrinkled jacket as he glared at his son-in-law. Jasper saw his rage, but also his weakness. His emptiness. How he had produced three daughters of substance and character, he had no idea. But he was certainly glad their apples had fallen so far from the tree.

"I understand you perfectly," Shelley said. "And you understand me, *boy*. You may do a little damage control with the money you obtained from marrying my daughter, but there is no forgetting what a scandal you are. And if you move on me, I can also make your life much more difficult."

He turned on his heel and stomped from the room. Only then did Jasper look at Thomasina and Juliana. They were huddled together, hands clasped. Juliana stared at the door where her father had left, her cheeks pink and her eyes bright with tears. But

Thomasina was looking at Jasper. Only him. And something in his stomach, something in his chest, stirred at her focused regard.

"I'll go speak to him," Juliana said softly.

Thomasina managed to jerk her gaze from Jasper and looked at her sister. "He will go to Scotland. He'll look for Anne at last."

Juliana nodded and squeezed Thomasina's fingers lightly. "At last we may know something of what happened to her." She glanced at Jasper briefly. "Thank you, my lord. I'll go help him ready to leave."

She exited the parlor, leaving Jasper and Thomasina alone. His chest hurt as he stared at her. She wanted so desperately to know about Anne's escape. And he had information. But it was so open ended, with such a lack of good news...*could* he share that with her without hurting her even more? She already cringed at the idea of Anne being harmed, being used. There was little he had discovered to ease her pain. To know Anne was with yet another stranger, another villain...it would only solidify that terror.

And it was more than that which made him withhold what he knew. He wasn't certain he wanted to give up what a villain his *own* brother had been. Because Solomon's failings were stamped all over every single thing he had uncovered.

He didn't have to decide. Once her sister departed, Thomasina stepped up to him, her hand extended. He watched as she folded her fingers around his and lifted his hand to her lips. She kissed his palm and his cock twitched in response to the seemingly innocent graze of lips.

"You didn't have to do that," she whispered.

He shook his head. "Yes I did. Truth be told, I should have done it a week and a half ago. The moment we discovered your sister's escape. I merely hoped he would do the right thing on his own."

"Because you judge him at the same level that you hold yourself," she said. "But he is not half the man you are."

Now those questions, those guilty feelings, rose up in his chest even higher in the face of her compliments. She offered him trust and he was betraying it.

"Thomasina," he began, uncertain how to tell her what he knew. But knowing in that moment that he had to do it. At least give her a kernel.

She lifted up on her tiptoes and brushed her lips to his, silencing him. He wrapped his arms around her, sinking into the pleasure and relief just the gentlest touch provided. Knowing he shouldn't surrender to her but needing it like he needed breath or water or food.

She was his sustenance.

She remained in his arms even as she broke the kiss and looked up into his face. He saw everything in her eyes then. Her trust, her hopes and her love. He saw that she loved him, and instead of frightening him, it gave him joy. He'd never earned the love of most of his closest companions. He'd sought it but never attained that moment of true acceptance.

And here it was, on her beautiful face.

"No one has been my champion for a long time," she said softly. "I didn't know how much I wanted one until you began to take on the role. But I have very little to reward you with, fair knight. Except to take you up to my bed and show you what it means to me to have you push my father beyond his most cruel and selfish desires."

His lips parted. Take her to bed. Let her connect with him the only way he fully knew how. And when it was over, he would tell her the truth. Or at least part of it. That was what he had to do. He could only hope that shocking love he'd seen on her face wouldn't be erased by the things he had to say.

Thomasina's hands shook as she shut the chamber door behind them and turned to face her husband. A week of pretending she didn't care, of distancing herself from him as he'd asked, had been nearly impossible. So many times she had wanted to go to him and curl into his life. So many times she had wanted to comfort him.

But now, after watching him put her father in his place at last, she couldn't hold back. She *needed* connection and this was the only way he would allow it. With a shuddering sigh, she moved to him. He opened his arms without hesitation and she stepped into the space there, loving how she fit against him perfectly, dreaming that was by design. His mouth found hers and she lifted into him, seeking passion and pleasure.

But he seemed to have other ideas. He cupped her chin and drew back so that his lips were only brushing hers. "Slow," he whispered against her mouth. "Please."

The *please* was what did her in. If he asked, she couldn't deny him. Not in this, not in anything else. She knew her own weakness. She could own it and revel in it.

She nodded, the act brushing their lips together. "Slow," she repeated.

He tilted his head, angling his mouth against hers. The kiss deepened and she drowned in it. Drowned in him as they stood like that for what felt like an eternity. His hands fisted against her back, his passion restrained, and she shivered against him in anticipation.

"Turn around," he ordered, his voice rough as he broke his mouth from hers.

She followed the demand, putting her back to him. She bent her head forward and he pressed a kiss to her hairline, then lower until he reached the edge of her gown. She pushed back against him with a gasp as sensation jolted through her. He made it all seem so easy to want him. To want *them*.

He unbuttoned her gown, continuing to kiss along the skin he exposed there, the silky fabric of her chemise. When he pushed the dress forward, she wiggled out of it and heard him let out a little groan.

She peeked over her shoulder as he cupped her hips, rubbing his hands over the fabric and her skin beneath, rocking her against him as he wordlessly looked at her.

"I'm never going to tire of seeing you like this, of touching you like this," he growled, suddenly possessive and dark.

Her eyes widened. "You can't promise that."

He slowly turned her so she faced him again. He cupped her cheeks and met her stare. "Yes, yes I can. I can promise that because I know that it's true. You will always be desired, Thomasina. I will always crave you and the only thing that will set me free is touching you. And watching you come. And feeling you around me and in my arms. Forever."

Her heart thudded at that vow, spoken as seriously as the ones that had made her his wife had been. Only this one was more personal. And while it might not be the declaration of deepest love that she secretly wished for, it was certainly a step she hadn't thought he would take and definitely not so soon.

Her hands shook as she lifted them to cover his. "And I will always set you free, Jasper. I will always welcome you."

She lifted to him and he met her halfway. Their mouths collided again, this time not slow or gentle as they had begun. This time she felt his need, she felt his desire...she felt a hint of desperation that she didn't fully understand. But she would take it. That hungry desire for her was something she would always take, even though she wanted more. But for now, it was what he gave and she had to be satisfied with that.

J asper's heart throbbed as he slid his fingers beneath the thin straps of Thomasina's chemise and dragged it down her body in one smooth motion. There was nothing more powerful than unwrapping the gift that was her body. And it *was* a gift, just as she was a gift that had been unexpected in his life but was most definitely wanted.

He stepped back as the chemise pooled at her feet with her gown. She wore no drawers beneath, so she was naked now. Naked and achingly beautiful. He reached out to trace a hand along the curve of her breast. When he stroked over her nipple, she arched with a hiss of pleasure.

The smile that curved his lips was not something he could control. She did that to him, along with so many other things. He was beginning to forget what his life had been like before all that. It was certainly a sharp demarcation in his life. Before Thomasina and After Thomasina.

He leaned in and swirled his tongue where his hand had been. Immediately her fingers went into his hair and she held him closer, gasping out his name with that hitch of breath that let him know he drove her wild. She drove him wild, too. He wrapped an arm around her waist and tugged her flush against his entirely clothed body. He loved how her soft curves flowed against him, molded to him. She shared her warmth and her light without asking for anything in return. He still wanted to give it to her.

"Lie on the bed," he rasped, rubbing his chin against her breast so she could feel the faint hint of whiskers abrading the sensitive skin.

She nodded and pulled from his arms, taking her place against his pillows. She watched as he divested himself of all his clothes, her pupils dilating and obliterating the green as her desire mounted. He kept his gaze on hers as he finished stripping naked and held out his arms.

"You do love this show," he said with a laugh.

She smiled up at him. "It is my favorite of all time."

His smile fell, for he knew it was the truth, even though it was said in jest. What a gift that was, to know what he meant to her. No one had cared for him as steadfastly as she did. He'd pretended he didn't want that.

Now that he had it, he didn't want to lose it. His mind fled again to all he knew about Anne's disappearance. All the times Thomasina had asked him for more information and he had pretended not to have it. All the times he'd lied by omission and distraction and failed to deserve the faith she placed in him.

"Oh, don't do that," Thomasina purred as she sat up and caught his hand, dragging him toward the bed. "Don't run away in your mind just when I can't wait for you any longer."

"I would never do that," he promised, pushing aside his troubling thoughts.

After, he would tell her. It was time to offer that vulnerability in the face of all she had given him. It was time to accept that she was his partner and deserved to be part of his search.

For now he kissed her ankle as he joined her on the bed. He dragged his tongue along her calf, hesitating as he rubbed his chin on her knee, stroking his fingers along the back. Her eyes squeezed shut and she shivered at that touch. One of many he had found drove her wild. God how he loved exploring them all, inch by inch.

He moved higher, parting her legs as he kissed a soft trail to the apex of her thighs. He could already scent her desire, sweet and heady. He opened her wide, draping her legs over his shoulders. She lifted to him, no longer shy or shocked by this.

"Please," she murmured.

"Always," he said as he licked her. Her flavor burst on his tongue, earthy and sweet, and for a long time he feasted on her flesh, stroking her with long, languid licks as she keened and murmured his name. Eventually those licks grew shorter and more focused as he slowly circled her clitoris and drew her toward release. She grasped the coverlet, twisting it until her knuckles went white. Her neck strained and he watched as she fell over the edge of her orgasm. Her sheath fluttered beneath his mouth and he drove her on and on, relentless in his pursuit of her pleasure even when she was twitching and begging with wordless murmurs.

His cock felt hard as steel, and at last he could wait no longer. He caught her hands, pulling her into a seated position. He sat back, wrapping her legs around his waist as he shifted her over his cock.

They were face to face now, as intimate as they could be. Her gaze held his as she took him inside, inch by wet, tight inch.

He could barely contain himself as he rocked her closer, fitting himself to the hilt in her still fluttering body. She massaged him, the perfect wet wrapping for his cock. And as she tilted her head and kissed him, licking her own juices from his lips and tongue, he cupped her backside and began to grind her over him in slow, circular thrusts.

Immediately he was on the edge. *That* was what she did to him. Excited him to a lack of control, tempted him like a green boy with his first woman.

She clung to him, grinding down in time to his thrusts, moving with him like waves on the ocean as they built together to climax. He felt it coming, saw it in the strain on her face, the squeeze of her body around him. He kissed her as it exploded, sucking her tongue as she moaned into his mouth and rode harder, faster, her sheath squeezing him and milking him to his own release.

He tightened his arms around her as he came, pushing up into her, as pleasure arced through his entire body, releasing all the strain and worry from his being as he claimed her.

And as they collapsed back together on his bed, he found a tiny bit of peace.

Thomasina lay on her side, gently tracing patterns on her husband's bare chest. Jasper had fallen asleep almost immediately after they made love. His face was now relaxed in slumber, his body no longer the coiled mass of tension and worry. She had given him that gift, she knew it.

She was proud of it.

And he deserved to rest after what he'd said to her father. He'd been a champion for Anne and for all who had been left behind by her foolish decisions. And when Jasper looked at her across the room, Thomasina knew without a doubt he'd done it for *her*.

She pushed to her feet and found the tangled mess of her dress. With a shake of her head, she tossed it back on the floor and instead caught up his shirt. She tugged it over her head and fastened a few buttons, loving how the scent of him clung to the fabric, sinking into her skin like his body heat.

She moved across his room, looking at all the little items that made this place his home. A few miniatures of his family, *Moll Flanders* by Daniel Defoe, and a candle worn down to the nub.

She moved to his dressing table. There were a few bottles along the top, tonics and waters. She touched the tops gently, wondering what he did with them all as he sat here preparing himself for the day. There were two small drawers in the table, and she tugged one open absently. A comb and a brush were within, with fine onyx handles.

She opened the other drawer and paused. There was a stack of letters there, and she realized she was intruding on his private items. Things not meant to be shared with her. She was about to close the drawer and back away when she noticed a name written in a firm hand in the middle of a sentence on the page on the top of the stack.

Miss Anne Shelley.

Her hands shook as she drew the letter from the drawer and turned it over to start reading from the beginning.

CHAPTER 19

J asper opened his eyes with a contented sigh. He rarely allowed himself a nap in the middle of the day, but after making love to Thomasina, it was impossible not to need the respite. Now he felt refreshed as he rubbed his eyes and sat up to find her.

When he did, his heart began to pound. She was sitting at his dressing table in just his shirt, the chair pivoted to face the bed. In her hand was one of the letters from Reynolds. The rest stacked beside her on the tabletop. Her face was pale, her cheeks streaked with tears, and she was staring at him as if she had never seen him before. As if she didn't know him at all.

And he knew in that moment what she had done, what she knew and what it had all destroyed. He leapt to his feet, completely uncaring about his nakedness as he took a long step toward her.

"What are you doing?" he snapped, far more sharply than he intended in the face of her utter censure.

She jerked from the chair and backed away from him. "You want to take that angry tone with *me?*"

"You ought not have gone through my private things," he said, fighting to gentle that tone. He'd always gone to defensiveness when he had done something wrong.

She shook her head. "Perhaps not, though that wasn't my intention as I dreamily looked at all the things in this room that define who you are. Including these lies." She threw the letter in her hand toward him.

He stooped to pick the item up and clutched it to his chest, as if he could undo the power of it. But he couldn't. Her rage and hurt and betrayal were all alive on her face. She was no longer trying to be pleasing when it came to him.

And she was beautiful. So beautiful in that moment that it hurt his heart to look at her and know she no longer trusted him. Especially when her expression crumpled a fraction and tears filled her eyes.

"I asked you about Anne," she whispered. "Over and over again. And you lied to me. I told you about my own search and you acted as if it didn't matter. You looked me in the face, you bastard, and you pretended like you knew nothing when in fact you had so much information about her."

"So much *terrible* information," he corrected, reaching for her. She jerked away. "I had snippets of terrible information and no real answers about her whereabouts. I thought it would hurt you if I—"

"Told me the truth?" she asked with a humorless laugh. "Or did you think me too stupid to understand it? Or too fragile to bear it? You, who doesn't even care to know me beyond the bedroom? You, who wants to keep as many barriers between us as possible for my *protection?*"

He turned his face at her accusation. It hit so hard in his chest because it was true. When she said the words out loud, he heard the cruelty in his actions. Heard the cowardice. He had withheld from her by telling himself he was protecting her.

But he'd really been protecting himself. From letting her in. From admitting how much she mattered. From allowing her to be his partner in every sense of the word and giving himself to her as her partner.

He had clearly been silent for too long because she huffed out a breath. "Well, now I know so there is no use trying to pretend anything any longer. I will take care of this myself."

He moved toward her. "Thomasina—"

She shook her head. "Don't. Just don't. Oh, and you needn't worry anymore about my feelings, my lord. When I look at you right now, the only one I have is contempt."

She pivoted and exited the room in only his shirt, slamming the door that connected their chambers and leaving him standing naked, staring at the place where she'd last stood.

His legs shook and he sank into the chair she had abandoned a moment before. He stared at the letter from Reynolds that had started it all.

And then he looked toward Thomasina's chamber again and knew he was utterly lost.

~

The rage that bubbled in Thomasina's chest was an emotion she had rarely allowed herself to feel over the years. It had always been crushed down, first by others who told her it wasn't right and later by herself because she had believed them. But now it boiled, threatening to overwhelm her.

She loved Jasper, but she'd also trusted him. *That* was the material fact. She'd had faith in him, and all along he had been lying. Not directly. No, he was too proper to lie to her face. He did it by omission. He did it by using their connection to turn her away from everything that mattered. *That* stung far more than it should have and inspired the cold words she'd snapped out in their bedroom.

His bedroom.

She shook her head as other, more comfortable emotions joined that anger. *Fear.*

No, not fear. That wasn't a strong enough word for what she felt. It was panic. Panic over what could be happening to Anne at this moment. Jasper's man of affairs had written to him about Ellis. That man seemed like a pure villain, and Anne had run away with him. Rook, the one she'd last been seen with, sounded slightly better, but only because no one knew a damn thing about him.

So where was Anne? Was she alone? Frightened? Injured? Dead?

Thomasina bent over as the thoughts bombarded her, clutching her stomach as the pain rose up and replaced everything else.

"I would know," she whispered, needing to say the words out loud. "I would *know* if she was dead."

The door behind her opened and she knew it was Jasper. She didn't turn toward him, though. She buckled and he caught her elbow, dragging her into his chest, gathering her into his arms and carrying her to the settee. She allowed him to hold her, despite how angry she was. She turned her face into his shoulder, feeling the cloth of his robe against her skin as she wept into his arms for a moment.

He merely held her, smoothing her hair with one hand. She waited for him to tell her to stop crying or to reassure her, but he didn't. He just let her *feel* in the safety of his embrace.

A safety that had been false. When she remembered that fact, she pulled away, inching to the other side of the settee.

"No," she whispered, all the heat gone from her tone. "No."

He nodded, as if he understood the betrayal she felt. The pain. He didn't try to defend himself, as he had a moment before.

"I'm going to tell you everything," he said.

Her gaze jerked up and she stared at his face, trying to read his expression and find the truth or the lie that she hadn't been able to identify before. Trying to decide if she could trust him even a tiny bit.

She wasn't certain, so she shrugged. "Oh, thank you for that, *my lord*." She heard the sarcasm that dripped from every word. He flinched at it.

Then he cleared his throat and said, "You read the letters from Reynolds, so you know a little. Here is the rest. My brother,

Solomon, was a wastrel and often a fool. There are rumors, of course, and his manner of death in a duel caused quite the stir in Society. They do not know the half of it. I didn't even know a great deal until this happened with Anne."

"He was involved with this Maitland person," she said softly.

He nodded. "He was. I have no idea how they found each other, but I have no doubt that my brother was an active and willing participant in every scheme Maitland presented to him. He clearly dug himself a snug little hole with a criminal."

The anguish in his tone was plain and everything in Thomasina made her want to slide back down the settee and offer him the same comfort he had just given her. She fought against those impulses and nodded at him to continue. "How does Anne come into it?"

"Maitland thinks Solomon betrayed him in some wretched deal they put together. In his mind, at least, there is a treasure that my brother had possession of. Withheld from Maitland. He wants it back. To do that, he made himself attractive to your sister. He thought he could make me bargain for her."

She leapt up. "But you refused? What kind of treasure could be worth more than my sister's life?"

He shook his head. "I don't know anything about a treasure, Thomasina. If I did, I would have given it to him by now. I've been trying to figure out exactly what he's talking about since the day I returned from Beckfoot. To find it."

She stared at him. "Beckfoot...wait, did you *meet* with this man?"

The color drained from his cheeks. His lips pressed together and for a moment she saw how much he wanted to turn away from her and her question. But he didn't.

"Yes," he said softly. "He called me to a meeting the day after she ran."

"Was my sister with him?" she gasped.

"I would have taken her by any means necessary if she were," he assured her. "You may believe many things about me, Thomasina, and some of them are true. But if I could have discovered your sister, I would have died to save her from whatever trouble she and my late brother have gotten her into."

She considered that a moment. She was angry with him for lying, but when she looked past that sharp emotion, she did know that he wasn't the kind of man to hurt someone else. Not an innocent.

"But you let this Ellis person escape," she said softly.

"There was little choice in the matter," he said, scrubbing a hand over his face. She saw his exhaustion there. His heartache. His sense of failure. He'd been carrying all of it alone. By choice, but still alone. "Reynolds stayed behind in Beckfoot, trying to determine more about Maitland. That's when he discovered that Anne had boarded a small vessel with another man."

"The other Maitland."

"Rook," Jasper said with a shake of his head.

"What kind of name is Rook?" she whispered.

"Probably a name he...he carries from the street."

She couldn't help the low moan. "The nickname of a villain. A piece on the chessboard that is secondary in importance only to the queen. What kind of man could he be?"

Jasper held her stare. "I'm sorry, I don't know. There's so little information about him. They share a name, but I don't know their connection in truth. Rook seems to have been involved in Ellis's schemes but little is said about him. I don't know where he is, where Ellis is, where your sister is. If I did, I would go there and bring her home to you, no matter the cost. But I don't. And I'm trying." He let out his breath in a long, shaky sigh. "I should have told you all of this from the beginning."

"Why didn't you?" she asked.

He ran a hand through his hair. "At first, I wasn't sure I could trust you. Then I didn't want to hurt you. And then I selfishly didn't want you to judge me."

She bent her head. Those reasons didn't satisfy her, but she understood them. This man, this proud man, wasn't accustomed to depending on anyone else. Certainly, he couldn't have pictured doing so with her.

She looked at him evenly. "*How* have you been searching for the truth?"

"Reynolds continues to work in Beckfoot and the surrounding towns. And I've been here searching my brother's journals and personal diaries, trying to find a connection between him and Maitland that could tell me *anything* about this supposed treasure and where it might be."

"But no luck," she said, her heart sinking.

"No," he admitted.

"Is that all of it?"

He nodded. "Yes. All I've done and kept from you. All I know."

She pushed to her feet and paced away from Jasper, going to the window, where she stared out at the pretty gardens below. He had been doing so much, in truth, while she stood by, wringing her hands and waiting...just waiting...for someone to take charge. It had been that way all her life, hadn't it? Assuming her father or one of her sisters would handle things?

Only now she didn't want to wait anymore. Anne was in serious trouble, worse than she had imagined, and Thomasina couldn't be angry at being kept out of the loop if she refused to do anything but dither about the problem.

For the first time in her life, she felt the strength to tackle it head on.

"I'm helping you," she said, her voice shaking as she turned from the window. "I'm not asking you for permission, I'm telling you that I'm doing it."

His lips parted in what she could tell was surprise. She waited for him to refuse her. But then he nodded. "Yes. Of course. I might do better with a person at my side who didn't know my brother. You could see things I am not capable of seeing."

She blinked at his acquiescence. At his implication that she could be a true partner in such an endeavor. She folded her arms so he wouldn't see how much that moved her.

"Don't lie to me again," she demanded.

He got up, a slow unfolding of all the beautiful muscle and sinew. He moved a step toward her and no farther. "I won't. I don't expect you to believe me. I know from experience that words mean nothing without action. But I will prove to you that I can be trusted."

"I hope that's true," she whispered, and meant it with all her heart. Right now she wanted so much to trust him again, but she had to keep herself at a distance.

He shifted. "That leaves me with a question. Will you tell Juliana and your father what you now know about Anne and her whereabouts?"

She drew back, for she had been so shocked by everything that she hadn't considered that question. Now she thought about it carefully.

"I...should," she said. "Or else I'll be as much a liar as you've been."

He nodded. "But it's complicated."

She knew that comment was directed toward her. An explanation. Worse, she understood it and him. If she told Juliana the truth, her sister would take all the responsibility on her shoulders, bearing the weight of all the pain. Juliana had been made that way, to fix.

If she told her father, she feared he might throw up his hands and abandon Anne entirely. It would be his last excuse to write her off.

She pressed her lips together. "Yes, it is complicated. I will wait a few days, no more, in the hopes that together we can find more information and give them both something solid."

He inclined his head. "I would not dream of interfering in how you manage your family."

She narrowed her gaze at him. "I see what you are doing, trying to absolve yourself of your lies."

"I'm not. Yes, I had my reasons. I believed them to be the right reasons to keep the truth to myself. But my intentions and the results of what I did are separate things."

She folded her arms. It was so difficult to remain angry with him when he was being so...so reasonable. She fought to do so. "They are."

He drew a long breath. "Let's get dressed. We can go to the library together and I'll show you everything I have there. Then we can decide what to do next. Together."

She nodded as she followed him back into his chamber to retrieve her gown. But even though the conversation about his lies was over, she couldn't shake the feeling of the betrayal. And wished that her husband had cared enough about her to tell her the truth.

CHAPTER 20

J asper should have been reviewing the handful of journals he had pulled out during his search, double-checking the notations that could relate to Maitland. But he wasn't. Instead his focus kept shifting to Thomasina.

She sat cross-legged on the big rug in the middle of the library, her head bent over one of the journals, her gaze flitting back and forth as she tried to find a truth within his brother's many lies.

Hurt still lingered on her face. Fear. Anger. She had always been so open in her expression of her feelings. There was no artfulness to her at all, no lie. He liked that. And yet it made *his* betrayal all the more painful.

But here she was, sitting in his parlor, helping him. For her sister, of course, but she had been...gentle when she hadn't had to be about Solomon and his bad acts. Jasper had been holding tight to those secrets for so long, he actually felt better now that he'd loosened his grip. Now that someone knew the truth about his brother's actions and the humiliation that lingered around every corner. He felt less...alone than he had been in years. Decades.

Ever.

She glanced up. "There is nothing," she said, and her disappointment was heavy in her tone.

He nodded. "That's the same conclusion I've come to over the past week or so. The diaries detail my brother's empty existence. But if Maitland is in these pages, he is hidden well. Which makes me think…"

He trailed off, because he could hardly say the horrors that lingered in his heart. The words that would take all goodness from his brother's memory.

"What?" she asked, pushing to her feet and stretching her back gently. "What do you think?"

He swallowed. "If Solomon hid his relationship to Maitland, it's because he *knew* what they were doing was wrong. He wasn't some imprudent fop Maitland played for a fool or tricked into action. Solomon was a full partner in their schemes."

Her brow wrinkled. "I suppose that is possible," she said. "But we don't know it for certain. I know the late earl didn't protect his reputation much, but did your brother care for his power? Lord his title over those around him?"

Jasper snorted out a humorless laugh. "God, yes. He loved to crow to me that I was only a second son, not as worthy as he was because he had our father's title and his lands. He loved being an earl over all else."

She shook her head. "I'm sorry he took pleasure in cruelty," she said, that kindness offered to him once again, even if he didn't deserve it. "But that might be just as much an explanation as anything else."

"What do you mean?"

She shrugged. "A man like Maitland was far below him in stature. If he put their meetings in his books, their apparently close bond might have come to light."

"He could have seen it as lowering himself."

"Perhaps."

"You are kind to offer me a lifeline in this sea of…" He looked around with a shudder. "…shit. But either way, Solomon continues to prove himself entirely unworthy. I wish I could shake him now, try to scream some sense into him."

Her expression softened. "I'm certain you do."

He turned away. "If the journals are of no use, I suppose you and I must plan our next move."

"Your letters from Reynolds mentioned that you had some of your brother's things stored here at the estate after his untimely death."

"Yes. And more than that, Maitland had expressed an interest in buying some of those things after Solomon's death."

Her lips parted. "You think he believes this…this treasure might be amongst the items?"

He nodded. "Perhaps."

"Then I think that has to be our next move," she said. "I'm surprised you didn't pursue it before."

He hesitated as emotions he didn't normally allow flooded his entire body. He cleared his throat. "I don't like to…to look at those things. I refused to do so after my brother's death. Reynolds took care of it all."

She stepped closer. "Too painful?"

"I would lie," he said. "But I promised I wouldn't do that anymore."

She reached out and took his hand. It was the first time she'd voluntarily touched him since she discovered his duplicity, and the warmth of her fingers on his was almost enough to buckle him. Somehow, though, he didn't and merely stared at their interlocked hands.

"You cannot avoid this, Jasper," she said. "You cannot hide from the truth of him, or the truth of your feelings anymore. Not when so much is at stake."

He caught his breath. *No one* saw him, not truly. They saw the shell, the protective wall he'd spent a good deal of time building around himself. *This* woman he had never intended to join his life with could see through him like he was made of glass.

She had jumped over his barriers without even trying. Now she stood within his life, pushing out the boundaries he'd told himself no other person would ever cross.

What was startling about that was that there was comfort to that fact. Comfort to the idea that this one person could come into his world and make herself such a part of it. That she could see his secrets and be willing to keep them. That she could touch those places he'd kept frozen for so long and melt them.

He loved her.

The thought raced through his twisted mind like an arrow on a straight, true course. It shocked his system and he staggered back, breaking the grip of their hands as he stared at her.

He loved Thomasina. His wife. He loved her. And more to the point, he recognized just as clearly that this wasn't a new sensation that burned in his chest. He had loved her for some time, piece by tiny piece, probably from the first moment he met her. Even when he was meant for her sister, he had been falling in love with her.

That was why he could recognize her and not her other sisters. *That* was why he'd been drawn to her. *That* was why he hadn't been upset by the idea that Anne had run and left him with Thomasina as his choice for a replacement bride.

He loved her. And he had destroyed everything they'd been building. He'd hurt her, not just by keeping the truth of her sister from her, but by distancing himself at every turn.

She stared at him now with empathy, yes, but also with wariness. A guarded quality that hadn't been there before.

In short, he had been just like his brother, selfish enough to decimate everything that mattered. And he might never get it all back. But he *wanted* it back. He wanted her trust and her sweetness and her gentleness. He wanted the bond they'd been building since their marriage. Now he would have to earn it.

"Harcourt?" she said, tilting her head. "Have you thought of something important?"

He jerked at her observation. "What—why?"

She shrugged. "You just looked like you were pondering something. I thought perhaps you had recalled a fact about your brother that could aid our search."

He almost laughed. For the first time in over a year, his brother's actions hadn't been at the top of his mind. She had made him think of his own life, his own future, and that was a gift in itself.

"No," he said, and when she frowned, he knew she didn't believe him. He caught his breath. "I wasn't thinking of Solomon or your sister, I assure you."

She hesitated, and then nodded. "Very well."

"But we should put our focus back on the matters at hand. We'll start in the outbuildings, I think. There's a storage building, and I know a great deal of Solomon's things were placed there. Only a few items were put inside the manor."

"Good," she said, motioning to the exit from the library. "Then lead the way."

~

Thomasina was trying to keep up her cool exterior, but it was difficult when she could see every ounce of pain and anxiety on Jasper's face. Where before he had kept himself so separate, he seemed to be remaining true to his word and revealing all to her now.

They walked along the paths down toward the outbuildings, away from the main house. It had rained several times in the past week, but today the sun was shining brightly, accosting her pain and fear with its beauty. She wished it would become stormy again instead, to remind her that the situation was tumultuous. To be a physical manifestation of her anger, even though she felt sympathy for her husband.

"Why do you think your brother involved himself with a criminal like Maitland?" she asked. "He had power and influence of his own."

Jasper shook his head. "And no limits. My father would not give him any because he, himself, did not subscribe to them."

"He was as wild as Solomon?" she asked, thinking of the soft rumors she'd heard whispered about the previous two earls once her sister's engagement had been announced.

"Worse, in a way," Jasper said, staring off into middle distance up the road. "My brother, at least, didn't have a bride or a family to destroy alongside himself. My father had two sons and a wife. Two wives, considering Solomon's mother died."

"How did she die?" Thomasina asked.

He pointed to a building just at the end of the lane. "There is where the things were stored." He sighed. "Er, my father's first wife? An illness when my brother was young. Solomon didn't even remember her. Our father used to talk about what a love match they were. He said it in front of my mother a dozen times over the years, I think just to watch her flinch."

Thomasina flinched at just the thought. "That is cruel."

"Well, he was that. He thought it was comical. He prized nothing more than a joke at someone else's expense. If you think my mother cold and distant, I think he made her that way. It is what I tell myself, at any rate."

Thomasina glanced at him from the corner of her eye. Jasper was so often accusatory of those in his orbit, seeking blame for all that had gone wrong. But he was willing to offer grace to his mother, even if she might not fully deserve it.

She didn't know many people who would do the same to a mother so cold and brittle with her children.

"He hurt your mother, often on purpose," she said.

"And my brother," he continued, bending his head. "He was abundantly cruel to my brother. He used to pretend as though he would include him on outings, to teach him to take his role.

They'd rub it in my face, laughing that it was for first sons only, but then my father would leave without my brother. He waved from his horse as he rushed out of the gate, laughing at *both* his sons. And yet Solomon kept trying to earn his love. Earn his regard."

Thomasina shook her head. She understood a little about never being able to earn a parent's love, but her father had certainly never been so abjectly cruel about it. "I'm so sorry that happened to you both," she said, fighting the urge to touch him, to comfort him with more than mere words.

"Here is the building," he said, digging in his pocket for a key he'd retrieved from Willard before they left the house.

As he fiddled with the rusty lock, she saw the worry line his face. He was truly afraid of what he would find here. She knew as well as he did it might destroy any small bit of goodness he recalled in his brother.

She couldn't imagine feeling that way about Juliana or Anne. She knew their hearts and characters. To lose that faith in them would crush her.

"You told me once you were separated from your father at some point," she said softly. "How did that happen?"

He pushed against the door with a curse and it slowly creaked open. She caught her breath. She'd been expecting a few trunks or items in the medium-sized building but it was filled with them. Boxes and piles of an entire life.

"Jasper," she breathed as he stepped aside to let her come into the room.

He stared at it with her, and his voice cracked as he said, "I didn't want any of it when he was dead. I didn't want it at all."

Now she couldn't deny herself anymore. She turned on him and wrapped her arms around him, drawing him against her. He let her for a moment, sighing against her shoulder as she smoothed her fingers through his thick hair. She felt him soften, releasing some of the tension he always carried. She took it, bearing it on her shoulders for a moment and praying it would give him strength to carry on.

But the moment passed, and at last he lifted his head and stepped away. "I don't deserve that kindness," he said softly. "After what I did." He turned away, cutting her off from his emotion and looked at the pile before them. "God's teeth, there is so much. Where to even start?"

She motioned to the back corner of the room. "From the back forward, I think. We can clear a bit of space away from the wall, go through each trunk and stack them afterward."

He nodded. "Yes, a very good idea. Let me move these things and give us a working space."

He stripped out of his jacket and unlooped his cravat, then rolled up his sleeves, took a long breath and went into the back corner of the room. She stood back as he moved around, pushing and lifting trunks and boxes without hesitation. As if he weren't an earl who could ask a dozen men to do this for him.

"You asked about why I was taken away," he said with a grunt as he lifted one trunk onto another. "One afternoon after church my mother and I came home to find my father in the midst of...er... some very amorous activities with my mother's lady's maid."

Thomasina slapped a hand over her mouth in horror. "Oh no!"

"Yes." He hesitated and his jaw tightened. "The countess was humiliated and angry. It was one of the few times I recall her mask of disinterest falling. They quarreled and my father laughed the whole thing off. Disgusted, she packed me up and took me away. He let me go, of course—he had his heir. He didn't need his spare. I never saw him alive again."

"How old were you?" she asked.

He swallowed as he motioned her forward into the space he had created. "Let's see...sixteen? My father died five years later, when I was twenty-one and Solomon twenty-six."

"You didn't see your father or your brother for five years?" she asked softly, again stricken by how utterly painful such an idea was to her. She was uncomfortable with Anne being missing for less than two weeks. To go years without hearing her voice or seeing her face?

That seemed unbearable.

"The next time I saw my brother was at our father's funeral service and he was a changed man. As irresponsible and wild as the earl who preceded him. We went out for a drink a few days later, to my club in London. My brother made a mess of things and got us both banned."

She shook her head. "Was he sorry?"

"No," he said simply. "He was never sorry. I cut myself away from him over time. I only saw him when it was absolutely necessary or when I bumped into him by happenstance. I worked hard to make my own reputation free of any ill repute in the hopes I could make something of myself and protect my mother some small bit. But Solomon's antics affected me. Kept me from position and respect."

He shrugged. "At any rate, it did me little good, and now I have a mountain to climb when it comes to reputation. I suppose that punishes you, as well."

She moved forward and crouched before a trunk, unlocking it as she said, "I've spent my life with my reputation tied firmly to Juliana and Anne. I recognize the unfairness of being held to a standard that isn't your own. I know you and I know you aren't like your brother."

"You know that despite what I did?" he asked softly.

She lifted her gaze to him. "I can be angry and hurt by what you did and not judge that you are an irresponsible person on the whole. Those are two separate things."

"What's in the trunk?" he asked, stepping closer as they closed the painful topic.

"Clothes," she said with a sigh as she picked up some of the items and held them out. She moved her hand through them and only found cloth. "Nothing that could be called a treasure unless this Maitland has a desire for waistcoats."

He smiled despite the tension on his face and relocked the trunk before he carried it to the corner. They worked like that for a while, silent except for comparing what they found in trunks and boxes. She found it was not an uncomfortable quiet between them. They simply focused on the matter at hand, both serious about what they might find here.

Had she not discovered his lies, she would have felt the silence, the ability to work together, was further proof of their growing bond. Only right now she wasn't sure if she'd seen the truth of that at all. She'd imagined they were coming together. Now they felt so far apart, and she was a fool to love him when he was hiding so much.

He stood up from a crouched position and wiped his brow with the back of his arm. "Dusty work. I apologize about the state your gown is in."

She looked down to find her dress was grayed with dust. It put her to mind of that night he had hidden under her bed from Juliana. She couldn't help but smile. "It will wash out," she reassured him. "Why don't we—"

She didn't get to finish the question, for the door to the cottage opened and a footman stepped inside. "I'm sorry to intrude, my lord, my lady, but Willard wanted you to know that it's seven o'clock. Supper shall be served at eight."

Jasper let out his breath in a frustrated sigh. "Thank you. We'll come up." The young man left and Jasper looked at her with a shrug. "Two hours of miserable work and nothing to show for it."

She tilted her head. "Is that what you think? It's only if you win your prize that you've succeeded?"

"Yes," he said. "Of course. How can you succeed if you don't win?"

"Well, you learn, for one thing," she said with a laugh. "Gracious, Jasper, we have gotten through ten trunks in what...a couple of hours? We likely only have fifteen left to examine, and then we'll know for certain that the items out here are not related at all to Maitland and his supposed treasure. That will close out this part of the search at least and let us move to another place in the investigation with a clear conscience."

He seemed to ponder that a moment, then nodded. "I suppose I've never looked at it that way before."

She forced a smile so he wouldn't see she, too, was disappointed in the lack of any evidence that could help them recover Anne. "Well, now you must. I command it."

A hint of a smile softened his expression. "Then who am I to argue," he said softly, and held out an arm.

She blinked as she stared at the outstretched arm. The hopeful look on his face. Once again, she was drawn to take his offering, to forget what she knew.

But she couldn't. She'd left her heart unguarded going into this endeavor, and knowing he'd lied to her crushed it. She wasn't ready to offer it again so swiftly, even if she could find empathy for her husband.

"We should go up," she said, pretending not to notice his arm as she swept past him. "To ready for supper."

He said nothing, but she felt his stare on her back as they walked up the hill to the house. Back to the place where they would each have to pretend nothing had changed when everything had.

CHAPTER 21

J asper sat at the head of his dining table, his wife across from him and her family between them. Thomasina picked at her dessert, and he had to admit he was no hungrier than she was as he thought of their thwarted attempts to find information on his brother and Maitland's blasted treasure.

"Where did you two disappear to this afternoon?" Juliana asked, oblivious to the tender subject she was wading into.

Jasper watched Thomasina flinch, but her fake smile was bright as she said, "We walked around the estate. There's so much to—to discover."

He appreciated her attempts to not lie directly. He supposed that was an accusation against him and he couldn't help but feel it.

"Thomasina was a great help to me as I've been putting off going through some of my late brother's items," he said.

Mr. Shelley tilted his head. "After all this time? I'd have thought you'd just fold them into your own life."

Thomasina cleared her throat. "What did you do, Father?" she asked, changing the subject, much to Jasper's relief. She met his gaze evenly and he nodded his thanks to her.

"I prepared for my trip to Gretna Green tomorrow," he said,

arching a brow in Jasper's direction. "As forcefully requested by your husband."

"I did the same," Juliana said as she glanced at Thomasina.

She jerked her gaze toward her sister. "What? You'll go with him?"

There was a lifetime of communication that flowed between the sisters in that moment. Jasper watched it, mesmerized by their connection, feeling, and not for the first time, all he had lost out on through his strained relationship with Solomon.

Juliana cleared her throat. "I think it best. I can help Father stay on task. You know how he depends on me to organize his duties."

Thomasina bent her head, her hand clenching on the table before her. How he hated she had to endure this. How both she and Juliana did, thanks to all those in their lives who they could not depend upon. It was patently unfair.

"Yes, having your sister there will be a great help," their father said, then he pushed his chair back. "But we must leave very early, so I will excuse myself. I won't see you before we leave, so goodbye. Juliana will write, no doubt, to keep you apprised of our search, foolish as it may be."

He pivoted and exited the room without so much as a warm glance to the daughter he was abandoning. Once he had gone, Thomasina looked at Juliana. "Will you be safe?" she whispered.

Juliana glanced toward Jasper. "Assuming the men your husband sends to accompany us are true."

"They are," he reassured her softly. "I'll give them special instructions to protect you and your maid at all costs. Will having you there truly keep him in line?"

"Him, my father?" she asked.

Jasper nodded. Juliana glanced again at Thomasina. "Yes. Of course it will. I can at least actually look for signs of Anne in truth, not just as some show to keep your wrath from coming down upon him."

Thomasina stood and moved to sit beside her sister. She

wrapped her arms around her, and Jasper watched as his wife shook with emotion. She was losing so much. Because of his family. His past.

He hated himself for all of it.

The two women silently held each other for a while, then Juliana pulled back, wiping her eyes. "Don't worry," she reassured her sister. "I'll be very careful and sharp-eyed. If there is news to be found of Anne, I will find it."

Thomasina nodded and squeezed her hand gently. "I will get up tomorrow to see you off."

Juliana glanced at Jasper and then shook her head. "No, leaving you will be hard enough. Let us depart in the morning without fanfare. It will be easier for me."

Jasper could see how much that request pained Thomasina, but she managed to jerk out a nod. "Very well."

Juliana pushed from the table. "I'll go up now, so say goodbye to me."

Thomasina bit out a sob as she embraced Juliana again tightly, whispering to her for a moment before they parted. Thomasina paced away to the window. Juliana's eyes were bright with tears as she walked to Jasper. She reached out and took his hand, meeting his eyes evenly as she whispered, "Be careful with her, my lord. Please."

He nodded and Juliana left the room. Left him with his bride, who was now shaking as she wept against her hand. He moved to her, turning her into his chest and holding her as he soothed her as she had soothed him earlier. And knowing that he could do nothing to ease her pain except everything in his power to bring Anne home.

And even then it might not be enough.

∾

Thomasina stood at her window, looking out across the moonlit garden behind the house. She had been standing there for almost an hour, thinking of everything this long, horrible day had brought. How much she had lost. How much she could still lose.

There was a knock on the door that led to Jasper's adjoining chamber, and she sighed heavily as she called out, "Come in."

He did so, stepping into her bedroom and leaning against the door. He had stripped out of his propriety just as she had and stood only in trousers that slung dangerously low on his hips. She turned her back so she wouldn't be moved by him.

She didn't want to be moved by him yet.

"I was worried about you," he said softly.

She stiffened, her fingers gripping at her sides. "You don't have to be. I'm fine. You ought to worry about yourself."

"No, I've worried about myself quite enough, I think," he said, and she felt him move toward her rather than heard it. He stopped just a foot behind her, and then he reached out and gently turned her to face him.

She stared up into his face, her heart swelling with love and pain and wishes that might never be fulfilled. He was being kind to her now, trying to make up for what he'd done before, and that was nice enough. But she wanted more than guilt or duty. She just couldn't ask for it.

It was as if he read her mind, for he tilted his head toward hers. "You've spent your life trying to please your father," he began. "Trying to please everyone and make all their lives easier. And when you were forced to marry me, you took on that role in my life, as well. Helping, soothing, giving, always giving and never expecting anything in return. You crush down your fear and your sadness and your anger so they don't trouble anyone else."

She bent her head. "I didn't crush down my anger earlier today."

"I was glad of it," he whispered. "I deserved it, for one, and also it made me think that perhaps you trusted me enough not to hide it from me. That we were bonded enough for you to show me the truth. Now I see you standing here, coiled like a spring about to pop, holding back all that you feel because you don't think you are allowed to share it. I'm asking you to share it with me."

She swallowed. She'd wanted him to tell her he loved her, she supposed. Not tonight, but someday in the far future when she had proven that it was a good bargain for him to take. But right here, right now, he was saying words that were far more powerful. Words that sank past the barriers she put up to protect herself, to protect those around her, and gave her permission to be...herself.

She straightened her shoulders. "Can I trust you?" she asked. "Truly?"

She expected his defensiveness at that question, his upset. But instead he held her gaze, steady and gentle. "I can promise you a thousand times that you can trust me, but that won't matter until I prove it. Which I intend to do, you know. For as long as it takes, even if it takes a lifetime."

"Why?" she whispered.

His lips parted and he shifted slightly. "Because I..." He broke off and shook his head. "You're my wife, Thomasina. And I want us to be happy together."

She wrinkled her brow, wondering what it was he was going to say before he shifted his tactic. Too afraid to ask him. Too exhausted to be rejected one more time.

"Right now," she said. "I despise my father. He forced Anne into the marriage bargain with you and he must have known it wouldn't be a good match. He didn't care about her, just as he proves he doesn't care about her now. She's lost her value by running away and he has moved on to his next plan."

"That must be difficult," Jasper said. She saw his hand flutter like he wanted to touch her, and part of her wished he would. Part of her was glad he kept the distance between them.

"You would know, based on your own past," she said.

He nodded. "I do understand, I suppose. Though I can't say I *know*, because your situation is different."

She blinked. He took no ownership of her pain. He didn't try to erase it or hurry her through it. He just stood there, offering her his ear and nothing more.

She shook her head as the pain heightened. "I have never been without my sisters," she whispered. Her voice broke with the depth of her heartbreak at that thought. "Never for more than a night at a time. And now they will *both* be gone."

"Should I go with him to Scotland instead and leave Juliana here with you?" he asked.

She gasped as she stared at him. "You would do that?"

"I think Gretna Green is likely a waste of time because I don't think Anne and Maitland ever truly went there," he said slowly.

"Nor do I," she agreed. "But why send my father there, then?"

"In order to cover that faint possibility and perhaps even shock him into understanding the gravity of this situation beyond the damned scandal." His fingers flexed at his side. She could see he wanted to touch her. Console her. He didn't out of respect to her. "But if you'd like to keep Juliana here, I would go in her stead."

She reached out and caught his hand, lifting it to her lips and pressing a brief kiss on his knuckles. "The fact that you would offer such a boon is meaningful beyond measure. But no. Juliana would go wild here, waiting for information. And the two of us wouldn't know what to look for in any search we made. It is better for her to go with my father and keep him on task. For you and I to remain and do whatever real work there is to find Maitland's prize."

He stared down at her, nodding slowly at her words. But she saw the shift in him. The desire that fluttered into his eyes just because she'd touched him. She felt a faint desire of her own calling back to him. A knowledge that if he touched her now it would erase the pain for a moment. It would begin to reforge the bond that had been damaged when she found those letters hours ago.

He lifted a hand into her hair, gliding his fingers along her scalp.

He tilted her face toward his and she let out a shuddering sigh as his mouth found hers.

He was gentle in the kiss. Almost like it was the first time. Perhaps it was the first, for their relationship had changed—they were renegotiating their future now. She parted her lips when he traced them with his tongue, drowning in his taste and the way his arms felt as they came around her and supported her.

But then she thought of all that had come to pass between them. All that had been said and unsaid. All that he had done to keep the truth from her even as she begged for it. And she gently shrugged from his embrace and backed away.

He let her, watching her but not pursuing.

"You told me once that I could withdraw my consent at any time," she whispered, her cheeks flaming as she dropped her gaze to the floor beneath her bare feet. "And I am doing that now. Not forever. But until my mind can untangle the truth from the lies."

She lifted her gaze to read his reaction. He could take what he wanted, not that she thought he was that kind of man. He could argue and cajole and seduce and get it through those means too.

But he didn't do any of those things. He took a long step away instead and inclined his head. "I understand," he said softly, the strain heavy in his voice. "I know I've lost any right to touch you. I know I must earn that back, as well. So I'll leave you if that's what you want."

"It's probably best for tonight," she said, and suddenly didn't feel as certain in that decision.

He moved for the door. He stopped there and turned back to her. "I'd like to start the search of the rest of those trunks in the morning, if you are up for an early day."

She nodded. "I'll be sure to have my maid wake me at a reasonable hour."

"Good." He shifted, running his fingers along the door absently. "Thomasina, I won't push you, but I want you to know that I *do* want you. I do need you. And when you are ready for me, I'll be here. Goodnight."

He left then. Left her to stare at the barrier he closed between them. Left her to ponder if she'd made the right decision by putting up the wall to protect herself.

Left her to miss the man who had come to mean everything to her.

CHAPTER 22

T he walk down to the outbuilding was as quiet as the one the day before had been, but this time Jasper didn't feel as high of a barrier between them. Thomasina might have refused him the night before, but today she talked a little easier with him. She dared a smile now and then.

Still, he felt her worry. Her fear for both her sisters, now that Juliana had gone with Mr. Shelley to search out some truth in Scotland. He felt how lost she was without those same sisters as her anchors.

How could he help her? How could he soothe those hurts? He didn't know because he'd never been close enough to another person to *want* to do that. He'd never been encouraged to embrace his more emotional side because of the fear he would become irresponsible and a wastrel like his father and brother.

Only loving Thomasina didn't make him feel out of control or less responsible. It took nothing away from the man he had fought hard to be. No, loving her added something to his life. Made him steadier, it gave him a compass and a center he hadn't ever had before.

So he had to learn how to be the man she needed.

"Thomasina—" he began.

But she wasn't attending. She grasped his arm and pointed, drawing his attention away from her face and toward the outbuilding where they were going.

"The door is open, Jasper!" she gasped.

"We locked it behind ourselves last night," he breathed. "And no one from my staff would have disturbed it."

They exchanged a glance and then both began to run toward the building a hundred yards away. When they reached it, she moved to enter, but he caught her, pushing her behind him.

"It someone broke into the building, they might still be inside. Stay back and let me look."

She caught her breath. "Oh, Jasper, no. Please, you must be careful."

He squeezed her hand. "I will be. If anything happens, run to the house."

Her eyes brimmed with tears, but she nodded and released him at last so he could push past the partially open door into the storage building.

Inside it was quiet. The remains of a candle were melted into the dusty wood floor. That had probably provided the light for the intruder who had come here after he and Thomasina left. He could certainly guess who that was. But the building seemed empty now.

But not untouched. Every trunk, every box, had been torn open, thrown about, the contents ripped through like an animal had been the one searching them.

"Jasper?" Thomasina called from the door.

He sighed. "Come in. Whoever did this is gone."

She entered and her hand jerked to cover her mouth as she looked around the chaotic room. "My God," she murmured.

"Yes. Maitland was driven to find this item, whatever it is," he mused.

She leapt forward a few steps. "You think it was Maitland? That means he's been watching the estate. It can't be a coincidence that he broke into this building the day after you and I began our search here."

"You're right."

His stomach clenched at the idea that Maitland had been watching them. Watching *her*. What had he said in Beckfoot? That he would find a pressure point to get what he wanted.

Anne hadn't been that for Jasper. But Thomasina was a different story. Thomasina was everything, and if Maitland discovered that, it might put her in grave danger. Jasper had to put a guard on her for the rare times they weren't together.

"If he's close by, do you think my sister might be with him? Or near?"

He hated the desperation in her tone. The lilt of hope and terror mixed in one. Especially since he couldn't give her that answer.

"I don't know," he admitted, driven not to lie anymore, even for a good purpose. "But we're going to look into it. Come, we must return to the estate and let my staff know of the break in. I also must write to my man of affairs, Reynolds, and get him back here."

"The kind of man who would do this…what if Maitland won't let my sister go?" she asked, her voice cracking as she bent her head.

He moved to her then and caught her hands, lifting them to his chest so she could feel the steady beat of his heart. "I will not stop searching until we find Anne. I promise you I'll never stop."

Her expression softened and she lifted on her tiptoes to brush her lips to his. "Thank you," she whispered. "Come, we must take care of this duty."

He took her arm and led her from the outbuilding and the mess made there. But as he took her to the house, he could only pray the promises he made were ones he could keep. For his sake, for hers.

～

Thomasina was with Jasper in body as they entered the house together, but her mind and her spirit were far away, dragged to terrible places by visions of the horror of what Anne was going through at present.

She blinked, trying to find focus as she watched Jasper bark out orders and jerk out messages across a sheet of vellum that a rider raced to deliver to his man Reynolds, wherever he was. He looked every inch the earl in that moment. Formidable, powerful, unwavering in his every action and word. Perhaps that might have encouraged her. Perhaps she should have sought solace in that face, but she couldn't.

Because in his eyes she saw fear. It was the same fear she had sensed down at the building when he realized it had been ransacked. It was the fear of a man who had underestimated his enemy and now realized what kind of foe he faced.

Tension lined the corners of his lips and wrinkled his eyes.

At last the servants had scattered to fulfill his every whim and he stared at her. His shoulders rolled forward a fraction, the earl dissolved away and the much more complicated man she called her husband reappeared.

She reached for him, needing to offer comfort as well as receive it. He was as damaged by this as she was now, the only other person who fully understood the thoughts tangling her mind.

She squeezed his fingers. "Do you think Maitland found what he was looking for when he ransacked the outbuilding?"

He sucked in a breath. "He tore at items that could hide nothing within. He kicked trunks until there were holes in them. He destroyed where there needn't be destruction. To me that says frustration. Desperation."

"He tore that place apart and ended in defeat. Which means the item he is seeking wasn't there, Jasper."

"Or well hidden," he said with a shake of his head.

"Was there *any* other place where you put Solomon's things after he died?" she encouraged softly. When he flinched, she already knew the answer. And hated that they had no time for him to ready himself.

He bent his head. "Yes," he admitted after what felt like the most pregnant of pauses. "There is just one trunk left, which Reynolds brought to the attic. It's filled with the most personal of my brother's items. But they are not of much value."

"Except to you," she said.

He lifted his gaze to hers and held there. "I value nothing my brother left behind. You know that."

"I know you tell yourself that," she said, lifting his hand to her lips and brushing them across his knuckles. "Jasper, why don't we look there? Please."

He released her hand and paced away to stand at the still-open door. The rider he had sent with his message thundered past, riding hard toward the gate. Jasper speared her with a glance over his shoulder. "Fine," he said, his tone harder than it had been toward her in a very long time. "We can waste our time with this. Come with me."

She gathered her skirt in her hand and followed him. Something in that attic made Jasper turn himself away from her. Away from himself. And she feared that as much as she feared the discovery of whatever supposed treasure had been hidden from plain view.

The attic rooms had once been kept for servants, back in his grandfather's day and before. Over time, they had been closed up, the servants moving into either lower level rooms in the estate or out to the dedicated servant quarters his father had built just after taking over the title.

Now Jasper stood at the door and felt why the family had made the change. It was bloody hot in the hallway. All the heat from the rest of the house lifted to fill this sloped ceilinged space. How generations of house servants had survived during especially warm summers, he didn't know.

He supposed he had to give his father some credit for not abusing his staff by making them continue to live in such conditions. He frowned as he led Thomasina up the narrow hall and to a closed and locked door at the end.

He hated giving his father even the slightest credit for his behavior.

"Here," he said, pulling the key from his pocket and taking a breath before he slipped it into the lock. There was a rusty click as the door creaked open slowly.

He stepped in first. Rude, perhaps, but after coming upon the ransacked remains of the outbuilding that morning, he wasn't about to let the custom of ladies first put his wife in danger. Or at least further danger. He feared she was already in some peril just by being married to him and sharing the title that had brought so much shame to so many.

The room was as dark as it was dingy. He withdrew the candle and flint he had retrieved from Willard a short while before and lit it, giving the room a rather eerie glow. Made more so by what it revealed.

There was only one thing in the room. One item that sat in the middle of the narrow chamber. A trunk. *The* trunk.

The last remnants of his brother's most treasured items. Reynolds had packed it up after Solomon's demise, assuring Jasper that he would be extra careful with any very personal items or those that had value. He'd tried to pass a few of the heirlooms along, but Jasper hadn't taken any. He didn't want anything to do with those things.

He still didn't and the sight of that trunk in the middle of the room, rather like a coffin arranged for viewing in a rotunda, turned his stomach.

He shook his head as he broke his gaze from the trunk. He looked around the room a bit more. "My brother locked me up here once," he mused, thoughts going back to his childhood. "I was five and desperately afraid of the dark. He was eleven and thought it was the best joke. I could hear him laughing as he walked away while I screamed. One of the servants found me a few hours later, huddled in the dark. Was it this room? Perhaps another—they look very much alike."

Thomasina bent her head. "I'm so sorry, Jasper."

He shrugged, though the memory meant more than he decided to let on to her. She knew it, of course. That was what she did... knew things. Even things he didn't want to share.

No wonder he loved her. No wonder the idea of that love was so...troubling.

"Let's get it over with, shall we?" he said, moving a step toward the trunk. He stopped, still three feet away. He stared again at the old, battered box, sealed shut by two rickety buckles that held heavy leather straps around the circumference of the trunk.

She tilted her head, watching him, then Thomasina stepped forward. Her tone was falsely bright as she knelt before the suitcase. "Why don't I open it and hold up each item for you to access? That seems a better use of my hands than of yours."

He grunted his acquiescence because he could find no other words. He held his breath as her delicate fingers loosened the stiff leather straps, sliding them through the buckles one by one and finally lifting the trunk lid.

It creaked like the door had, signifying the lifetime this case had been here. Or was it only a year? It felt like a lifetime. Everything always felt like a lifetime when it came to memories of his brother.

She reached into the trunk and withdrew the first thing she found. He flinched, turning his head.

"My brother's pocket watch," he said, and when he shut his eyes, he could see the intricately etched gold case and the carefully built face of the watch. Even though it wasn't wound, he could hear the echo of its tick as the seconds passed by.

"It's lovely," she said, turning it in her hands. "Was it something Solomon bought for himself or a family heirloom?"

"Family heirloom." He choked on the words as he allowed himself a peek at the watch as it rested in her delicate hands. "My great-grandfather purchased it near the end of his life. It was some kind of statement, I suppose, to wear one then, versus the kind on chains that were looped around the neck." He shook his head. "My father treasured it and my brother used to crow to me about receiving it as part of his legacy. I'm shocked he didn't gamble it away during one of his low points."

She drew a handkerchief from her pocket and gently wrapped the golden watch in it. "It seems he still saw the value in it, beyond what he could get for it."

"What are you doing?" he asked, feeling every muscle in his body tighten.

She glanced up at him. "It *is* a family heirloom, Jasper. If you do not wish to carry it, that's your choice and I respect it, but I think it deserves more protection than to be kept in a hot, dusty attic. I will put it in my jewelry box. Perhaps one day we will pass it to a son or grandson."

He caught his breath at that idea. Of course he would have children with this woman. The expectation that he carry on his father's line was very great. But he hadn't pictured those children until now. With her smile. With his hair. With her eyes.

He could imagine handing over the watch to one of them, and to his surprise, there was no pain in that idea. His son or grandson would have none of the bad memories of Solomon or Jasper's father to go with the piece. The demons that went along with the watch would be gone by then.

And that was comforting.

She took the next item from the trunk with a gasp. A thick book. "Your family Bible," she breathed.

"Neither my father nor my brother followed it, it was all for show," he said. "And I fear my faith has been shaken too much to not be a hypocrite by placing it in a spot of honor."

She nodded slowly. "Well, perhaps there will be a time for faith again, in the future. If not in the church's doors, then in your own."

He took those softly spoken words in. And realized they were already true. He had found faith. In her. And that was more powerful than any sermon he'd ever heard in a chapel.

"Take it down with us," he suggested. "We'll place it in the library. For those same children you believe will want that old watch."

She smiled slightly at his tone and placed the Bible on the floor and the wrapped watch on top of it. She moved into the trunk again. She pulled a heavy fabric from the trunk. It was thick and black, and he stared.

"What is it?" she asked, staring at it in confusion.

He moved forward at last and touched the corner of the fabric that she held up for his inspection. He had a flash as he did so, of his brother's coffin, draped in black. He shook his head. "This looks like the fabric on his coffin. It must be the extra bombazine from the roll and for some reason Reynolds—"

He cut himself off as he stared down into the trunk and his gaze found the next item within.

"Reynolds what?" Thomasina asked as she bundled the fabric up and placed it aside.

He couldn't answer. He had no words. Not when he was looking down at a reminder of childhood that froze his heart. *Broke* his heart.

"Jasper?" she whispered, and her gaze flicked to the trunk.

She saw the toy bear he was staring at and gasped. "Oh. What is it?"

"Solomon's bear," Jasper whispered. She reached for it, but he shook his head. "No. No, please don't touch it."

She drew her hand back and looked up at him in concern. "Jasper?"

He gasped for air, trying to draw it in when it felt impossible. The button eyes of the toy held his, accusing, reminding him of something he had forgotten. Someone he had convinced himself didn't exist.

"He was too old for the bear, my father said," he whispered. "Twelve, I think, and he kept it hidden under his bed. I think he slept with it sometimes. My father took it. He said he was going to burn it."

Thomasina recoiled at the cruelty Jasper described. He could see Solomon's face so plainly, young and frightened and so angry. So filled with righteous hatred for the man who had half-heartedly raised them.

"It seems he saved the toy after all," Thomasina whispered.

"No," Jasper said, his voice cracking as emotion overwhelmed him, crashing over him in a wave more painful than anything he'd ever felt before. "I saved it," he whispered. "I saved it for him."

And then he buckled at the knees and collapsed to the floor as a thousand tears he'd not let himself shed overcame him.

CHAPTER 23

The sound Jasper made as his knees hit the floor was unlike anything Thomasina had ever heard before. It was the howl of an animal in intense pain. The grief of a man who had never let himself feel it.

She crawled across the scant distance between them and wrapped her arms around him, drawing him to her chest, stroking his hair as he wept out all he had concealed for such a long time.

She felt it all as it flowed through her. His mask was gone, all his accusations quiet. That hate that had protected him had been taken by a child's toy and he was no longer able to use it as a shield.

They sat like that for what felt like an eternity. He clung to her without apology or attitude, and she prayed her strength would be enough to buoy him through this storm that threatened them both.

At last she smoothed her hand along his cheek once more and whispered, "Talk to me."

He jolted at the words, as if they made him realize where he was and with whom. He straightened, turning his face as he wiped his eyes with the back of his hand. "Forgive me," he said. "I'm weaker than I thought."

She wrinkled her brow. "No, you're not. You have suffered and survived. That makes you so very strong. But that doesn't mean you don't *feel*. If you didn't, you wouldn't be human." She cupped his face again and he let her. "Please, won't you tell me?"

There was a long, charged moment where she could see he was fighting the idea of sharing with her. How could she blame him? Cutting himself off from his emotions had been his way to save himself from a rocky, difficult childhood. She understood barriers, boundaries to keep others from seeing inside.

But she had shared parts of herself with him that no one, even her sisters, understood. She wanted so desperately to be the same shelter for him now. If she wanted any kind of life with him, she had to win that battle.

But not by forcing it.

He cleared his throat, lifted his gaze to hers and whispered, "My father had thrown the bear into the parlor as he dragged my brother off to scream at him. I snuck in and took it. I hid it so the earl couldn't destroy it."

"What did you father do when he couldn't find it?" she asked.

"He assumed one of the servants had thrown it out with the rubbish, I think, since he had shouted so long and hard about destroying it. Went off to drink with his cronies and forgot the whole thing."

He shivered, and in that moment she knew he wasn't with her anymore. He was back in time, a little boy trying to save his brother. Trying to save them both from the kind of man who would punish a child for seeking comfort.

She didn't push him, but let him live out that memory, watching as his eyes swelled with tears again, but this time they didn't fall. This time he choked out, "I went to Solomon's room that night. He was crying, I think I remember him crying. I showed him the bear."

"He must have been pleased," she whispered, looking into the box before her with its evidence that the late earl had kept his child-hood toy close to him for a great many years.

"He was not," Jasper corrected, his voice rough. "He shouted me out of the room, telling me he didn't need baby things like I did. He said he'd burn it himself."

She shut her eyes, feeling the laced, tight pain of her husband's words. Feeling the rejection of his brother at the core of that kind act. And seeing the truth of it in the box in front of them.

"It must have been hard for him to go against your father," she suggested gently.

He nodded. "I'm sure it was. As a child, his words hurt, but as a man I can understand it more."

"Understand *him*, despite all he did."

He was quiet a long moment, and then he sighed, "You know, I have spent so long hating my brother. Loathing what he became and what he did with his power. What he forced me to undertake when he so selfishly died." He leaned in and she watched as he reached for the bear, then pulled away like he feared touching it would conjure some demon. "But looking at this ugly, battered child's toy, I remember a thousand laughs and smiles. A thousand happier memories that I forced myself to forget when we were separated."

"The good ones," she said.

He jerked out an unsteady nod. "Yes. I wish I had recalled them earlier. Before—"

He cut himself off and got to his feet. He walked away, pacing the small room absently. She watched him as she stood, not approaching even though she so wanted to do that. To comfort again.

But he didn't want that. She could see it. He might need it, but in a different form.

"Before he died," she offered, filling in the gap in the sentence that hung between them.

"Yes." He rubbed a hand over his face. "I hadn't spoken to him in a year before. He hadn't paid some men and that kept me from being able to arrange a financial situation for myself. I confronted Solomon and we fought over his lack of self-control. I meant to reconcile. I thought we would. And then he was...gone."

"Oh, Jasper." The words were barely spoken loud enough for him to hear them, but he still flinched at them.

"Now I'll never see him again," he continued. "And as much as I have hated him for all the ways he failed, that is nothing compared to how much I hate myself for failing him."

She stared at him, pain raw on his face as he looked at her and let her see down to his very soul. She knew that was a gift, painful as it may be. After all, this man held himself so stiff and proper and unyielding so much of the time. He wouldn't show his broken heart to just anyone.

He'd chosen her. Not at first, perhaps, but in the end. And she wouldn't let him down.

She moved toward him, watching his every reaction, carefully as if she was approaching a wounded beast. When he didn't turn away, she caught his hands and tried her best to allow any strength she had to flow through herself to him.

"Life is so complicated, Jasper," she said softly, choosing each word with the greatest of care. "We all have pains and regrets. But I think you've carried this one long enough, my love. Set it down."

He shook his head. "How can you say that?"

"Because if your brother ever had any love for you, if he contained a fraction of the goodness you now recall about him and grieve, he wouldn't have wanted for you to torture yourself. He would want you to release these weights on your shoulders."

He turned his face, staring at the trunk across the room. "How can I when I've taken over what was meant to be his life?"

She touched his chin and drew his gaze back to hers. "But it's not his life, Jasper." When he jolted and tried to look away again, she held firm. "No, please don't. Look at me. It is not his life anymore. It's *your* life. If you don't make it what you desire for yourself, you will be as lost as you think he was."

He let out his breath in a long, shaky sigh. She released him then and turned, walking toward the trunk. She paused there. "Let him go, Jasper."

She bent to pick up the bear, to return it to him in the hopes that the act of holding this thing that represented his loss would help. But as she lifted it, she gasped.

He had been staring at her as she moved, watching her every move, but now his brow wrinkled in confusion. "Thomasina?"

"It's...it's heavy," she explained, switching to hold the old toy with both hands.

She moved toward him as she turned the bear, examining it to try to determine why it was as weighty as it was. It had to be more than half a stone, far too much for a child's bedtime toy.

She paused as she turned the item upside down. There, hidden amongst the matted fur of the toy, was a strange seam, something that had been hastily sewn by a not particularly skilled hand.

"Look," she said, holding it out toward him. "Was this always there?"

"I-I don't know," he murmured. "It could have been."

She bit her lip and examined the scar along the base of the toy. "I'm going to tear it," she said, looking to him for approval.

He hesitated a moment, then nodded.

She balanced the toy with one hand and tugged with the other. After a few tries, the seam began to give way. She wedged her hand inside the space, rending it further. Her fingers brushed something hard in the old fabric and she jerked her hand out as she brought her gaze back to Jasper.

"There's something inside," she whispered.

He nodded and held out his hands. "Let me steady it as you tear."

She gave him the bear and his eyes widened at the weight she had described but he clearly hadn't pictured. He held the toy in his palms, and now she used two hands to rip the seam the rest of the way open. Inside, where the toy's stuffing should have been, was hard marble. She pulled it out and gasped.

"A statue," she whispered.

∾

J asper stared at the beautiful bust perched in his wife's hands. On the base was marble, with a terracotta sculpture of a woman perched on top. It wasn't particularly large, but the detail was lovely.

"Is it a family heirloom?" she asked as she handed it over to Jasper.

He set the now-empty shell of the toy aside and took the sculpture, weighing it in his hands with a shake of his head. "No, most definitely not. I've never seen it before. There's only one reason he would hide this in that toy, Thomasina."

She nodded, for she had thought the same thing. Hoped she was wrong, but not believed it. "This is the treasure Maitland wants so badly."

He flinched. How he wished he could deny that. How he wished he had found something to prove his brother wasn't as connected to that villain as he obviously had been. Instead there was this. This proof of just the opposite.

He carefully handed the statue over to her and walked across the narrow room. He felt caged in now, both by the size of the space and the chains that his brother had created through bad decisions and equally bad friendships.

"What the hell was he thinking?" he muttered.

Thomasina brushed her fingers over the details of the clay lady's face as she shook her head. "If he and Maitland stole this, if it is worth so much that it could cause this kind of chaos, it would have been difficult to find a buyer, wouldn't it? The robbery might have been reported."

"They'd have to go underground," Jasper breathed.

Thomasina worried her lip as she stared. "I know this belongs to someone else. It isn't ours to use as a bargaining chip. It certainly isn't Maitland's. But Jasper...my sister."

He pivoted to face her and saw her crumpled expression. She

wasn't certain he would put her family first. Put *her* first. He hadn't yet proven himself to her. And that broke his heart as much as anything else he had uncovered in this dark and dingy room.

He moved toward her, shaking off his own concerns for the moment in trade for hers. "Of course we are going to help Anne if we can with this item. I don't love that it is stolen and that I will be party to keeping it from its rightful owner, but the life of your sister is worth more."

She wobbled slightly at that declaration and her eyes filled with tears. "Thank you," she whispered. "So what is our next step then? How do we use this to find Anne and bring her home to us?"

Jasper stared at the statue and the unblinking lady's gaze, with all its accusations. "I'm not sure. We already know Maitland is close by, watching."

"Because he ransacked the storage building just after we searched it," she said.

"You said that it wasn't a coincidence and I happen to agree. Perhaps we can draw him out." He shook his head. "But I'm not the expert here. Reynolds would be the better person to help formulate this plan."

"Your man of affairs. You sent someone to fetch him." She shifted. "Jasper, every moment we wait I feel my sister's life is in danger."

He set the hated statue down on the floor beside himself and caught her hands. "I understand, but Reynolds is but a handful of hours' ride away on a fast mount with a skillful rider. And I'm certain he'll return as swiftly as possible once he gets my message. I think we can safely expect him by morning. It's only a short delay, Thomasina, and then we can be more ready. The last thing we want to do is be as reckless as Maitland is."

"You think that if we're calm, we'll have the upper hand."

"I know we will. Reynolds will be pivotal to any plan. He's spent the better part of a week looking into Maitland. If anyone would be able to guess his movements and next move, I think it would be him."

She dipped her head back in frustration, but also acquiescence. "Fine. I won't argue the prudence of waiting."

For the first time since they had begun this search that day, Jasper found himself smiling. Because that was what Thomasina did. She brought light to the darkness.

He touched her cheek. "I thank you for that. For now we will put this statue in the safe in my study. And we wait."

She leaned against his palm. "And discuss our next move? I would assume that includes planning how we intend to parlay with this villain once we make contact."

Jasper stared at her. They had been speaking in terms of "we" when it came to their plans, but he hadn't ever imagined bringing Thomasina into the dangerous endgame he would certainly face if he met with Maitland a second time. The very idea of exposing his wife to that bastard made Jasper's skin crawl.

"I'm happy to discuss strategy with you," he said. "But I want one thing to be perfectly clear: I'm not taking you to meet with him."

Her mouth dropped open and she looked genuinely shocked by that declaration. "What do you mean you aren't taking me? It is my sister we're trying to save. I most definitely want to be part of this!"

"He is a criminal," Jasper said, throwing his hands up. "A man willing to steal and lie and…"

He trailed off because he didn't want to pursue anything else Maitland might have done, not when Thomasina was already concerned about Anne's whereabouts.

Thomasina's cheeks burned crimson and she pivoted away from him. "You would cut me out, then? Let me stay here, terrified not just for my sister but for you if you were to meet with this person? This desperate, terrible person? That's wonderful, Jasper. I'm so pleased that you only use me when you need me. That you don't see me as a partner."

She didn't give him time to answer her accusation. She simply exited the attic chamber in a flounce of green gown. He stared at where she'd left. He should probably leave it be. Let her steam and stew at him if doing that kept her safe.

But he found he couldn't. So he followed her.

CHAPTER 24

Thomasina was halfway down the stairs from the attic to the family wing of the house when she heard Jasper's footfalls behind her. Her heart leapt despite her anger with him, her frustration at the situation, her fear of being left out of its resolution.

"Thomasina," he said from behind her.

She chose to ignore him, tears stinging her eyes as she turned toward her chamber down the long hallway.

"Thomasina," he repeated, this time louder. "Please stop."

"Why?" she asked as she reached for her door handle. "What else is there to say? You have determined I've used up my usefulness, haven't you, my lord?"

"No!" he snapped, his tone sharp as he reached out and covered her hand with his on the door handle. His tone was softer as he forced her fingers to loosen their grip on the iron handle. "Please."

She huffed out her breath as she stared at the door before her, felt his fingers against hers as he held her hand. She was being unfair, perhaps. Letting her emotions, her fears, make her reactive in a way that didn't take into account what he feared.

But damn it, hadn't she spent her whole life taking everyone else into account? Hadn't he asked her not to please, but to ask for what she wanted?

She pivoted. "What do you want to say?"

Her breath caught because he was so close now. He leaned a hand on the door beside her, and suddenly he felt very warm and very close as he stared down at her with all that coiled intensity. All that palpable heat and power.

Why did he have to move her so much?

"My not wanting you to be a part of any confrontation with Maitland has nothing to do with not trusting you or valuing you as a partner. I have never had a better one in my life, Thomasina. I've never understood how much I needed one until you crashed into everything I've built and made me question all of it."

Her lips parted. "That—that doesn't sound like a compliment."

He smiled a fraction. "It is the *best* compliment. My life needed crashing. But the reason I don't want you to be near Maitland is that it terrifies me. Thomasina, I—"

He broke off and his cheeks flushed slightly. His gaze darted away. When it returned, she could see the struggle in him. The barriers that remained between them. Lower now, so much lower, but still present.

"You?" she encouraged.

He leaned closer, until she felt his breath on her skin. She shivered with it.

"I have never wanted to have something to lose. But I have that now, in you." His voice was low, rough. It skated across her skin like a kiss. "And if you were to be hurt by Maitland in any way, I wouldn't survive it. I would be focused on you and your safety for every moment we were with him."

She stared at him. "Are you saying you...you...care for me?"

He hesitated, but then he nodded slowly. She couldn't breathe as he leaned in, his hands gliding up her arms, his lips brushing hers. She caught his lapels, gripping them for purchase as he kissed her. It was light at first, gentle, but then the power and passion of that connection of their bodies grew. His mouth opened, he dragged her tongue inside, sucking as she lifted on her tiptoes to get closer to him.

She was drowning in him, lost to everything but him. Perhaps that was his plan. She wasn't so foolish as to think he wouldn't use her desire against her to keep her from going against his wishes. But in that moment she didn't care. She wanted to be comforted by his touch and offer the same comfort to him. The past few days had been so painful...they both deserved a little pleasure to soften the edges.

But he didn't ask for that. Instead, he drew away, releasing her gently as he tried to catch his breath.

"Why?" she gasped.

He smiled. "It is not for a lack of wanting, I assure you. But last night you withdrew your consent. I respect that barrier and your reasons behind it."

It was evident he wanted her by the expression on his face, not to mention the patently obvious erection straining his trousers. But he didn't pursue because she'd asked him not to.

Only she didn't want that anymore. She wanted connection. She needed it, and she knew he did too. She cleared her throat and opened her chamber door. "Lord Harcourt, I want you to come into my room. I want you to come into my bed. I want you to come into my body. Right now. Tonight. All night." She shifted as the discomfort of demand washed over her. "Please."

He tilted his head back with a low chuckle that seemed to work its way through her very bloodstream. "Can't help that last part, can you?"

"No, it's my nature to ask rather than demand," she admitted.

She backed into her chamber and he followed, his shoulders back, his chest forward, like a beast stalking her rather than a very proper earl. She liked the beast.

"You did a very good job demanding," he whispered as he shut the door behind them.

She moved to him and he caught her in his arms, grinding his mouth down without the sweetness or hesitation he'd had in the hallway. He consumed her and she burned in the fire of his desire even as she stoked it with the fuel of her own. She had never needed something as much as she needed this man. She'd never wanted something more.

She wasn't about to let tonight end without getting exactly that.

She forced her hands between their tightly pressed bodies and found the buttons on his jacket. She twisted at them in frustration, opening some, popping others away as he laughed against her mouth. She pushed the jacket aside just as he spun her around roughly. He yanked her backside against his pelvis, rotating them together as he walked her toward the bed.

She couldn't breathe as he kissed the side of her neck, sucking hard enough for a flash of pleasure-pain to make itself known in every sensitive nerve ending in her trembling body. He unfastened her with far more finesse than she had used, and once the gown was open she tugged it away so she stood only in her chemise.

He backed up, the warmth of him no longer curling against her. She looked over her shoulder to find he was unbuttoning his shirt, but watching her with a speculative expression.

"Put your hands on the bed," he ordered, softly but firmly.

She edged closer to the high mattress and fisted each hand against the coverlet. She heard his shirt hit the floor and gasped at the sound. He would take off his trousers next, and her legs shook at the thought of him naked behind her.

"Touch me," she whispered. "Please, please touch me."

He was silent a moment. "You want me to please you?"

She glanced at him over her shoulder again and nodded. "Yes."

"I very much intend to do so, and myself in the process," he promised as he moved forward and tugged her chemise down her arms. He lifted each hand off the bed in turn so he could pull it away.

She lifted her backside against him out of instinct rather than knowledge, and he grunted out a curse beneath his breath that turned her ears crimson, then gripped her hips and ground himself against her. Through his trousers, she felt the hard ridge of his erection press against the valley of her backside, and sucked air in through her teeth at the sensation.

His hand wedged between them and she felt him unfasten his trousers. Now his hot flesh touched her rather than the rough fabric. His cock nudged her from behind as he reached around to curl his body around hers, to cup her breasts, to pluck her nipples. She pushed back and he entered an inch. They sighed together, and he stood a little taller as he thrust his hips and claimed his prize in one long stroke.

She gripped the coverlet tighter as he withdrew and slammed forward again. Her sheath fluttered at the hard invasion, which hit her body in new ways thanks to the position. He leaned in and bit her shoulder, gentle but possessive, and she cried out with unexpected response at the harsh touch.

He caught her hand, tangling his fingers with hers. She clung to him through a few strokes, but then he moved, guiding their combined hands between her legs. He settled her fingers there, against the wet warmth of her sex.

"Please yourself, Thomasina," he said, his voice rough.

She looked back at him, saw the desperate need in his eyes. The driving desire and passion and somewhere beneath it all, something else. Something deeper than the physical. Something close to everything she'd ever dreamed of.

She found her fingers moving as he stroked again, pushing aside her outer lips, brushing against the root of his cock as he took her. He let out a garbled moan and gripped her hips harder, grinding in shallow circles as she found the right spot for her pleasure. Her clitoris was already hard there, and she stroked it, letting the hood come back to find the exquisitely sensitive nub beneath. She gasped as she ground against him, ground against her own hand.

Sensation mounted, the combined power of their joined bodies and her seeking fingers. Already she was close to orgasm, reaching for it as she panted out moans that mingled with his, as she pushed back against him to drive him faster and harder. His hands held her so tightly, she knew she would have bruises. She wanted them. Marks to prove that she was his.

And that he was hers. The fingerprints of his passion would be left on her body, and she longed for that.

She arched against her hand as the sensation arced out of control. A few more strokes and she was flying over the edge, gasping for air as she flopped on the bed, her fingers still rubbing madly, her hips still rising to meet his rapidly increasing strokes. Their skin slapped together, mingling with the sounds of their pleasure, and finally he cried out her name and arched his back, his seed pumping deep within her as the final waves of her orgasm faded.

He flopped down against the edge of the bed over her, his hands sliding over hers, his body still joined with her, his mouth against her neck as he whispered gentle words of pleasure and warmth and gratitude on her ultra-sensitive skin.

Together they crawled up on the bed. He lay on his back, she sprawled across his chest, and for a moment every other thing, every other anger, every other fear in the world faded and there was only them.

And even though she knew that couldn't last, she reveled in it, reveled in him for as long as he would let her.

CHAPTER 25

After a long night of making love, Jasper was asleep. Deeply asleep, if his long breaths were any indication. Thomasina rolled on her side, watching him in this brief moment where he couldn't put a barrier between them. Even in sleep, the toll of the previous day's events was on every line of his face. His mouth was pulled into a frown, his fist clenched at his side, his eyes darting beneath his lids in a dream or nightmare.

Was it about his brother? Or her sister? Or the title? Or the man who threatened all of it, all of them, Ellis Maitland? It was hard to say.

After all, Jasper had carried all that weight on his back, along with a good deal more, for a long time. There had been no one in his life beyond perhaps his man of affairs who he could truly depend upon. Not his father, his brother, his mother. Not a lover. So he didn't know how to put the weights down and let someone else bear some of them.

No matter how frustrated she'd been the previous night after their search of the attic, she was fully aware that his past was why Jasper shut her out. He feared for her safety, certainly that was likely true. But he also doubted her ability to help him. To support him. To be a true partner.

She slowly pushed from the bed and walked to the window. Outside day was breaking, sending just a sliver of golden light into the room. She leaned against the glass, taking in the garden in that soft paleness of dawn. And if she looked just to her left...there was the first of the outbuildings down the hill. Including the storage building where Maitland had made his search for the very statue they had found the night before.

She wondered if that villain had searched the trunk upstairs, if it had been with the others instead, if he would have found the bear and the bust it held. After all, it had been a good hiding place. If she'd picked the bear up in an armful of items, she might not have noticed its extra weight.

Which made her wonder if Solomon had hidden *other* things in careful places like that. Outside were there other clues to his dealings with Maitland, hidden carefully amongst the mess the villain had left behind?

More to the point, were there items that could ultimately help in their search for Anne?

She glanced again at Jasper, asleep in her bed. He would probably be annoyed if she went down to look for herself. He'd growl and mutter and tell her she was being foolish and even reckless. But how reckless could such a thing be if there were guards down at the outbuilding? She knew Jasper had arranged for there to be armed men watching there at all times, she'd heard his stern command the day before.

If she went, she might spare her husband more of the pain he'd experienced when he saw Solomon's old toy and realized just how far his troubled brother had sunk into the mire. If she found something useful, she might be able to use it as leverage to convince him to allow her to help in his continuing search for her sister.

She folded her arms. That was all there was to it. She was going down to the outbuildings. She was going to look for more clues. She moved to the attached dressing room, shutting the door carefully behind herself, and opened her armoire. She picked a gown she could fasten in the front and dressed herself swiftly. She pulled her hair back and pinned it in place. She didn't look like a countess, but it wouldn't matter.

Then she slipped from the chamber and went downstairs. She found Willard in the foyer, talking to a housemaid about some bit of business. As she entered the vestibule, he nodded the young woman off. "Good morning, my lady. We did not expect to see you so early. May I have your breakfast brought, or were you planning an early morning constitutional?"

"A constitutional," she said with a smile for the butler. "I'll wait for the earl to rise to eat. Willard, do you know if there were guards stationed overnight at the building that was burgled?"

Willard's expression hardened. "Yes, my lady, of course. We did just as the earl requested and our largest footman, Parks, was stationed there overnight with stern instructions not to let himself fall asleep. You will not find anyone allowed to harm this family again."

She warmed at his passionate defense of the family. Her family. Certainly Jasper was a good master to his staff, for they were all fiercely loyal to him. "I'm sure no one would dare shirk his duty with you around, Willard. You are doing a fine job."

"Thank you, my lady," he said, and his cheeks glowed with true appreciation at the compliment.

"Well, I shall be off then," she said, making no other reference to the outbuilding. The butler certainly didn't need to know her whereabouts and he had answered her only concern in regards to her own safety. Now she could go along to the building without fear of consequences and tell Jasper she had been careful.

She slipped from the house into the increasing morning sun and headed toward the building at the bottom of the hill. It was a bright day, cool but with the promise of a warmth to come that made her smile. She did love this estate. After Anne was found, she truly looked forward to exploring it without worry and with Jasper by her side.

In a few moments, she reached the lower buildings. In the distance, she saw the storage building and a chair set up beside its door. But there was no footman perched there.

She slowed her gait as she reached the building. Nothing looked out of place. There was a tin of coffee or tea sitting beside the chair and a half-eaten biscuit, as if the young man had been interrupted in his snack. But not by an enemy.

She moved to the door. Maitland had kicked it in when he came before, so it wasn't locked. She pushed it open and stepped into the dimmer light, letting her eyes adjust as she looked around.

"Parks?" she called out, wondering if the young man had come inside. Or even been asked to reorganize the items that had been ransacked two nights prior. It looked like someone had been setting things to rights since then.

"Parks?" she repeated, a little louder this time.

"Yes, my lady?" came a voice from the back of the room.

She sagged a little in relief and moved toward the sound. But as she stepped behind a row of boxes, she came to a halt. There was a man standing in the room, but it wasn't a footman to her home, of that she was certain. No, he was tall, broad-shouldered and very handsome with his rakishly long hair and a smirk that made a dimple pop in his cheek.

As he stepped forward, she realized there was another man behind him. Prone, bound at the wrist and ankle, and dead.

No, not dead, she realized with relief as she watched his chest rise and fall. Parks.

"Who are you?" she whispered as she backed toward the door, even though she knew she wouldn't escape.

It seemed the intruder did, too, for he smiled at her with indulgence. "Handsome Ellis Maitland at your service, Lady Harcourt. What a pleasure it is to meet you at last."

She pivoted to run, but he lunged and caught her arm, holding her in place effortlessly.

"Let me go!" she screamed. "Help!"

He let out his breath in a sigh. "Great God, cease your shouting. No one in the house can hear you. No one is going to come. Now come along and sit down."

He punctuated that last order by dragging her into the back of the room and hurtling her into a chair. She hit the seat with a thump and glared up at him. He smiled back and then threw his head back with a chuckle.

"God's teeth, you three really do look like an exact replica of each other. Even more so up close. I suppose I was lucky I picked the right sister to woo."

"You are talking about Anne," she whispered. "An innocent woman you seduced in order to exact your awful plan."

Maitland shrugged. "No one was seduced," he said with a wrinkle of his brow, as though it was a distasteful suggestion that he would take advantage. "I must say your sister isn't as predictable a lady as I thought, however."

"One of her best qualities." Thomasina held his gaze evenly. "Where is she?"

He shifted. "Due time, my lady, all in due time. Now you tell *me*, where is my damned treasure?"

There was a worry to the way he asked the question. A wildness to his expression that made Thomasina lean a little closer. It wasn't madness. No, the man seemed in full control of his faculties. There wasn't cruelty, though his tone was harsh. But there *was* desperation on every line of his handsome face. And *that* could be just as dangerous.

"We have what you seek," she said, being careful in the words she spoke.

He jerked, that desperation multiplying. "Where? Tell me now and all this can be over."

Her heart leapt, pounding so hard she feared he could hear it as he loomed over her.

"I-It's in the house," she said. "Which is filled with dozens of people. You'll never get to it."

He jerked away from her, clenching his fists at his sides. His defined jaw was tight with frustration as he paced away. "Damn it! That earl wasn't worth the fucking trouble. I never should have trusted him. What the hell did we get ourselves into? Why the hell did we involve such a bastard in our dealings?"

She tensed. He was talking about Solomon when he said the earl, that was clear. But it seemed like he was talking about someone else, too. She didn't understand it, but she had to remain calm, just as Jasper had said the previous night. Calm would help her in the face of this man's lack of control.

"I *can* get it for you," she said softly.

He pivoted to face her, eyes narrowed. "How?"

She swallowed hard. "Just let me go up and—"

He threw his head back and laughed. "Oh no, my lady. I may look young, but I was not born yesterday. You go up there and I'm certain the guard will greet me, not my treasure, when you return." He paced for a moment, glancing at her with every turn. "I hate this. I hate it. It's not who I am."

"Then who are you?" Thomasina whispered, hoping that getting him to talk would help.

He shook his head. "I used to know. But things change. I need leverage, and now I have it, much as I despise all this. Harcourt obviously cares for you. He'll do anything to keep you safe."

Thomasina shifted in her seat. Maitland was right, of course. Jasper had spent a great deal of time last night trying to explain how much he feared she would be in the exact position she found herself in now. If her husband heard she was in trouble, he would race to rescue her, treasure in hand. He wouldn't care about the cost or the risk.

He cared for her. Maybe it was more than that, even if he

wouldn't admit it yet.

"And I'll do anything to keep him safe in return," she said evenly. Calmly, and for that she was pleased. At least she didn't sound as terrified as she felt. "What do you want me to do?"

"Not you," Maitland said, and leaned down to the servant on the floor. "Hey. Hey you, Parks. His name is Parks, right?"

Thomasina nodded. "Yes, the name of the man you tried to murder is Parks, Mr. Maitland."

He looked at her again. "I didn't try to kill him. A man in my position learns how to take out a threat without hurting him permanently. I cut off just enough blood with a choke to put him in this state, and nothing more."

Thomasina shook her head. This man wasn't how she'd pictured him when she imagined a great, terrible villain. Maitland was... charming in his own way, despite the horror of what was happening.

"Parks!" Maitland repeated as he lightly slapped the cheeks of the servant.

At last the poor footman groaned and his eyes fluttered open. "You bastard," he grunted. His foggy gaze slipped to Thomasina. "My—my lady?"

She nodded. "It's all right, Parks. Are you well?"

Parks rubbed his neck as he sat up slightly. "Aye, my lady. Just a headache."

She let out a sigh of relief. "Please do anything he says. Don't put yourself in more danger than you already are."

Maitland smiled at her. "Good, listen to Lady Harcourt. Seems she's a reasonable person after all. I want you to go up to the house. Speak only to your master. Tell him I have his wife and I want my treasure. If anyone else comes down here with him, she..." He trailed off and shifted slightly as his gaze flitted to her. There was hesitation there. Anguish. "I don't want to have to hurt her. I don't want to have to hurt *anyone*."

Parks' gaze slipped to Thomasina and she nodded slightly.

"Do it."

He struggled to his feet. Maitland spun him around and cut his binds on his ankles and hands. He held the blade out, as if poised to strike as Parks kicked away the ropes and rubbed his wrists. "You have fifteen minutes to bring him back, you understand? Hurry!"

Maitland glanced at Thomasina, almost apologetically, she thought. What the hell was going on with this man? He was no hero, after all. Driven by greed and whatever other terrible things made men steal and cheat and lie and not care about any other person they hurt.

But he also seemed hesitant about physically harming her. And perhaps she could use that to her advantage. To Jasper's advantage. To Anne's advantage. But only if she used her wits.

Maitland waved Parks toward the door and then he returned his focus to Thomasina.

"Your quarrel is with Solomon, not Jasper," she said softly. "But you know that."

He shrugged. "I don't care which Harcourt brother gives me what I want. I just want it." He ran a hand through his hair. "Solomon created this situation, you know. I'm just living with the consequences."

Her brow wrinkled, for she didn't understand what he meant. But she ignored that for the moment. "What about my sister? Your pawn to get Jasper to do your bidding? Did you harm *her*?"

Maitland's gaze darted away, almost like he wasn't proud of his situation with Anne. "I did what I had to do. But when I last saw her, she was fine."

Thomasina straightened. "Last saw her?"

He glared at her. "Shut up, my lady. We're done talking. Until your husband shows up, we have nothing to say."

She clamped her lips shut and watched him as he paced the room, checking his watch every minute, waiting for Jasper. He was a trapped animal, that much was clear. And who knew what would happen once Jasper entered the room and confronted him?

CHAPTER 26

J asper rolled from the bed and looked around Thomasina's empty chamber. Despite the dire nature of the situation he found himself in, he still smiled at the rumpled sheets, the scent of her in the air. Whatever else happened from now until the day he took his last breath, he had her in his life. To have, to hold, to protect and to be protected by.

He flexed his shoulders back and moved to his room. He intended to dress and then find his wife. They could continue the search for clues about Maitland until Reynolds arrived from Beck-foot, and then they could determine how to reach out to the bastard with an offer of parlay.

He entered his chamber and rang the bell. In a moment, his valet, Hoffman, entered. "Good morning, Hoffman," he began. "I'll wear the—"

He didn't get to finish the request, though. The door to his chamber flew open and one of the footmen, Parks, rushed in with Willard behind him and Reynolds on their heels. "What in the world —?" he began.

"I must speak to you alone, my lord," Parks burst out, red and sweaty. Jasper stared disheveled nature of the young man's hair and clothes. His gaze was a bit unfocused. "Please!"

"Come away, Parks," Willard said, grabbing for his arm as Reynolds reached for the other. "Thank God Mr. Reynolds returned just a few moments ago in time to help me deal with this. I don't know what madness you discovered during your guard shift, but we do not allow drinking on this staff. You will be dismissed for—"

Jasper pushed forward. "Guard duty?"

"He was at the outbuildings, my lord. Though he must have been imbibing to behave thus. I only hope Lady Harcourt wasn't bothered by him on her walk."

His world screeched to a halt at those words. "Get out. Everyone but Parks, get out."

The rest of them looked at him in confusion, but Reynolds directed them out. He shot Jasper a meaningful look and shut the door.

"What is going on?" Jasper said. "And I swear if Willard is right—"

"He's not. I was sent on guard duty to that old outbuilding last night. It was uneventful until someone grabbed me from behind and nearly choked the life out of me," Parks said. "I woke up and *he* had Lady Harcourt."

Jasper's knees nearly went out from beneath him at that sentence. He'd intended to put a guard on Thomasina whenever she was alone, but he hadn't planned for this contingency, that she'd go to the storage building alone before he woke. And now she was held captive and it could only be one villain who would be so bold.

Parks touched his head and flinched. "I don't know who the bastard is that done it, but he's going on about treasure. He said you had fifteen minutes to get down. I ran fast as I could being so dizzy."

Jasper was already stripping out of his robe and tugging on a pair of trousers and boots. "How long ago did you leave them?"

"Eight minutes, maybe ten? I lost track when everyone tried to stop me."

"Is it just Maitland?" Jasper asked, trying to focus on the matter at hand, not desperate images of Thomasina in danger. Thomasina alone with a man who would hurt her to get what he wanted. "Just the one man?"

Parks nodded with another wince of pain. "That's all I saw was just the one man. He said you should bring the treasure."

Jasper froze. He had meant to bring the statue down the night before, but when he and Thomasina had argued, he'd all but forgotten it in the attic.

"Go upstairs, to the attic. There is an open chamber. Bring me the statue there in the middle of the floor. Then get yourself looked at, with my thanks. Hurry now."

Parks bolted from the room, and Jasper shouted after him, "No one stop that man or you will deal with me. Reynolds, get in here."

His man of affairs rushed inside, looking rather road-worn himself. "What is going on?"

Jasper shook his head as he pulled a pistol from the bottom drawer of his wardrobe and loaded it with shaking hands. "I called you back to find Maitland, but he found us. He has Thomasina and he wants his treasure."

"Do you have it?" Reynolds asked.

Before Jasper could answer, Parks reappeared, the marble-based statue in his hand. "This?" he asked.

"Yes, good man." He grabbed it and motioned to Reynolds to follow. "This is it, we think. He wants me alone. You'll need to conceal yourself. If I give the word, come running."

"What's the word?" Reynolds asked as they rushed past the stunned staff.

"Call for the guard," Jasper called out. "And tend to Parks, he's a damned hero."

As they exited the house and headed for the outbuildings down the hill, he thought of Thomasina. Of her life being in danger. Of the time that was sliding through the hourglass even now.

He thought of what he'd have to tell her if things went wrong. What she needed to know more than anything.

"If I tell her I love her, we're in trouble," he said. "And you come running. Save her, do you understand? Save her before me."

Reynolds caught his breath. "You do love her."

"I do." Jasper motioned to a side path where they would separate so Reynolds wouldn't be seen from the building. "And I hope I can confess that in better circumstances."

"Good luck," Reynolds said, squeezing his arm before he rushed off to take the longer route to the building.

Jasper moved along the main path, cresting the hill where he saw the building. He and Thomasina had come here together twice. Once when she was so angry with him and yet still supportive and caring. It was not in her makeup to be anything less so.

And now he might lose her.

A great swell of panic rose up on him at that thought, but he tamped it down, drew a long breath and entered the outbuilding.

He saw them immediately. Maitland stood behind the chair where Thomasina sat, her hands clenched in her lap. He had a gun in his hand, not pointed at her, but too close for comfort. Jasper was relieved to find she looked unharmed.

"My lord," Maitland said with a shake of his head. "Welcome to our party."

"Are you injured?" Jasper asked, ignoring Maitland.

She blinked at the tears in her eyes. "I'm fine. I'm sorry that my coming down here created this."

"I should have guessed you'd be undeterred in your quest to save your sister. To save me even if I don't deserve it. And *you* didn't create this, he did."

Maitland edged closer to her. "Enough. If you do what you are told, there is no reason you two couldn't live a very happy life together. Now where is my treasure?"

Jasper had been holding the statue behind his back, but now he drew it out and held it up. "I think this is your prize. Let my wife go and tell us where to find her sister, and you can have it with my blessing."

Maitland stared at the statue, utterly silent for what felt like a lifetime. Then he came around to stand beside Thomasina's chair. "What the fuck is that?"

Jasper blinked. "The treasure. We found it hidden in my brother's things. What else would he hide but the treasure?"

"That's not my treasure," Maitland barked. "Put it down."

"What?"

"Put it on the ground," Maitland roared, shaking the gun without intent or care. "I don't want you using that as a weapon."

Jasper eased the item to the floor. "I swear to you on my life, Maitland, that is all we found."

Maitland was trembling now. He swore a blue line and then pressed a hand against his forehead as he stared at the statue and back to Jasper. "You—you swear on your life, eh? Do you want me to test that?"

Jasper noted he didn't turn the gun on him or Thomasina, but his heartrate increased nonetheless at the threat of an armed man.

"He's not lying," Thomasina gasped, gripping the edge of the chair until her knuckles went white. "Please!"

Jasper came forward a step, hoping to keep Maitland's attention on him. "Listen to me. I want to help."

"You bloody liar, you don't want to help me." Maitland shook his head. "You have no idea what is at stake here."

"Then tell me," Jasper said, meeting Thomasina's gaze evenly. Hoping he could soothe her as she had done so many times. Thinking of all he would lose if she were taken from him. Of all he would have left unsaid if he were the one with a bullet through his heart today.

"Let *us* help you," Thomasina whispered.

The gun shook as Maitland fought to catch his breath, like he couldn't find it. "No one can help me."

Jasper realized this was the moment he could strike. When Maitland was emotional, when he was falling apart from whatever desperation had driven him to this. But he needed help.

He looked at his wife, her eyes wide with terror. And he cried out, "Thomasina, I love you!"

Her eyes went wide and then she swiveled in her chair. She kicked Maitland's left knee with all her might and he toppled forward. The trigger depressed and the gun fired. The bullet ricocheted past Jasper, lodging in the wall instead.

Jasper dove forward, grabbing for Thomasina and yanking her from the chair as he heard Reynolds' shouting as he entered the door. Maitland swore as he pushed some of the boxes and trunks down around them, and then there was the crashing of glass as he hurtled himself through one of the back windows and ran.

"Go after him!" Jasper shouted to Reynolds as he kept his body over Thomasina's, protecting her with all he had, all he was and all he ever would be.

~

"Jasper," Thomasina said, her voice muffled against Jasper's wrinkled shirt, muted by the pounding of his heart as he lay across her body, trembling.

He didn't move and she pushed gently. "Jasper," she repeated.

He looked down at her, his eyes widening. All his fear was plain on his face then. But so was his love. He'd said he loved her, a sentence shouted in the heat of the moment, perhaps. But now that she looked into his eyes, she knew it was true.

"Are you unharmed?" he asked as he rolled off of her, pushed to his feet and helped her up. She stretched and smoothed her hands across her body, checking herself for injury and finding only a few bruises from hitting the floor.

"I'm fine," she reassured him, but then the reality of what had just happened hit her. She relived that awful moment when Maitland had fallen and the gun had fired. "He could have shot you," she whispered, and fell against his chest.

He smoothed his fingers through her tangled hair. "But he didn't, love. You saved me. We saved each other. I'm fine now, please don't cry."

She lifted her head from his chest and stared up into his beautiful face. "I didn't know he'd be here. I thought I was safe when I came down to look at the trunks. I thought it would keep you from having to relive more unhappy memories."

He nodded. "I know. And why would you know? How would you possibly think that Maitland would return to search this place again? He must have been truly desperate."

She sucked a breath. "He was. Not mad, but there is more to this story than we know. He's not what I expected. And Jasper, I don't think he knows where my sister is. When I asked about Anne, he said something about the last time he saw her, like it had been a while."

"Then she might have escaped him," Jasper said. "That would partly explain his reaction. His plan was falling apart."

She clutched her fingers against his chest. "She might try to come home."

"I hope so," he said, and put an arm around her to guide her out of the building. Reynolds was coming down the path, and Jasper lifted a hand. "Anything?" he called out.

Reynolds shook his head. "He had a horse waiting. He was gone through your gate before I could mount to make chase. Luckily the guard was coming in just as I began my exit. I turned them back to follow him, but he's long gone, I think."

"Go manage them then. We'll be up in a moment," Jasper called out. When he had disappeared over the hill, he turned her to face him in the path. "I want to talk to you about what happened a moment ago."

She flinched. He was talking about his confession of love to her, said at the most heated of moments. It was possible he wished to take it back, even if he meant it. To rebuild those walls he constantly kept up to protect himself. But she couldn't let him. Not ever again.

"Please don't say you didn't mean those words," she said, lifting her gaze to him. "Because I love you, Jasper. I have loved you probably from the first moment I met you all those months ago. Even when I knew I shouldn't, even when you were my sister's fiancé, I loved you. And today I came painfully close to losing you. So I won't ever hold my declarations back again and I hope you won't either."

He stared at her, blinking in what seemed like utter shock and disbelief. "You—you loved me all along?"

"Of course I did," she said with a laugh.

He shook his head. "I suppose after spending most of my life either watching love be twisted into something ugly or avoiding the pain it might cause, I am not adept at recognizing it. I never dared to hope that you could love me from the beginning."

"Well, I do. I know that love is frightening to you. I know why it would be so, considering what you went through. But you can't run from it all your life. It is too powerful and lovely and beautiful to avoid."

"You think I'd like to avoid it?" he asked. "Avoid what I declared to you?"

"Under duress, and now you might be trying to think of a gentlemanly way to take it back, even if you might mean it deep in your heart." She touched his face.

"Now it is you who is blind to the truth." He turned into her hand and kissed her. "What I was going to say, *wife*, was that the last way I wanted to admit my feelings for you was in a moment that might have been our last together. But I knew I would say those words to you. I've known for some time, actually, that my heart belonged to you."

Her mouth dropped open at that easy confession, not hindered by drama or withholding or fear as she'd thought it might be. "You have?"

"Yes. And like you, it probably began happening the moment I was introduced to you. You have become the greatest light in my darkness, the path that leads me home, the person I wish to see first in the morning and last before sleep steals me. You are my heart and my life. And that has *nothing* to do with duress. It is just the truth. You have bewitched me and I have never been so happy to surrender to a spell in my life."

She blinked. "I am having such a hard time with this. I thought I would have to fight you and draw you to me and convince you that love is worth having and sharing."

"Well, you could still do that if you'd like." He smiled. "I would very much enjoy being the recipient of all your focused lessons on love."

He leaned down to kiss her. The kiss was brief and shockingly chaste, but no kiss before had ever been sweeter. No kiss had ever been so powerful. Because no kiss had ever been given or received with the knowledge of her heart and of his. So it was like the first kiss, and he reveled in it before he drew away.

"We must go back to the house now. There will be the guard to manage and the household to calm," he said. "We will be expected to be the earl and the countess now, but I want you to know two things."

They began to walk and she rested her head on his shoulder with a content sigh. "And what are those?"

"First, that I will put every resource into uncovering your sister. I'm certain she must be trying to get back to us. I'll send for you father and Juliana. They've probably only just reached Gretna Green and they need to be on the lookout for her if she's trying to go home by road. Hell, I'll go to Scotland myself if I must, and knock door to door on every path that might lead Anne to us."

"You would do that for the woman who left you almost at the altar?"

He glanced down at her. "No, for the woman who met me there instead."

She turned her face to his and brushed her mouth to his cheek. "And what is the second thing?"

"That once we clear all these interlopers out, once we start all my resources onto the task of finding Anne, I plan to take you upstairs and prove my love to you. Without words. For as many hours as we can both stand."

They had reached the top of the hill now, and he was correct that the drive teemed with strangers and servants all talking at once. Looking for a leader. Looking for her husband.

"I cannot wait," she whispered as they moved toward them. "And to prove the same to you."

CHAPTER 27

T wo *Days Later*

Thomasina looked up from the brimming plate of breakfast delights and smiled as her husband entered the room. An expression that fell when she saw his long face.

"What is it?" she asked. "Word from Reynolds?"

"No," he said, and set a slim folded sheet of paper before her. "From Anne."

She yelped out a cry and jumped to her feet, tearing open the seal. She scanned the words and then read them out loud:

My dearest Thomasina, Juliana and Father,

I must start by saying I am unharmed. I made a foolish mistake in believing the words of a charlatan, but I have been punished for it, I promise you. I am safe now and will be returning to Lord Harcourt's estate by Tuesday. I hope I will be welcomed. I love you all so much.

Your Foolish Anne.

She handed the letter over to Jasper as she clutched her hands to her heart in relief and joy. "She is coming home!" she burst out. "My sister is unharmed and she is coming home!"

Jasper frowned as he folded the letter. "And it seems she has a tale to tell. There is no direction on the envelope, so I cannot take you to intercept her. But Tuesday is tomorrow—we will see her soon, assuming she will be on time."

"And Juliana and my father will be here this afternoon, so we will all be here to greet her." She blinked at tears. "I cannot wait to touch her and know she is real and whole."

He reached out and brushed her cheek with his fingertips. "I understand entirely."

She stepped into his arms and held him as her joy overflowed within her. Joy that Anne would be home safely soon. Joy that she had found so much love in the midst of chaos and helplessness.

"Reynolds did send word earlier," he murmured into her hair. "He has lost Maitland's trail. He's still out there. But I promise you I will keep you safe."

She pulled back enough to look up into his eyes. "We'll keep each other safe," she whispered. "Forever."

"Forever," he repeated, and then he kissed her.

EPILOGUE

Ellis Maitland stood in the copse of trees at the western edge of the Harcourt estate, watching as two horses entered the long drive toward the house in the distance. He recognized one rider immediately and his stomach clenched. His cousin, Rook Maitland, was in the lead. And the other was Anne Shelley.

So his plans had been foiled, though he couldn't say he was entirely disappointed. Taking Anne had been the most unpleasant bit of trickery he had ever pulled off. Seeing the terror of her sister a few days before made it clear what a villain he was.

But he needed the treasure Harcourt had. He *needed* it. If he didn't find it, others would be harmed. Just as innocent. Someone would *die* and it would be Ellis's fault. So as distasteful as he found the entire endeavor, he couldn't stop.

He *wouldn't* stop.

Not until he had the prize that would free him from a prison of his own making.

EXCERPT OF A RECKLESS RUNAWAY

THE SHELLEY SISTERS, BOOK 2

Preorder Now - Available February 4, 2020

Anne's hands shook, but she gripped them into fists as she reached the end of the dock and what seemed like a very small boat. An older gentleman was sitting in the back near the oars. He had a glowing lantern on a hook mounted beside him, and he was glaring at her and her new companion through the fog as if he had schedules to keep and they were intruding upon them.

"Good evening," she squeaked in his direction.

He glared harder and she dipped her head as terror overcame her. She was in danger. That was clear. She had been in danger from the moment she slipped from the warmth of her fiancé's home and took off on this madcap adventure.

Perhaps she'd been in danger even earlier than that, when she'd first agreed to meet with Ellis even though she knew it was wrong to do so.

And now here she was in God knew where, watching a handsome stranger with an odd nickname get onto a rickety rowboat. He set her bag down none too gently and then pivoted back to stare at her. He extended a hand slowly to help her on board.

She glanced back down the dock, toward where she'd last seen Ellis. Somehow she'd thought to find him in the milling crowd, watching to determine she'd safely gotten on the craft. But he was gone.

She shuddered and turned back to the boat, staring at Rook's extended fingers for a moment. That rough hand, big and calloused from work, could be attached to a murderer for all she knew. He could be a great many terrible things and have a great many terrible plans in store for her. And yet what choice did she have but to go with him?

"Stupid girl," she admonished herself beneath her breath as she took the hand he offered.

She wasn't wearing gloves, she'd forgotten them in her excitement to escape on this adventure gone wrong. When her palm touched his, she felt a thrill of something, a hiss of awareness that shot up her arm and through her body.

She stepped into the boat and snatched her hand away as she settled onto one of the hard benches in the middle of the boat. Rook Maitland took the one facing her. He was so big, his knees pushed into her space and their legs almost touched no matter how far back she tried to tuck them. She huffed out a breath at this new invasion and tried with all her might to make her mind go somewhere else. Anywhere else but here.

Only it wasn't so easy. Not when her mind kept taking her back to her family. She had to assume that Thomasina would have returned to her chamber after the ball. She would have found the letter Anne had left. The one filled with hopes for a future with Ellis that now seemed so faded and far away and foolish. What would her sister have thought? What would Juliana think? Would they be able to manage their father's outrage together? Would Harcourt's fury lead to untold punishments against them?

She bent her head as the consequences of her selfish action washed over her like the bouncing waves that occasionally crested over the edge of the boat as they rowed farther into the heart of the Irish Sea. In the dark.

She lifted her head and found Rook Maitland watching her. He was hardly more than a shadow outline in their captain's lantern light, but his dark gaze glittered as he held it on her.

"How far must we go?" she asked as the sea bobbed heavier.

He was silent for what felt like an eternity, but at last he grunted, "It will be a few hours, yet. It's a long row to Scotland."

Her eyes widened. *Scotland?* She had thought that idea was abandoned when Ellis sent her off with this man. But if they were crossing the sea after all, perhaps that meant Ellis wasn't the villain he had seemed to be. Perhaps he would return for her after all and this could be resolved just as she'd planned from the beginning.

She clung to that hope and nodded. "What town?" she asked.

"You have a great many questions," her companion said softly. "Why didn't you ask Ellis about his plans for you, as he is your love?"

She bit back the retort that she didn't love Ellis and shrugged. "I thought I knew the plan," she said. "So I didn't ask. And here we are."

He nodded slowly. "Yes. Here you are."

She realized he hadn't answered her question about the town, but she was too exhausted to ask again. She would find out soon enough, she supposed. And if he was reticent to share with her, perhaps that was for the best. He wasn't going to be her companion for very long. It was probably best that an unmarried lady didn't attach herself too strongly to a very handsome cousin of her intended. People would talk, wouldn't they?

God, people would already be talking. She knew that. Her running away was too big a secret to keep, especially with the wedding planned for less than a week from now. When she didn't appear for it, when it was all canceled, there would be no stopping the tale that would rip through Society.

"You look like you have some regrets, Miss Shelley," Rook said.

The little boat careened into a wave and Anne gripped at both sides of it, clawing to retain purchase. "No," she lied. "Of course not. I know what I'm doing."

But she heard the lilt in her tone, the terror and the pain. His expression didn't change. If he heard it too, it was clear he didn't give a damn. But why would he? He'd been sent here to collect her, and he didn't seem particularly pleased by that.

She wouldn't give him any more reason to be annoyed, nor to judge her more a fool than he clearly already did. She sat up as straight as she could and did her best to focus on a point just behind him rather than at his handsome, frowning face. Of course that point was the disappearing light of the distant town, of England vanishing into the fog.

And she gritted her teeth as moments bled to almost an hour of rowing through the endless night. At last she shivered as the air pierced her thin wrap and tugged it harder around herself. The boat rolled endlessly on the waves as their captain rowed on, seemingly unfazed by the cold splash of the sea water or the blowing wind that caused the spray to soak her face and hair and clothes.

She would not cry. She would *not*, even as the fog swirled around her, making her colder than ever.

Rook had been silent during the time they rowed, his gaze fixed behind her, toward whatever their mysterious destination was. But now he suddenly moved, shrugging out of his great coat in one smooth motion. The action revealed a crisp linen shirt beneath that seemed to strain against broad shoulders and chest.

He held the coat out. "Here, you'll catch your death otherwise."

She blinked at the offering. His coat, which had just been around him. It seemed very intimate to accept the offer. Too intimate.

His brow wrinkled. "Take it before it loses its body heat."

Body heat. She inwardly groaned, but it was too cold to argue. She took the woolen coat, sliding her arms into the sleeves and fastening it around her waist. It dwarfed her, for he was far bigger than she was. The sleeves came over her hand by at least a few inches and it was more like a shapeless cloak around her shoulders than a fitted coat like it had been on his.

But it was warm. He was right about that. She felt his body heat curl around her like his arms were there. And his scent lingered on the woolen fabric. It was a nice scent. Something woodsy and clean and masculine.

Once again her stomach clenched with an awareness she shouldn't have felt, and she bent her head as she muttered, "Thank you."

He didn't respond, but nodded, and his focus shifted away from her again. She glanced at him now that he wasn't looking at her. He had a hard line to his very defined jaw and an equally tight quality to his clamped lips. They were full, though. She could tell that despite the annoyance that lined his face.

He didn't seem troubled by the roiling of the boat. Her stomach rose and fell, but he didn't even have an increase in breath. Damn him. She really didn't want to make more of a fool of herself than she already had, but nausea was rising by the moment as the sea grew heavier and wilder away from the coast.

It had been such a long night, filled with such disappointment and fear. She had hardly eaten anything since afternoon tea and now all she could think about was that food and how much she hated everything she'd ever put into her mouth.

Rook cocked his head and looked at her. "Miss Shelley?" he said softly.

But she didn't answer. All she could do was lean over the side of the boat and cast up her accounts as she cursed every decision she'd made since three o'clock that afternoon. Including the ones that had put her in the boat with a stranger, vomiting in front of him.

Preorder Now - Available February 4, 2020

ALSO BY JESS MICHAELS

~

The Shelley Sisters

A Reluctant Bride

A Reckless Runaway

A Counterfeit Courtesan (coming March 3, 2020)

The Scandal Sheet

The Return of Lady Jane

Stealing the Duke

Lady No Says Yes

My Fair Viscount

Guarding the Countess

The House of Pleasure

The 1797 Club

The Daring Duke

Her Favorite Duke

The Broken Duke

The Silent Duke

The Duke of Nothing

The Undercover Duke

The Duke of Hearts

The Duke Who Lied

The Duke of Desire

The Last Duke

~

Seasons

An Affair in Winter

A Spring Deception

One Summer of Surrender

Adored in Autumn

The Wicked Woodleys

Forbidden

Deceived

Tempted

Ruined

Seduced

Fascinated

The Notorious Flynns

The Other Duke

The Scoundrel's Lover

The Widow Wager

No Gentleman for Georgina

A Marquis for Mary

To see a complete listing of Jess Michaels' titles, please visit:

http://www.authorjessmichaels.com/books

ABOUT THE AUTHOR

USA Today Bestselling author Jess Michaels likes geeky stuff, Vanilla Coke Zero, anything coconut, cheese, fluffy cats, smooth cats, any cats, many dogs and people who care about the welfare of their fellow humans. She is lucky enough to be married to her favorite person in the world and lives in the heart of Dallas, TX where she's trying to eat all the amazing food in the city.

When she's not obsessively checking her steps on Fitbit or trying out new flavors of Greek yogurt, she writes historical romances with smoking hot alpha males and sassy ladies who do anything but wait to get what they want. She has written for numerous publishers and is now fully indie and loving every moment of it (well, almost every moment).

Jess loves to hear from fans! So please feel free to contact her in any of the following ways (or carrier pigeon):

www.AuthorJessMichaels.com
Email: Jess@AuthorJessMichaels.com

Jess Michaels raffles a gift certificate EVERY month to members of her newsletter, so sign up on her website:
http://www.AuthorJessMichaels.com/

f facebook.com/JessMichaelsBks
twitter.com/JessMichaelsBks
instagram.com/JessMichaelsBks

Made in the USA
Coppell, TX
28 April 2020